Mrs Rochester

Hilary Bailey was born in 1936 and was educated at thirteen schools before attending Newnham College, Cambridge. Married with children, she entered the strange, uneasy world of '60s science fiction, writing some twenty tales of imagination which were published in Britain, the USA, France and Germany. She has edited the magazine *New Worlds* and has regularly reviewed modern fiction for the *Guardian*. Her first novel was published in 1975 and she has since written twelve novels and a short biography. She lives in Ladbroke Grove, London

Mrs Rochester

Hilary Bailey

POCKET BOOKS

LONDON · SYDNEY · NEW YORK · TOKYO · SINGAPORE · TORONTO

First published in Great Britain by Pocket Books, 1997
An imprint of Simon & Schuster Ltd
A Viacom Company

Simon & Schuster Ltd
West Garden Place
Kendal Street
London W2 2AQ

Simon & Schuster Australia
Sydney

A CIP catalogue record for this book is available
from the British Library

ISBN 0-671-51672-8

Typeset in Sabon 10/12pt by
Palimpsest Book Production Limited, Polmont, Stirlingshire
Printed and bound in Great Britain by
Caledonian International Book Manufacturing, Glasgow

Chapter I

Here in my calm, light room at Thornfield Hall, I sit on a window-seat writing, sometimes looking down on to the broad swathe of lawn below, my pen and inkwell on a small table beside me. It is May now and the orchard in the walled garden to my left is in bloom. Soon, there will be roses. Looking up into the cloudless blue sky I know content; I am safe again after storms.

Yet in my mind I am not fully here in the magnificence of the restored Thornfield Hall. I dream, recalling those last happy days at the manor of Ferndean, thirty miles away. I remember the September of last year at Ferndean, dear Ferndean, my Paradise, my shelter, my joy during the first ten years of my marriage.

Let me go back in memory to those September days.

Years of love and patience had transformed that formerly gloomy house in its wooded valley into a calm and delightful home, surrounded by a garden, made with my own hands, full of scent and colour. Small as it was by the standards of the great, it was large enough for us. Who, living with those they truly love, will wish to be separated from them by a spread of imposing rooms and great lengths of gallery and corridor? Such distance may end in distances of the hearts, I believe. For my husband and myself, the small pretty dining-room, one charming drawing-room and an even smaller study and library sufficed. When we were alone in the evenings by the fire, my husband would look about him, lean back in his chair and tell me often, 'My dear Jane – you could make a home in a desert, of that I'm sure.'

'I am so glad you are pleased with me, sir,' I might then tell him, in jest. 'Is there aught else I can do for you?'

Then, 'Well,' he might return, 'first you might bring me my book and then you might bring me yourself and then sit near me while I read to you.'

How I recall the closeness we had then, and the quiet activities which filled our days in that little house where began my happiest years, those of my marriage. This thought comes to me seldom during the daylight hours, but at night I dream of Ferndean, nestling in its hollow, its red brick gleaming in the sun, the old mulberry tree under which we used to sit.

I recall so well the quiet routine of our days there. Each morning Edward and I would breakfast quietly together, talking of the pattern of the coming day, little varied, it must be said, from day to contented day. Oh the delight, the joy of seeing that dear face across the table from me each morning.

Then Edward would go into his study to conduct his affairs, for, apart from his estates, he had business interests to occupy him. Later, I would bring him some refreshment – Edward looks up from his desk – huge Pilot gets up from his position by the desk, wagging his tail and I, with some tea or lemonade on a tray in my hand, go to my husband, and, laying my hand on his shoulder, ask him, is there any help I may give him.

Sometimes he would say, 'Well, little scribe, can you find the time from your household tasks and garden, and the school and all your other multifarious businesses, to act for a time as my secretary? Will you make fair copies of these letters for me? Will you add up these figures and check the totals? Play the lady of business?' And then I would set to at the little desk opposite his own and gladly do what I could, rejoicing in the opportunity to assist and to understand the progress of his affairs. Knowing all his dealings, I was able to keep in tune with his movements and his moods. At other times, though, he would refuse my help, saying, perhaps, 'No – I am managing well enough without my handmaiden. But will you take Pilot about your business with you, for he pines for activity.' And I leave the room, Pilot at my heels. (This was not the old dog, now long dead, but some son or nephew of his.)

All this while, my boy would be at the rectory, receiving his lessons from the curate with his two young companions, the sons of our vicar. Often I would walk my little Jonathan there in the mornings, not because he could not find his way down the lane to the rectory, but for the pleasure of being with him at the start of the day. On his return we would all, Edward, Jonathan and I, take our midday meal together, talking of what we had done that morning. My time during the afternoons was for my dear son.

How well I recall these last, happy, Ferndean afternoons. Picture us both: I, so small of stature that already my boy came almost to my shoulder, walking hand in hand with him through the orchard, heavy with fruit, then through the fields and down to the river bank. There I and the bright-haired child who had gladdened my life for every moment of each day of all his six years, walk the river banks, which were fringed with trees on either side, their leaves just beginning to turn from green to red and gold.

As we stroll we see all manner of things to exclaim over – a red squirrel leaping from branch to branch, an otter slipping smoothly from a rock into the water, gliding off, its friendly brown head just above the surface. Then Jonathan scrambles down the bank, through the brambles and bushes, clutching a little pail, and, keeping a precarious balance above the fast-moving stream, mercifully shallow, begins to pluck the juicy black fruit. Then, we wander home together, where he hands his pail to Mary, in the kitchen. She will be sure to make a pie of his fruit for supper, or say that it was made of all he had plucked, even if the amount had turned out to be insufficient.

Jonathan settles to his milk and bun in the kitchen, and afterwards wanders forth to help the gardener, the coachman or the groom with his labours – his, I say, for these important functions are all carried out by the same man, Jeremy, son of Mary and John, our loyal housekeeper and her husband.

Meanwhile my dear Edward and I are taking our tea in the late sunshine of the day at a rustic table I have had put in the garden, beneath the old mulberry – Ah, dear Ferndean, how I loved those last, peaceful days we spent there – all the dearer, for they were so soon to end.

There may be some who will protest – this woman tires us with her continual affirmations of her own peace, happiness and contentment. What has she to say to us, who are leading lives of effort or challenge, ever

attempting to respond to situations not of our making?
What has she to say to those who are over-busy in the
wide world, who have the care of large families, who are
afflicted by sickness or anxieties of many kinds?

To this I respond, my life had not always been as
it was in those days. Imagine me, ten years earlier, at
eighteen, the small, dove-grey figure of a governess, hair
tidied away to invisibility, hands doucely folded before
me, eyes downcast, betraying no expression, a creature
like some timid woodland animal, seeming to seek only
concealment. Imagine this subdued figure. Imagine the
torments within. I was passionately in love, yet knew my
love was impossible, that the object of it could never be
mine. Then imagine that love returned – magnificently
returned. Then think of hopes dashed, desolation, a state
of despair making death seem almost better than life.
Think of flight, loss, poverty, near starvation and then,
almost by chance, the recovery of love . . .

It was through this, tribulation that I, once Jane Eyre,
came to be Jane Rochester, Mrs. Edward Rochester.

I had come to Thornfield Hall – the old Thornfield
– as governess to Adèle, Edward's ward. He did not
appoint me himself; that was done by his housekeeper,
a kinswoman of his, Mrs. Fairfax. I knew nothing of my
employer's existence, nor he of mine, until he, a proud
man on a high-stepping horse, came across me, standing
quietly by a stile.

He has said I was beautiful then, but if so, I did not
know it. In my own eyes I was a slight and insignificant
figure, a veritable mouse. Yet he has told me since, 'I saw
a lovely girl, little more than a child, with great compelling
eyes, full of subdued life and thought (which, though you

tried, my dearest, you failed to conceal from me). This girl's dear face had a delicacy of form and feature such as I had never seen. And I thought, the man who overlooked that face, that form, would be he who would put aside the finest of water-colours in favour of a great daub of an oil painting.'

Yet my Edward says I am better now than in those days, that I have more colour, a flush in a healthy cheek, my brown hair gleams, those grey eyes of mine have more lustre than they had all those years ago. Well, I believe that ten years of happy marriage will make a beauty of any woman, but even now I can see nothing remarkable about myself. 'I would have you continue to believe yourself plain and insignificant, my Jane,' Edward tells me, 'for if you did not, who knows, you might decide to start going out in society and cutting a great figure in the world, and then farewell to tranquillity, farewell to the domination of Edward Rochester over his wife.'

As if he could ever occupy anything but the first position in my heart! As if I could ever seek out the world! I am by nature retiring. Better, I maintain the pleasure of well-loved friends and members of the family than loud and noisy gatherings of people not necessarily loved or admired. At Ferndean our chief visitors were few – our good clergyman, Mr. Weatherfield, and his admirable wife; the worthy Miss Crane, a lady who lived quietly in our village and was the main teacher, other than myself, of the little school I had begun there for the sons and daughters of the rural people. Others were Edward's trusty friend Sir George Lynn, my cousins Diana and Mary and their excellent husbands, Captain Fitzjames and the Revd. Mr. Wharton.

This was all the society we craved, or needed. After we married, at first Edward was too ill to wish for much company – later, when he was recovered and I questioned him as to whether he required more society and entertainment, he replied that the pleasant quietness of our lives had become so agreeable to him he could not contemplate an alteration. Gone was that restlessness which in old days had taken him from place to place, country to country, and which had filled his house with a throng on the rare occasions when he honoured Thornfield with a visit. No longer was he fleeing despair, seeking noise and movement in an attempt to dull an inner pain; now he was a happy man.

And for myself – I wonder, what need has a happy woman of constant society? Certainly I had no such desire – my husband and child were all in all to me, their company all I required for perfect happiness, Indeed, I must confess that after a long visit even from my dear cousins or the best of our friends my heart would begin to yearn again for the quietness and uninterrupted company of my two dear ones.

But I digress. I must bring myself to tell of the past, though it pains me to relate it again. Yet I must, for my own sake and disarm my imaginary critics, those who might be impatient of a catalogue of benefits, rolled out seemingly without thought or consideration for others whose lives are more troubled or difficult, whose burdens sometimes threaten to overwhelm them. Let me return to the painful contemplation of the past, return to when I first met my employer. I did not know him to be so, then discovered he was indeed Edward Rochester, the man with whom I was destined to share a roof during those times when he chose to be at home.

What can I say of that house, Thornfield Hall, where I found myself? It was stately and imposing and yet, from the moment I entered it, I felt some apprehension. Befriended by the worthy Mrs. Fairfax I was ever astonished by the menacing presence of the servant Grace Poole, whose sewing-room, an eyrie on the top floor, was seldom allowed to be entered or approached. I knew nothing, only sensed mystery.

I came to love Edward Rochester, despite his brusqueness and rages, but knew I must hide this from others, often wishing in my heart I could hide that love also from myself, hopeless as it was. Yet there were other times when, bearing within me a love I knew could never be returned I still rejoiced – that Edward was at Thornfield, that there I might see and speak to him daily – simply – that I loved him!

I had believed he could never return that love – yet he did! And confessed his love; we planned to marry. And then came tragedy.

My poor Edward – he should not have tried to deceive me, yet what choice had he? He told me, when he returned home after years of wandering, he found a good, bright creature, clear-eyed, clear-headed, one who, he knew immediately, was capable of reviving his jaded heart, who could help him towards a new life. But this girl, whom he needed so greatly, was forbidden him by law.

Locked in the house guarded by Grace Poole, was the wife he had married when young. She was mad, a bestial creature, unclean and raving, her only thoughts of doing violence to any she came near. I did not know of her existence, nor did even Mrs. Fairfax, but others did, and those included her brother and his representatives. Edward and I were on the verge of marrying, in the church itself – when one stepped forward to denounce the wedding as illegal. Edward had a living wife.

Edward offered me a life as his mistress; I could not accept. I fled into the world, friendless and in despair. I know now how easily I might have perished. But Providence led me to friends, to relatives of whose existence I had not known, even to a modest fortune. And thus I prospered and began to renew my life, though I knew I could never feel joy again, having lost him whom I held most dear.

And then I found him again. I searched, found Thornfield Hall a ruin, burned to the ground by the madwoman. Edward, gravely injured in the fire as he attempted to rescue his wife from the flames, had gone to Ferndean, blind and lacking his right hand. He had decided to end his days there, in a kind of death-in-life. It was at Ferndean that I found him, and vowed never to leave him whether he willed it or not – and there we married and made our lives. So I will tell those who may say I have dwelt too much on my own happiness that it did not come easily. We both, Edward and I, suffered much, before we found content.

That is the past. What had we made of ourselves since, during our ten years at Ferndean? Edward calls me beautiful, and, be that true or false, so long as I am beautiful to him, what matters the rest? I live in his light. Without it I would be plunged in utter darkness.

And Edward, Edward Fairfax Rochester, my Edward? Well he had not lost his dark look; he could even still be harsh, as once he was, but that was seldom those days. When I asked him playfully not long after our marriage why he no longer cried out impatiently or gave his orders in a loud and demanding tone, he said, 'What need, when a man is contented as I am?' That happiness lasted the length of our time at Ferndean.

The house, as I have said, was small, which meant we were prevented from employing any more than dear Mary and John and their son to serve us. I was able therefore to carry out many small but useful tasks myself, taking care of my boy, tending those few precious articles I brought with me on my marriage, an old writing-table from the last century, a set of precious teacups and saucers, fragile as eggshells, which I loved, some old volumes I felt only my own hands could dust and preserve. These tasks I loved.

It was I who planned the garden and planted much of it and later, when my boy was toddling, I began the little village school, where I and good Miss Crane taught by turns. How my heart soared when I saw the children begin to blossom and considered how their lives would be changed by their acquisition of learning.

So diligent was I, even from the first days of our marriage, that one evening, as we sat peacefully in firelight, Edward took up my hand and looked at it, a little reproachfully, I thought, and said gently to me, 'Though I see no signs of harsh toil here, my little dove, I must ask, do you feel truly you must always be working? Sometimes it is your garden, then you will be sewing a shirt for me, now I see you frowning over the accounts. There are days when I wake with the nervous fear I shall walk out to find you on the roof, attaching tiles! I must ask – do you believe Mrs. Rochester must earn her bread by labour? For if you do, I must disillusion you. Mrs. Rochester has no need to earn her bread. She keeps her place by love, by being – just – Jane.'

I smiled, yet I felt a pang. At that time Edward was still a little blind in his one good eye, though his sight was returning. I knew, too, he felt the loss of his right hand, so badly burned when he tried to rescue Bertha Mason from the inferno at Thornfield, that amputation was the only recourse. Edward Rochester, master of Thornfield, was not then, in his own mind, the proud land-owner and mighty figure he had been before.

For this reason, I hastened to tell him, 'Oh, Edward, I wonder, what would you have me do? Should I sit merely enjoying my happiness in a world which has given me so much, or try to make some little contribution to it – sew, or plant a rose bush which will bloom to delight us in a year or so? But if you wish me . . .if you feel' – and here I began to falter. I feared that in my zeal I had not pleased, but indeed had begun to injure, the man to whom I owed all my happiness, he who had created afresh the person I now called Jane. I had been Jane Rochester a year, and, from the moment when I assumed the name, I had begun to transform. That name had brought me out of darkness, loneliness, enforced self-containment into light and warmth. But was I causing distress to the man who had given me so much, my husband?

But all he said to me, smiling, was 'How could I expect you, my Puritan maid, to be happy if you are not useful and active?'

'Do you think I neglect you?'

'Jane,' he said soberly, 'you have been my eyes. You saved me from solitude and misery like to have ended in my death. Now my good eye improves, and my strength and spirit return. You, my heart, would not help me by hovering over me and pressing on me attentions I do not desire, or, if I think I desire them, I do not truly need. The Rochesters have ever been a sturdy, stubborn race. Ask yourself, is it likely that I, their last representative, would be any less so? No, Jane. It was not for a nurse that I married you. Do all you wish. I am recovering. I need you still and will always need you, but I would not have you a slave to me.'

I wept, understanding again the man I had married. Perhaps I had partly feared him in the old days. Now, refined by his suffering, he was that truly great thing, a man strong as a rock and because of that very strength able to be gentle as a woman. He was peering at me through the mist which I knew was always before his eyes. 'I think you weep,' he said. 'You believe you can hide it from a blind old man.'

'You are wicked, Edward,' I told him. 'And what shall I do with you when you recover so fast?'

And he did, indeed, recover quickly, aided by his own strong will. The sight in his eye improved until it became as keen as ever before. He learned, with patient, manly effort, to use his left hand as well as he had once used his right. And gradually the memories of the past faded – their obliteration, I believe, came when the self-styled 'last representative of the Rochesters' discovered that he was no longer entitled to make that claim – when he became himself father of a son.

I ask myself now whether, lapped in happiness and contentment, we should not have spoken more of the past we had both in our separate ways endured. In the pleasantness of day-to-day life, in our constant communication, our shared interests, our delight in each other, it was easy to forget. Yet perhaps there is a price to be paid for turning one's back on those parts of life one would rather ignore. Perhaps when trouble came upon us we were less well equipped to face it than we would have been had we not, for the best of reasons, so firmly put the past behind us.

Mrs Rochester

Were we right in choosing to forget what it would have spoiled our happiness to summon up? Did we purchase a decade of unalloyed happiness by turning away from that which we would have done better to have confronted?

Chapter II

There have been Rochesters at Thornfield for five hundred years. The family had lived in the same house for more than two hundred years before it burned down.

After the fire it lay derelict during the ten happy years of our marriage until, one summer day, Edward said to me gravely at breakfast, 'Jane – will you help me?'

He never said, 'Will you help me?' Often and often I had chided him for this; often and often he had told me he was nothing if he must keep on calling out for help to his wife. Therefore, on hearing his words I smiled, knowing that in reality he did *not* want me to help him. But – 'No, I am in earnest when I say I desire your help, or, at any rate, your company. I plan to go back to Thornfield and wish you to come with me.'

Even then a little chill ran over me, I knew not why, except that the very word Thornfield brought back a flood of memories, countless recollections which, like a river in spate, brought all, twigs, branches, leaves, portions of the river bank, along with it, roaring and tumbling.

I said, 'Is that all the help you need? Too little. Of course I will come. When should you like to go?'

'Now,' he said. 'I have a fancy to go now.'

I rose. 'I will tell Jeremy to harness the horses.'

He smiled up at me, that sweet smile always so surprising in that dark and gypsy face. 'Bless you, Jane. Get some food put up. We will picnic in the old garden.'

That was where, by moonlight, he had vowed his love for me.

And so it happened. Half an hour later we were setting out for Thornfield. Just after midday we were there.

We stood in the tangled, overgrown grass of what had been the stretch of lawn before the house, gazing up at the roofless mansion. How dreary it all was, its destruction and dereliction seeming, perhaps, even sadder under bright sunshine. The back wall only was intact, and a corner and part of another wall. Grass and weeds grew from cracks in the smoke-blackened bricks.

The interior of the house was heaped with bricks, beams and other masonry, in piles as high as a man. These were the rooms, galleries and passageways where once we had trod. Grass grew from the piles of rubble. Through the clumps one could see, here, the charred end of a beam, there, a black rag of cloth which might once have a curtain or a hanging, elsewhere a fused and charred mass of brick, a heap of broken roof-tiles, blackened by smoke.

The last time I had seen Thornfield I had been too concerned for Edward to comprehend, truly, the sight of this destruction. The last time I had seen it, too, the damage had been fresh. Now the ruins of almost a decade seemed even sadder and more pitiful. I had not always been happy at Thornfield, but the sight of its present state filled me with melancholy.

Through these rooms little Adèle had run, curls flying. Through those often overpowering rooms I had paced, a girl trying to achieve womanly dignity at that time when the girl must surrender to the woman she is to be. In that house my dearest Edward had grown up. I turned from the ruin with a tear in my eye gazing, in an attempt not to weep openly, down over the lawn and across to the walled garden. That wall had broken down over the years, or perhaps been plundered for bricks. Through it I saw the overgrown beds, barely recognisable now as such. I noted the little statue of Cupid which stood by the pond, streaked and dirty now. Yet the trees in the orchard, visible over the unbroken portion of the wall, were green and vital and there were ripening apples, plums and pears on their branches. It was here, at dawn, that Edward and I had walked, and he had declared, to my joy and incredulity, his fatal, impossible love.

'Ah, Edward,' I said. 'Look, the apples are ripening in the garden.'

He smiled down at me. 'I saw your tear,' he said, 'the tear you tried to hide from me. Yes – the trees thrive in spite of neglect in that garden where you told me you loved me and I confessed my love for you. You were happy, were you not?'

'Oh yes, yes, Edward,' said I, remembering only his warm gaze upon me, his tender kiss, and not the later hurt.

He embraced me. 'You weep for Thornfield. Yet you need not. You have only to say the word,' he murmured into my hair.

So close to him, his arm about me, my face turned up to his, I realised his intention. Of course he wished to rebuild Thornfield, his family's ancestral home. To do so would be not just the indulgence of a personal desire but an act of family duty, of piety towards the dead, a promise to the living. Yet I knew, clearly and absolutely at that moment, that I did not want to return to Thornfield. I knew, too, that so great was my husband's love for me, I might succeed in influencing him not to rebuild the house.

'You would like to come back here?' he asked. 'Back to Thornfield?'

I replied, 'Of course, Edward. If you wish it.'

'No, my dearest. Not because I wish it. You must wish it too, or the pleasure will be gone.'

I knew that what he said was true, that his happiness depended much on mine. If I opposed his plan, for reasons I would hardly be able, candidly, to state – for how could I tell him how sad and frightened I had been at Thornfield, without reviving that past we had silently agreed to forget? – he would do as I asked. He would leave the house as it was, or cause the ruin to be demolished. But he would be disappointed, would see my opposition as a whim, not worthy of me. He might judge me not only as a wife failing to assist in the revival of the family grandeur, but as a mother depriving her son of his part in it.

In one moment, I saw all this. And knew that, above all, I did not want to disappoint my husband. Against my will I must support the plan to rebuild Thornfield. Yet even then I could not lie to him. I tightened my arms about him and gazed into his black eyes. 'Wherever you are, my darling, is my home.'

He put me away, to arm's length. 'Modest Jane,' he laughed. 'Will you ever demand anything for yourself – for yourself alone?'

'Only your love,' I pronounced boldly.

And there outside the ruined shell of the house Edward Rochester of Thornfield kissed me.

And it was done. Plans were drawn up, master craftsmen found and instructed. In a little over a year after the work began, the house was almost ready. My husband had caused it to be rebuilt, stone by stone, brick by brick, beam by heavy beam, an exact replica of the house as it had been before.

Before the year ended we would be living in that grand house, ready to entertain more widely, to cut a figure in the county, become, in very truth, the Rochesters of Thornfield.

Yet, I confess it, throughout that perfect late summer and early autumn at Ferndean, while they brought in first the hay and then the corn, while we culled our fruit and rejoiced in our late-blooming roses, my heart sank lower and lower in my breast. It was not the thought of entering into a grandeur I had never sought or wanted, nor of the entertainments which would be expected of us as owners of one of the great houses of the county. No, what afflicted me was a dread of returning to Thornfield.

What was Thornfield to me? It was the house where I had experienced terror, despair, loneliness, hopeless longing, then great hope, which alas had been followed brutally by equally great despair. I had entered that house a young and inexperienced girl. At my first sight of it I felt a chill, awed by its great size and sensing it contained something to fear. I had put these feelings aside as a fantasy, but alas too soon learned that Thornfield contained mysteries, the worst of them being that upstairs, behind a hidden door, was kept in concealment that dangerous woman, Bertha Mason. I seldom call her Edward's wife, give her the name I proudly bear, that of Mrs. Edward Rochester. Yet, it must be told – as a young man he had in the Caribbean married this inheritor of a family madness, not knowing enough of her or her family.

Poor Edward – lonely sufferer of an unbearable marriage. The fault was not his, but that of the law, which will not allow a man or woman to rid themselves of a partner hopelessly insane and with no possible hope of recovery. A man may be shackled to a wife as they chain convicts together. She may be insane, no true wife, her very presence abominable to him, yet he cannot get free, must live alone, without the consolations of marriage, until death releases one or the other of them.

If he loves, the only fulfilment open to him is to turn the woman who should have been his bride into his mistress, and the children who should have been his pride and borne his name into creatures of shame. And all this in the name of indissoluble vows taken before God. We may ask, what kind of a God it is who will permit one spouse to live all his life in wretchedness because the other is afflicted?

And yet – how often in the long lonely days after I fled the house did I not find myself secretly, regretting, that that marriage service, mockery as it would have been had not taken place without interruption. For then, wrong though it would have been, we should have been together, come what may. But once I knew we were not permitted to marry the hard choice was mine. Was I to become a creature little better than the depraved Céline Varens, mother of Adèle, and sustain perhaps in the end a fate like hers, a slow slide down from depravity to depravity, ending in the gutter? Or was I to preserve that female integrity which is more valuable than life itself? If so, I must go into the wilderness, the dark, the cold, which was all life without Edward Rochester could offer me. And I forced myself to go.

Such were my memories of Thornfield. I could not look back on those days with pleasure and contentment. True, they had brought me, ultimately, my happy marriage, the ideal life I led. But oh, the agonies of the past!

Though all storms were over and calm happiness prevailed, I could not rid myself of my superstitious fear of the return to Thornfield though I made every effort to conceal my doubts and fears from my husband and I truly believe he did not detect them.

As the house went up I continually reasoned with myself; the old days were over and could not return; in any event, this Thornfield was not the old one. Though it was a replica of the original building in every respect, it was brick, stone and beam, entirely new from its roof to its cellars. The walls of that little room at the back of the house in which I had slept alone at Thornfield no longer contained their stony memories of the secret intrusion of the madwoman on the very night of my wedding – the wedding that was not to be – and of her rending my veil as I lay, half waking, half sleeping. The upper storey where she had been kept prisoner, the very battlements from which she had thrown herself during the fire were not the same. The fabric was new, all new. The furnishings would be different – chosen by me to suit my taste; even the books on the library shelves would be different. The old poisons had gone when the house burned – so I told myself.

I reminded myself of the many compensations the move to Thornfield would bring – the chance to select new furnishings, hangings, paints and papers for the house, the old garden to restore, for it had grown wild over the years the house had stood abandoned. Yet, all the same, my heart failed me. Might we, I had timidly suggested to

21

Edward, at least rid the thorn field beyond the garden of some of those gnarled and twisted hawthorns, some forty of them, which crowded it?

Beyond the house and its pleasant garden, aromatic in summer with scents of flowers and ripening fruit, there lay a four-acre field, stony and rising. There grew the trees I have described, stunted and wind-bent, their grey trunks patched with brown. It was, of course, the prevalence of these harsh trees in the locality, and their age-old colonisation of the field adjacent to the house, that gave the house its name. In spring the branches were frothy with blossom, in spite of their age, in summer they were a dense green, but in winter, their stark and twisted forms were bare, the scoured trunks and branches under moonlight, seeming almost malign, the bony branches coming out at accusing angles, like pointing fingers. That field was ever a sore sight to me, though it was visible from the house only from a few windows at one side. Still I knew it was there, stark and angry, mocking joy and hope.

I even submitted to my lord, like some aspiring manager of the estate, a plan to clear the thorn field and lay it out with broad-leafed trees, to divert the stream to make a pool. But, 'No, Jane,' said Edward when I suggested my plan. His voice was tender, but firm. 'Plain, nay, ugly as they seem, those trees are the very spirit and essence of Thornfield Hall. It is from that field the house gets its name. In the old days they were used to say that if the trees were ever to die or be destroyed, it would mark the end of the family at Thornfield. Those trees are the symbol of our origins in older, harsher times which we must not forget. Long ago, they say, one hard winter after a succession of bad harvests the family only sustained itself by collecting from the branches of the thorns wool the sheep had left behind, and by cutting some of the trees and burning them as fuel.

'You see, Jane, a great family has the habit of remembering its noble deeds – this lord killed in the Crusades, another a prized servant of old Queen Elizabeth, another a general under Wellington. Such recollections are right and natural. But it behoves such a family to remember its poorer, harder times and therefore, my love, I must keep my thorny field as it is so as to retain my humility and ever remember the blessings heaped upon me – not the least of which is you, Jane, my little Jane.'

And with that he embraced me so warmly, and I was so struck by the reasons he gave for not doing as I wished, that I put aside my desire to see the stony field emptied of those twisted trees. I acquiesced, thinking, well, at least I will cover those windows which overlook the field with heavy net and damask. I will make sure little of it can be seen from the windows of the house.

However, as I have said, I allowed, none of my thoughts concerning the thorn field or of the house itself to escape me, seeing only my husband's great desire to reside again where his family had lived for generations and to pass it in turn to his son, my Jonathan. For his sake, I knew, I must become the contented mistress of Thornfield and do the position honour. A small price, I reflected, during that last happy time at dear old Ferndean, to pay for all my other contents.

Let us in imagination leave me there, at Ferndean in that long, low, warm-bricked house, on the lawn below the mulberry with my dear Edward – leave me at that moment when I was happy (and I had then, in early autumn, even more reason, or so I was beginning to believe, for happiness). Leave me in sunshine, with the birds going to roost, and Edward's hand straying across the gap between us to join with mine; leave the lengthening shadows across the lawn. Let me now take you to people I did not then know and to scenes where I was not. Over the last months I have painfully reconstructed this story for myself, until now I feel as if I had indeed been there to witness the arrival in England of two persons, two women, whose coming was to have such a strange and dreadful effect on our lives.

Chapter III

There were two ladies alone in the private cabin of the ship making its crossing from France to England on that September night.

The crossing had been rough. One of the passengers lay, very pale, on the red plush couch as the ship pitched, her white hand, which bore a large ruby ring, pressed to her brow. This ring was the only colour about her. On the heavy coils of jet-black hair was a small lace cap. She wore a dress of black silk, of very good cut. Her face was oval, her nose long, her eyes, gazing now into those of the other woman, very black, fringed with long dark lashes.

The second lady sponged the brow of the first and murmured to her consolingly in French, 'Not long now, Justine, before we shall be in port.' This woman's hair was loose over her shoulders and russet in colour. In comparison with her companion, she seemed like some exotic bird in her long, loose gown of dark red brocade.

The sea voyage which had so badly affected her companion appeared to have given her vigour – there was a flush of colour in her cheeks and her almond eyes, set in a charming, oval face, were very bright. She gently raised her friend's head from the pillow and gave her a sip of water.

A third woman, by her dress a maid, came in and spoke. 'Did you hear, Justine?' said the lady in red. 'Marie tells us they say we will be at Dover in an hour.'

'And thank God for it,' said the other feelingly.

Nevertheless, by the time a faint light was appearing in the tumbling skies to the east she evidently felt well enough to go on deck. The two, cloaked together under a long sable belonging to the woman in red, stood by the rail, looking forward, the deck rolling under them.

'There – see!' cried the black-clad lady, Justine. She pointed with her long, white hand, on which the ruby seemed to gleam in the darkness. 'See! The famous white cliffs of Dover.'

'Soon we shall be in England. And I wonder what fate that very strange country will bring us.'

'For you it will be fame, my dear,' said the lady in black. 'Of that I am sure. As for me, all I require of England is – justice.' She spoke the word with passion.

The other drew the cloak a little more firmly about them both. In her low, clear voice she said warningly, 'Yes, my dear. But – and however much I sympathise with your natural desire for justice against the man who has wronged you so deeply – I pray you, do not confuse justice with revenge.'

'Sometimes,' responded the other, 'I think in reality there may be very little difference.'

Morning saw them speeding through bright countryside by train. In London they parted, one to begin what was to be a triumphant season on the London stage, the other to go north and settle in Hay, a village not two miles from Thornfield Hall.

Chapter IV

That fatal voyage marked the beginning of the bad times which came to us, like a sickness or a plague.

While we were yet at Ferndean Edward went away to Manchester on business – and with a commission from me to search out the purveyors of some rare and beautiful fabrics of which I had heard. It was then that I decided to go to Thornfield for the first time since the rebuilding had begun. I went not because I would, but because I must.

I knew I must summon up my courage and visit the nearly completed house before the day when we were to move into it. I must face this alone in case my first sight of the new Thornfield caused me to flinch or seem unhappy. I could not let my husband, ever attentive to my moods and thoughts – until sometimes I would have sworn him a gypsy or a mind-reader – see anything but joy on my face as I took in the sight of our new home. Therefore I resolved to make my first visit a solitary one, to prepare myself.

Remember, I had seen the house only twice during the previous ten years. The first occasion was when I had gone to Thornfield to get news of Edward – to be confronted by the sight of the house gutted by fire and learn that he had nearly lost his precious life there.

The second time was when Edward told me he wished to rebuild the house. And now – it was nearly ready.

Early that morning I ordered Jeremy to harness the carriage, kissed my boy farewell and set out, summoning up all my resolution. By midday we were passing through Hay and taking the narrow road to Thornfield, two miles further on. As we progressed I told myself, this Thornfield Hall is not the old one. This Thornfield will be the home you, Jane, make for your husband and children. Leaving the carriage at the foot of the drive I walked up to the house and stood on the overgrown grass of the lawn.

There it was – Thornfield, in every particular the same house I had timidly entered, on my first day as Adèle's governess. I found myself gazing at it searchingly, hoping to discover changes – but changes there were none. Thornfield was the same. In response to some alarm no doubt, the rooks in the elms behind it went up, whirling and cawing in the blue sky above the trees.

The trees in the orchard to my right were losing their leaves. Far behind the house, nearly a mile off, I could see the long grass on the foothills was browning. A wind began to blow and I pulled my cloak about me.

I knew that, inside, the house was virtually complete. Yet I did not, now, want to enter it and see whether the effect of lightness and freshness I had planned was working to cheer the intimidating grandeur of the place. The old Thornfield had been impressive, but formidable, creating an atmosphere in which it was impossible to imagine children growing up healthy and happy. This melancholy effect had been offset by the efforts Mrs. Fairfax, had made to mitigate its gloom, but no effort could, I think, have changed the atmosphere of the house sufficiently. And then there was Grace Poole, the servant set to guard the madwoman in absolute secrecy. What household containing that strange, surly woman, carrying her secret burden all the while, could have been truly at ease?

My eyes went involuntarily towards the third storey of the building. Though smaller than the rest of the house, being under the roof, it was by no means an attic floor; the rooms were too large to be so described. There was a corridor there, on one side of which the servants had slept. On the other side had been Grace Poole's quarters and her sewing-room. Behind the sewing-room there had been a door masked by a hanging – and behind that hidden door the madwoman was kept. There she had crouched, filthy, her hair hanging round her in disorder, for she would not suffer it to be touched, living like a beast as furious thoughts of violence circled in her disordered mind. The servants must have known of her existence, or of the existence of something in that room. But Mrs. Fairfax, I am sure, had not.

I had recently written to her in her place of retirement, where she lived on a small pension supplied to her by my husband. In my letter I requested her to become, once more, housekeeper at Thornfield. I asked this because I considered I would need her to help me manage this new and far greater household, where we would certainly be entertaining more often and on a far grander scale than at Ferndean, and there was another, more important reason – and that was that I believed by next spring my time would be less my own than I had thought. Yes – I hoped, but dared not hope, quite yet, that the dearest desire Edward and I had entertained since the birth of our son was about to be fulfilled, that Jonathan would soon be blessed by the presence of a brother or sister. As high summer turned to autumn I had begun to wonder whether this most wonderful gift had been given to me, if I was to be a mother again. Now, I was almost sure.

I hoped my dear Mrs. Fairfax would leave her chosen seclusion and come back to Thornfield with me. I would need her, I thought, and her company while Edward was away. For, little as he wished for any separations, he was sometimes obliged to leave to attend to his business affairs in Manchester or on some occasions travel as far as London. I had known fear in that house before and, though reason told me all cause of fear had gone, some little superstitious feeling made me crave a friend to rely on when my husband was compelled to be absent.

From inside the house came the sound of banging. Two men emerged from the front door carrying a ladder. They observed me, nodded and called a greeting, imagining, no doubt, I was some curious person come to see how work on the house was progressing. They did not know me, nor did I make myself known. I had come to prepare myself for the sight of the new Thornfield and I had done so. That was enough.

The men put the ladder up to a ground-floor window and began to paint the woodwork around it. Meanwhile I stood, as if transfixed, the wind growing chillier, gazing at those mournful upper windows behind which had lain that creature who had caused me so much pain. And I suddenly felt her malignity blowing about me again, like another wind, and thought that, even though she was dead, something of her remained at Thornfield. I reflected that never, in all the ensuing years, had I wondered where she was buried. She should have been consumed in the flames of the house she burned, I found myself thinking, burned on the pyre she had made for herself.

It might have been the strength of this feeling which caused me to shudder – it might have been the chill wind. At all events I determined to return as soon as possible to the kindly safety of Ferndean.

Thornfield had risen from the ashes, sound and renewed. Yet one may enter any house, be it grand or humble, and find within it a cold grate, a savage dog, an enemy. Suddenly I felt Thornfield was awaiting me like a fierce beast poised to spring. Jane, Jane, I admonished myself, this house's past is done, you and you alone will create its future. So I encouraged myself and then thought, yes, yes, I will – I will make the new Thornfield as I wish. And in this mood I left, unrecognised by any as the future mistress of the house, and found my carriage waiting at the foot of the drive.

One further pilgrimage lay before me. Asking Jeremy to wait, I took the rough road leftwards, away from the village, and stood by a gate in a hedge, looking into the thorn field.

They had cut the hay. Rough grass was growing up through the stubble. I looked up that large and sloping field where, scattered as they had grown, were the forty twisted thorn trees, still in leaf. Not a bird or a beast stirred. The rising wind sighed and shook the branches of the trees and, as if to emphasise the desolation of the place, a cloud came across the sun.

To one side of this field lay the oaks and elms which edged the wall of the Thornfield gardens. Higher, where the clouds were creating long fingers of light and shade across the high hills, were mountains. Gazing over the thorn field, I could not prevent myself from imagining it in winter when those white trunks and branches, twisted and spiky, were without the masking of leaves, when the grass below the trees was sere and the sky black overhead. I shuddered. If only, I thought ruefully, in years gone by some old Rochester had taken it into his head to cut down the trees – but he had not and now, tradition being what it was, no man could, nor woman either. I turned away and walked back to the carriage, not happy, but braver for having confronted and taken the measure of the house and that ancient thorn field.

Great as was my desire to return to the comfort and welcome of Ferndean and see my boy again, for at that time we were rarely apart for many hours, I could not leave the neighbourhood without calling on the clergyman in the village of Hay, some two miles off. I did not look forward to the encounter with Mr. Todd, for though he and I had long been acquainted, for he had paid some visits to Ferndean, the acquaintance could not have been described as a happy one. For my part I found him too little a man of the parish. He was a plump man, always in a good black coat and spotless linen, greatly fond of vestments and decorated altars, a man more easily to be found dining at a good table in the neighbourhood than visiting the poor in their cottages. He was unmarried; a housekeeper, Mrs. Willows, presided over his comfortable household and his well-supplied table.

I must confess, though, I was uncertain how much of my cold feeling towards Mr. Todd stemmed from what he must have heard of that most terrible of days, when his predecessor stood at his altar, ready to conduct my first, sad mockery of a marriage, attended by no friends, no relatives, no neighbours – and cruelly interrupted by Bertha Mason's brother and his lawyer, making the hideous revelation that she was alive and concealed, mad, at Thornfield.

Oh, my poor, desperate Edward. In the first years of our marriage he told me, 'You could not, thank God, even imagine the kind of life to which a man with a wife such as mine was tempted to descend. I started on that path – that vicious path – I could not go on. Only you, Jane, could save me.'

And mercifully, that is what I was able to do, if indeed I did, and I am absolutely confident that he saved me, from loneliness and desolation and gave me a life happier than I could ever have dreamed.

How different was my true wedding at Ferndean. We took the quiet walk through summer lanes to the flower-decked village church, Edward and I together, I on his strong, good arm, and he leaning towards me, for I was at that time his eyes. A quiet wedding we had. I had no attendants; he no groomsman. Mr. Weatherfield and his clerk alone were present. I myself gave my hand in marriage to Edward, for there was none other to do so.

My only male relative, St. John Rivers, was in India on missionary work – had he not been, perhaps he might have wished to give me to Edward. St. John had himself offered me marriage before he left for India, while I was still separated from Edward and did not, in fact, know where he was or even if he lived. But my feeling for Edward Rochester transcended all – even if I had known for certain he was dead, the fact that he had once existed, that I had loved him, would have prevented me from marrying my cousin St. John.

And so we walked to church on that sunny day and were married by the good Mr. Weatherfield. We returned to a modest wedding breakfast at Ferndean, all laughter and good humour. How happy I was! I believed I could never be more happy; yet, next day, joy was transformed into ecstasy, an ecstasy which in quieter form has been with me ever since, every day of my marriage. What can one say of such loving companionship, such passion, such loyalty and meeting of minds? The bliss can scarcely be made real to those who have not experienced it, yet so it was between myself and Edward.

And at Hay I knew I must confront the man who must have been aware of all the details of that attempted marriage which destroyed all my hope, and, so far as I knew then, had destroyed it for the rest of my life.

Now, however, we were to return. I was to be mistress of Thornfield and I had reasons to compel myself to visit the Reverend Mr. Todd.

Hay is reached from Thornfield by a road of no merit, in winter scarcely better than a track. Halfway from Thornfield the land rises and then one can see from the eminence the village itself strung out along the road and spreading on one side halfway up the hill. On this rising ground are a few poor farms and some of the lead-miners' cottages. To the other side of the road, where the land is level and richer, lies the better part of the village. This doubles back towards Thornfield, on a road which is like a kind of horse-shoe, and includes some good smallholdings, substantial houses, the rectory and, of course, the church itself. The church, lying halfway between the village and Thornfield Hall, can be reached either by the road or by walking the lane across the fields from the house. This path, though, I would not take. It was the way we had walked on my first wedding day. I did not wish to revive the memory.

So I drove to Hay, where the return of my coach caused

as much excitement – coming to cottage doors, turning, staring – as it had when we went through on the way to Thornfield. Two little boys, black from their heads to their bare feet, stood, dirty fingers in their mouths, to watch us go. A woman with a flapping hen clutched by its scrawny legs stood and stared through her open door. There were little children round her feet on a mud floor. As my carriage passed, one man in a group outside the inn spat on the ground.

I was pleased to round the corner that would take us to the pleasanter pastures of Lower Hay. We passed a well-kept farmhouse, a tidy field of sheep, then a small collection of neat cottages, with well-tended gardens, full of vegetables, brightened by a few Michaelmas daisies. We reached the village of Lower Hay, which consisted, on one side of the road, of a post office and a small general store. There were also several good houses opposite the church, which was itself surrounded by a well-kept churchyard. Next to it lay the rectory.

This was a commodious house of red brick with a large garden in front and, I believed, half an acre of useful ground at the back. As we drove up I noted the portly figure of Mr. Todd, who was talking to his gardener and gesturing up at the elms which separated his dwelling from the church grounds. Seeing my carriage he broke off and hurried towards it. The blue eyes in his red face opened wide as he watched Jeremy open the carriage door and help me down. At first, I believe, he could not quite credit what he saw. Then recognition dawned and, his mouth opening in an 'Oh', he hurried forward to greet me, little Jane Eyre, once humble governess at Thornfield, now Mrs. Edward Rochester.

I advanced, smiling as composedly as I could. Mr.

Todd, his heavy chin quivering above his clerical stock, arranged his face hurriedly and began to beam, coming towards me with hand outstretched. 'Mrs. Rochester! Mrs. Rochester – I cannot believe this! I am honoured. Do, please, come into the house with me. We are not ready for you, alas. If only you had let me know – but nevertheless, how delighted I am that you chose to call. You will overlook our shortcomings I am sure. Enter, I pray you.' And he bowed me in, all smiles and civility, smothering me, as we went through his charming little hall into his drawing-room, with honeyed words and compliments.

I entered, responding as agreeably as possible, for I knew I must maintain good relations with Mr. Todd if I was to fulfil my coming duties as mistress of Thornfield. And that was the reason for my visit.

For do not believe I was unmoved by the wretchedness in Hay, or wished to take my ease at Thornfield as if I had nothing better to think of than upholstery, invitations and dresses. I would be leaving the school I had founded at Ferndean in the capable hands of Miss Crane, but no power on earth would stop me from using my position to help the folk of Hay to the best of my poor abilities. In order to do this it was necessary to be on good terms with Hay's vicar.

Mr. Todd urged me into a seat. He called for Madeira and biscuits, though I requested only a cup of tea, and he begged me to remain until luncheon. He made no allusion to our past, merely saying, 'I am so happy to see the great position you have been called to.' Then he exclaimed with joy at the prospect of our removal back to Thornfield.

I sat on throughout, saying little but what politeness demanded, Mr. Todd making up for both of us in the way of conversation. Some might term me hypocrite; certainly I would always desire complete frankness and confidentiality among friends; anything less makes for a life without value. Yet, as I have said, though Mr. Todd was not my friend and I did not conceive that he ever would be, what politeness I showed him was a means to a higher end. For the sake of the future I felt I must put all thoughts of the past, as well as my mistrust of him, behind me.

There was want, distress and ignorance in Hay and, although much can be done by the mistress of the neighbourhood's most important house, even if the vicar is no friend, a great deal more can be achieved if they are on good terms. Consequently I made myself as pleasant as I could. It was plain that Mr. Todd desired to dine at Thornfield when we returned. I extended that invitation. He glowed with pleasure. I returned his smile. What a difference ten years of happy marriage will make – what confidence it imparts. Even the confidence to play the hypocrite, thought I, wryly. I was on the verge of making my farewells when a maid came in, somewhat excited, and said, 'Sir – I am sorry to interrupt you but Mrs. Willows thought you would like to know folk are moving into Old House.'

'Good Heavens!' Mr. Todd exclaimed. 'How astonishing! That house has stood empty for ten years. I knew nothing of this.' He took a pace towards the door as if unable to prevent himself from rushing out to look, then pulled himself up and told me, 'Old House is the residence opposite to this. It has been empty since the gentleman who owns it went to Italy for his health.'

I stood up. 'Well, let me not detain you any longer, Mr. Todd. It has been very pleasant to visit you, and no doubt we shall be seeing much more of each other once we are back at Thornfield.'

'I look forward to it,' he said, half bowing, but I detected still his restless desire to see what was afoot at Old House, as a child will drop one toy, eager to play with a newer one. He would have done better, thought I, to have gone out among the lead-miners, who were probably nearly as ignorant of the Gospels as any Indian my cousin St. John was attempting to convert. Or getting up a fund to provide shoes for the barefoot children of Hay. But there, Mr. Todd was a shallow man.

In the street outside the rectory a dispute had begun between Jeremy and one of the drivers of two heavy drays. This man was trying to draw up his vehicle outside Old House, which I now perceived to be a large and graceful building with long, plain windows on either side of a porticoed door, after the Georgian style. The present difficulty was that one dray was already stationary outside the house, while the second man wished to pull up his own waggon alongside the first. This was prevented by the presence of my waiting carriage. I put a stop to the dispute by shortening my farewells to Mr. Todd and ascending into my carriage, ready to depart. Even as I did so, he glanced over my shoulder to see what goods were being removed from the dray already being unloaded outside Old House.

We had gone only a quarter of a mile down the road back to Hay, when round a bend in the road a handsome black open carriage drawn by two fine horses came racing towards us at a cracking pace. This apparition was startling – Jeremy uttered an exclamation – but to my eyes the most astonishing feature of the scene was that the driver aloft on the seat above the horses, wielding her whip over their backs – most expertly, so far as I could tell – was a lady! Dressed all in black, she wore no bonnet, but had a piece of white lace over her head and tied about her throat and this streamed off behind her as she came. I saw an erect figure, swaying with the vehicle and not at all discommoded by the speed at which she was travelling, the line of a long and emphatic nose – then no more.

Jeremy had been forced to pull our horses over on to the verge of the road to let the lady and her carriage go by. When I swung round I saw only the rear of her vehicle disappearing in a cloud of dust. As Jeremy drove the horses back on to the road I wondered, was this bold creature the new tenant of Old House?

And so I returned to the refuge of Ferndean. But safe refuge it was no longer.

Chapter V

Dear Ferndean stood in darkness as I descended from my carriage and approached the door. While I was disappointed that Edward had not yet returned, I was glad that when he did so I would be there to greet him. Mary, opening the door to me reported unceremoniously, 'There's soup and cold meat for you in the dining-room and master sent word he'd be home in an hour.'

'And Jonathan?' I asked.

'Been a lamb all day, bar falling in the stream deliberate, and now sleeps the sleep of the just,' she told me.

'The stream?' I questioned.

'That weren't no accident, though he fibbed and said it were.'

'Well,' said I, 'we shall speak of this in the morning.' I gave her my cloak.

My heart was leaping at the thought of Edward's return. How absurd it seems for one to await the return of a husband of ten years' standing with all the excitement of a girl attending a lover, yet that was what I ever did when Edward was away.

Only an hour, and he would be back, thought I with

delight, and then crept upstairs to my son's small bed-room.

And there he lay, my Jonathan, one soft hand beneath his soft cheek, and spread across his face a lock of golden hair, which I gently moved. How strange it was that dark Edward and I should have for a son this apple-cheeked cherub, golden of head and blue of eye. In one hand he clutched a small, carved wooden horse, his friend and familiar, the favourite toy from the collection of farm animals he loved so much.

I stood for a little while beside his bed, my heart filled with joy at his existence and rejoicing more that if my hopes were fulfilled next year my dearest boy would have a brother or sister, my husband another son or a daughter. For a long month and more, I had been checking my own hopes but now, I thought, now, surely I could say to myself, would be able to tell Edward – yes, yes, it is true. We will have another child. Was any woman ever so blessed? thought I, and with one last look at my sleeping child I went on to the landing.

I paused, thinking I heard Edward's voice in the hall. I decided he must have come in when I was in Jonathan's room but evidently rather quietly. His usual manner was to enter the house like a hurricane, calling for me as soon as the front door was opened to him. Instead I heard Mary say, in a low tone, 'I'll take your coat, sir,' and a muttered response from him.

Surprised, I ran to the head of the stairs calling, 'Edward!' and started to descend rapidly.

But although I had heard my husband's voice it was not Edward who came out of the shadows of the hall and advanced to the foot of the stairs, gazing up at me with dead, expressionless eyes. Oh, those eyes, how well

I remembered them! There below me, as I looked down in utter shock, was a figure horribly familiar from earlier days, even from the nightmares which had haunted me during the early years of my marriage, until daily love and security quieted my fears.

How bad she looked – standing there in a hempen dress which fell in skimpy folds over her wasted figure, the uneven hem revealing rags of stockings and boots cracked across the top. She had a miserable, worn tartan shawl about her shoulders. Some of her hair, knotted roughly at the nape of her neck had escaped and hung lankly on her shoulders. She was the very figure of a beggar in the street, and in that pale and sallow face her great, pitiless eyes burned like coals. I saw she hated me.

My head spun – why was she here, back to haunt me? It was Grace Poole standing at the foot of my own stairs at Ferndean. I was dizzy. I fell.

Chapter VI

I lay in my room for four long weeks after that, seriously ill and in danger of losing my child – perhaps, said the doctor, even my own life.

A fortnight passed, during which I was conscious only occasionally of the attentions of my good Mary and the nurse brought in to care for me, and of my dear Edward, patiently beside me. But oh, my nights were tormented by thoughts of that dreadful vision of Grace Poole, standing in the hall, her eyes blazing upwards into mine. Sometimes I thought it had been nothing but a vision, precursor of my illness. At others I knew, all too well it was no vision: the woman had indeed been there that night, in my house.

Yet slowly, weakness, fear and bad dreams abated. One morning, I awoke a little better, to see sunshine coming through my window, and hear reassuringly the sounds of the household coming to life below. I thought of Edward, who had been so loyally attentive during my illness. I luxuriated in the sensation of recovery. All might yet be well with me and my coming child, I thought. But then, what of Grace Poole? Even as I asked myself that question, there came a quiet knock at the door and in she stepped, bearing my breakfast-tray. She was still gaunt and pale, but now wore a plain dress and white apron and her greying hair was neatly arranged. My head swam; I turned my head on the pillow closing my eyes. Awful recollections filled my head of that spare, intimidating figure, severe and sinister, haunting the house at Thornfield. I remembered her standing by as the dishevelled madwoman attacked her own brother.

A voice, hard and level, was in my ears. 'You seem better, madam. Will you take some food?'

'No. No, go – leave me,' I murmured.

'Very well,' came that unsympathetic voice. And she went.

Dear God, thought I, what can she be doing here?

Later Edward came. Accustomed, I suppose, to seeing me very ill, barely conscious of my surroundings – though never, I think, during the course of my illness was I completely unaware of him during the hours he spent at my bedside – he was surprised to see me look at him, smile, speak, utter his name. 'Edward – Oh, my dear love. Edward.'

He bent over me, seized my hand and bent to kiss my brow. There were tears in his eyes as he sat down beside me still holding my hand.

'You are better! Oh, Jane, the worst is over, is it not?'

'I believe it is.'

For a little while, we spoke of our son and Edward told me of all the small events which had taken place while I was ill. So delighted was I to be well and united again with Edward in spirit that I had no heart to ask about Grace Poole, scarcely thought of her. The nurse came then, and bustled my husband from the room.

'Do not let Mrs. Poole come to me, though,' I said. 'I will have Mary and only Mary.'

'These instructions will please Mary – John, too,' the nurse quietly told me. 'For Mary dearly wished to attend you, and said none would do but she, but Mrs. Poole would not have it.'

'And so Mrs. Poole has been with me over these weeks?' I asked, and I am sure there was dread in my voice.

'Yes, from time to time, though never when you were conscious of her presence, so far as I know,' responded the nurse.

'Henceforth let it be Mary alone,' I commanded and then, overtaken by weakness, knew no more for a time.

Later, the doctor came and pronounced me better, though still frail and in need of much rest. I had insisted on being raised up on my pillows and had seen my boy, and now Edward came again. I almost dreaded to ask him what Grace Poole was doing in the house as a servant and moreover giving instructions to the others. Plainly she was there because he had ordered it. But why? I asked myself. Surely the last thing he could ever have wished was for the presence of that woman, a reminder of the dark days of the past.

So, we spoke of the progress at Thornfield – nearly ready, he said – and of our boy's latest escapade (he and Mr. Weatherfield's son chased by a bull!) but he said nothing of Grace Poole and nor did I until, timidly, I asked him, 'But, Edward – why is Mrs. Poole here, in the house?'

He replied earnestly, 'Jane, I found that poor woman in a street in Manchester, starving. After leaving Thornfield she went back to her brother, who, as you know, was in charge of an asylum, and there got employment. But when he died the new incumbent took a dislike to her and discharged her. She sank, Jane, she sank and finally, savings gone, became destitute. I was riding towards the mill when I saw her plodding along, in the rain, a pitiable figure indeed. I stopped merely to give a stranger, as I thought, something, a few coins, to relieve her immediate wants. Imagine my horror to find my old servant ragged and starving, utterly forlorn! Of course, Jane, after the fire and when gravely injured, I had not thought of Mrs. Poole's fate. But now – I ask you, Jane, what could I do? What would you have had me do?'

I murmured, 'I do not know. But she was hardly true to her trust, when she was your servant, Edward. It was through her negligence the tragedy occurred.' I said no more, unwilling to violate our unspoken agreement not to refer to those old, bad times. Nevertheless, Edward knew well, as I did, that it was Grace Poole's liking for drink which had caused her, more than once, to fall asleep and allow Bertha Mason to escape her room. In reality she had been the cause of the fire at Thornfield and the agent of my husband's injuries, for had she not permitted the madwoman to escape there would have been no fire, and therefore no attempted rescue of the madwoman by Edward and no injuries to him. Though Edward might generously overlook this, I could not.

'Come, Jane,' he told me. 'It is unlike you to be so unforgiving.'

'It is the injuries to you I cannot forgive,' I told him. 'For had she done her duty—'

He stopped my words with a kiss. 'That was long ago. And now we are happy.'

What was he telling me? That we owed our happiness to Grace Poole? In logic, of course, we did, for had there been no fire Bertha Mason might still have been alive and had she been alive, we could not have married. True, all true, but a truth too hard to contemplate.

I said faintly, 'It was your choice what to do about Grace Poole, whether to help her or not. I would never question your judgement, as you know. But to me it seems you have appointed her as a servant here, over John and Mary who have been so faithful over the years.'

He then said something terrible to me. 'You will need a housekeeper at Thornfield, Jane. It is a large establishment and you will be occupied with other matters.'

'But I have written to Mrs. Fairfax,' I told him.

'Sensible Jane, but perhaps not sensible enough. Mrs. Fairfax is old; the burdens of conducting affairs at Thornfield might prove too great, even if she were willing to assume them. I will write and tell her so, if you will permit me.'

'Yes, yes,' I concurred, but only so that he would leave me – leave me to my tears.

And, as soon as he had left the room, I sobbed. I could not understand Edward's appointing Grace Poole without consulting me. I could not understand why he did not take into consideration my obvious reluctance to have her as a servant. Now, she had settled like a black cloud over the house, and would be with us at Thornfield, as housekeeper. It was horrible, horrible.

As I sobbed, there came a tap at the door. In the doorway stood the black-clad figure.

'Madam!' she exclaimed. 'What ails you? I will tell Mr. Rochester. He must call the doctor.' And she was gone.

Not half an hour later the doctor came to me and composed a draught, which, when I had taken it, caused a heavy sleep. What had been said to him I do not know.

All I know is that from that moment on Mrs. Poole came to me twice a day, at morning and evening, and gave me medicine. I would gaze into that impassive face, take the potion from her long, cold hands, always with the sensation that she was giving me something damaging. Yet I had no choice; I could not assume the responsibility of defying the doctor's orders, when the consequence might have been to lose the child I so dearly longed for. This medicine made me sleep away my nights and days. And so another ten days passed until at last I received permission from the doctor to cease the drugs, and his reassurance, 'You and the child are out of danger now, Mrs. Rochester. But you must be careful in future not to indulge in any excessive physical or mental exertion. I have told this to Mr. Rochester. There will be henceforth some danger both to you and the child – all will be well, though, if you are most careful.'

'And that I shall be,' I assured him fervently. After giving me his further instructions, he pressed my hand and was gone.

However, during the ensuing days it became plain what a heavy burden the doctor's orders imposed on me. Edward continued to sleep in another room, as he had since the commencement of my illness. This parting – for we had not spent a night apart since our marriage – had afflicted me during my illness, and now became harder to bear. Yet there was no help for it. We must stay apart. A further grief was that my weakness precluded any domestic activities but the least taxing.

Edward came to me one evening and said, with an air of satisfaction, 'Well, my dearest, I am assured that all is in order for the move.'

I had almost forgotten the move to Thornfield. 'Could

we not delay it a little, perhaps until after Christmas?' I appealed.

'It will be better to manage the thing now, while the weather is fine and the days still fairly light,' he declared. 'A move in winter can be gruelling, even for one in perfect health which, alas, you are not. Even now we are making efforts to warm and air the house for you before we take up residence. Mrs. Poole has ordered the main fires to be lit and kept lit from now on. Rest assured, my dearest, nothing – nothing – will trouble you about the move. All will be done. You will need only to appear when the move is over, and become mistress of the house.'

This was not what I wanted. Yet how could I explain my need to be in charge of our translation to Thornfield, to order all the arrangements myself, to understand all the workings of the house from its inception? How could I explain this to Edward? What man could understand it? Be reasonable, Jane, thought I, or if you cannot be reasonable, seem so. And I answered, 'I hope this incapacity of mine at such a time is not too burdensome for you, Edward.'

'My dear,' he said, 'nothing is too much trouble. Your health and that of our coming child are my only concern.' He added, 'There's nothing at all to concern you – Mrs. Poole has the whole thing in hand.'

And so my sadness at leaving Ferndean, and my dear servants John and Mary, was increased by the knowledge that the move was to be presided over by that hard, cold woman, associated in my mind with all that was foul and gloomy, that woman who, I was sure, hated me. It was she who was to pack my belongings, even my most precious things, she who would ordain where they were to be placed.

Next day a letter came from Mrs. Fairfax. She told me she had received Edward's message to her, written during my illness, telling her that my invitation to return to Thornfield as housekeeper was revoked as he had recently come upon Mrs. Poole in very poor circumstances and had offered her the appointment. He had concluded by inviting Mrs. Fairfax most cordially to visit Thornfield at the earliest opportunity, as a guest. My dear Mrs. Fairfax ended her letter by saying she had been most concerned to hear of my illness and added, in a guarded manner, that she had every respect for Mrs. Poole and she dearly hoped I would be happy with my new housekeeper.

I must own to a sinking of the heart on receipt of this kindly communication. Of course Edward had done nothing but what was necessary in my illness in writing thus to Mrs. Fairfax, yet I felt a perhaps foolish melancholy that this matter had been taken so firmly out of my hands and Mrs. Poole's position so speedily and determinedly established.

I took heed, too, of the cautious tone Mrs. Fairfax struck on the subject of Mrs. Poole's services, for it confirmed my feeling of dread at having her in my house. And still I wondered – why did Edward, whose life had been blighted by the negligence of this woman, allow her now to be so close to us?

Chapter VII

And so the move to Thornfield took place.

    One gusty October day, when the leaves were being whirled from the trees in clouds of red, gold and brown, our waggons left Ferndean. But as they rolled the thirty miles to Thornfield I was obliged to remain in my chamber at Ferndean, first listening to the thuds and bumps as my possessions, those objects – chairs, china, my little desk – I had tended so carefully, were carried from the house while downstairs, I knew, Mrs. Poole presided over all. Then came the rolling of the wheels, then silence, an awesome silence, the silence of a house emptied of its furnishings, its inhabitants, its very function.

    Upstairs, I sat in my chair alone – my nurse, though still at Ferndean, being elsewhere in the house – gazed over my dearly loved garden, the lawn where leaves now blew and lifted in the wind. The borders were in decline now, and only one rose, always late to blossom, threw out its brightness. Later, Edward would return with the carriage and carry me to Thornfield. Meanwhile I sat waiting, picturing the empty rooms below me, the fragments of the last ten years left behind. I compelled myself to consider with optimism our new life at Thornfield, that more spacious life which was due to my husband and son.

And all the while, in the house was that deep silence, and from without came the sighing of the wind.

Soon enough, my nurse arrived and then came the sound of Edward's carriage wheels. His face was alight with pleasure when he entered. 'All goes well at Thornfield,' he reported. 'Now what remains is to install the mistress of the house.' He tenderly wrapped a shawl about me. 'Already Jonathan is running from room to room, just as once I did, my dearest – just as I did as a boy.'

Edward and the nurse helped me down the stairs. It was a month since I had left my room. Now, below me, I saw the hall, lacking any table, any pictures on the walls, empty and abandoned. Slowly, we left the house, I leaning on Edward's arm. The front door of Ferndean closed behind us for the last time, and I silently bade farewell to my garden, to the old mulberry tree under which we had sat together summer after summer, to the house itself. The sky overhead was blue, the wind fresh, whirls of leaves came from them like coloured clouds – and we departed for Thornfield Hall.

As Mary and John's son, Jeremy, who was coming with us to Thornfield, set the horses off, I had a strange sensation, as if I were now without volition, as if I were in a dream. And so we took the road to Thornfield.

Chapter VIII

This strange trance-like state held me as we left our fertile valley and mounted, passing through the reaped fields, where stubble stood in rows, and went on, gently upwards until the vast outlines of the mountains emerged to the right, and the fields became rougher, marked off from each other by stone walls, which carried on, up and up into the mountains.

And so we came to Thornfield, travelling up the drive between the tall elms, and there on its slight elevation lay the great bulk of the house. Outside, the big furniture drays stood ready to leave, their huge horses standing patiently in the traces. Behind the house rooks swirled in the tall elms. The front door stood open.

I felt Edward's hand in mine as we approached, yet – and I believed it to be a result of my illness and my new exposure to the world – I felt – and how difficult it is to describe such states of mind – as if I, Jane Rochester, were somehow a little removed from the scene. I had left this house in a torment of emotion, as Jane Eyre. I returned as Jane Rochester, mistress of Thornfield and yet I thought I dreamed.

I leaned on my husband's arm as we passed under the

portico and into the wide hall. All was as I had ordained it – the black and gold wallpaper, the pale paint, the portraits of two earlier Rochesters, he in doublet and hose, she in ruff and farthingale, which I had discovered in an attic at Ferndean. All was well done and I might have rejoiced had it not been for Grace Poole standing there in front of me, in a black silk dress, hands respectfully clasped. Bright new keys, the keys to Thornfield, dangled at her waist. Her black hair, streaked with grey, was tidily arranged, her face very pale, her dark eyes stern as ever.

My heart sank. I was so weak, and here in my own hall was Mrs. Poole, full of strength, cold, controlled, almost as if she were mistress of the house, standing ready to greet a guest. She advanced; I shrank against my husband's shoulder. He felt the movement and said hastily, 'The journey has tired Mrs. Rochester. We will go straight upstairs, Mrs. Poole.' She moved back and we progressed towards the great staircase which ran up through the centre of the house.

And so I reached my bedroom at Thornfield, that elegant great chamber in which, had I but known it, alas, I was destined to spend so many weary hours alone during the coming months. But this I could not know, and at that time I was delighted by the sight that met me, once we had climbed the broad treads of the staircase and turned along the gallery. All was exactly as I had hoped. The room stood at the end of the gallery, occupying the corner of the house and having therefore windows on two sides. Those at the rear of the room looked out on to the elms behind the house and then over foothills of green to the mountains behind. On the other side the view was of the walled garden and its trees. That the view included, beyond the far wall of the garden, a portion of the field of thorn trees was a misfortune, but a small one in this light-filled room, with its pale sprigged wallpaper, long brocade curtains and charming furniture. Flowers stood on a table; all had been beautifully arranged.

I was to lie on a couch, placed beneath the far window, for as yet the bedroom furniture from Ferndean, which had stayed in place until I left the house, had not arrived. The drays now leaving Thornfield were to collect it and bring it to the house.

Mrs. Poole, assiduous as ever, was in the doorway, as Edward laid me gently down. 'Will you take some refreshment, Jane?' he asked, glancing at the black-clad figure in the door.

I had a little tea and bread and butter, while Edward sat by me on a chair, and we conversed with our usual freedom and confidence.

'Is all to your liking, Jane?' he asked, desiring I should share in his joy at the restoration of Thornfield.

'Yes, indeed,' said I. 'All is new, clean and fresh. We have all the advantages of the old Thornfield with many new ones also. Indeed, I have a burning desire to come downstairs now, to examine my domain.'

'You are whimsical,' he said, with a smile. 'Let us take a sounding.' He turned to my nurse, who stood by. 'Nurse, what do you think of the suggestion?' he asked. 'Is my wife well enough to come downstairs?'

'I should say no,' replied the woman. 'For I fear too much excitement will harm her.'

'I assure you I shall be more excited if forced to lie here wondering how my plans and stratagems for the house appear in reality,' said I.

Mrs. Poole had arrived for orders and overheard these words. She now said, 'I assure you, Mrs. Rochester, that everything below is in perfect order.'

'I am sure of that, Mrs. Poole,' I said. 'But it is the impression, the atmosphere, about which I seek to reassure myself.'

To this she said nothing, but gave me a long, level look. My nurse, meanwhile, was taking my pulse and having done so said doubtfully, 'You may go downstairs, but you must be carried and restoratives given.'

Mrs. Poole, trying not to frown, said, 'I will fetch the man from the stables.'

'Have we no manservant in the house?' I asked.

'I did not wish one,' explained my husband, though to me it seemed strange for a house of such a size to have no male servant living in. However, Jeremy was summoned from the stables, which had been newly rebuilt with good accommodation, and I was carried ceremoniously downstairs to the drawing-room.

This room ran the full length of the house – which, on the ground floor was arranged round the large, square hall with its fireplace and pillars – and was thus some twenty feet long; the dining-room and breakfast-room ran along the back of the house. I had ordained that the salon should be divided by large doors, which could be opened for large entertainment and closed when more intimate surroundings were dictated. I had determined, also, that the old beauties of this room should be preserved, yet enhanced. There were the grand mirrors and imposing chandeliers, the snowy carpets with their pattern of wreathed roses, the pale marble fireplaces and the lamps and other ornaments of ruby, dark green and blue, to add points of intensity to the lightness of the room. This effect was created by three long windows at one side, curtained in pale brocade patterned with stemmed roses.

The effect was, to my eyes, lovelier than I had believed it might be and as for Edward – he stayed in the doorway, drew in the spectacle and embraced me even as I stood there saying, 'Jane – Oh, my Jane. I knew you for the composer of the charming cottage, Ferndean, but you have now designed an elegant grand salon, fit for a king! How happy we shall be with such a room in which to entertain our friends. Come, let us go to the dining-room and see what splendours you have arranged for us there.'

But I protested I was tired and so I was arranged on the couch near the fireplace, in which a bright fire burned, while Edward went to check that every detail was perfect for when I should be strong enough to see it.

My nurse bustled off to fetch me medicine, declaring this move to have been all but too much for her patient, and I lay there, indeed very tired, yet, in some part of my mind, remembering the old Jane, she whose strength had once supported her though so many trials at Thornfield. But the old Jane had not been a woman expecting to become a mother in spring and that was all the difference.

As I dreamed, suddenly Mrs. Poole was at my side, startling me, 'Is all to your liking, madam?' she asked me in that deep voice, almost like a man's, and I told her, 'Yes – yes, Mrs. Poole, it is.'

Then Edward was back, exclaiming, 'Just as it was – the house is exactly as it once was – yet somehow, better. How can this be?' I smiled a little at that, knowing exactly how such things can be achieved, when a woman has determined they should be.

'The library will be a sorry sight,' I told him. 'For books are something we cannot buy by the yard.'

'That will be our pleasure during the winter, to select what we should like for our library shelves.'

I smiled, imagining how happy we would be sitting by the fire discussing with delight what books we should select, how keenly we would await their arrival, the pressure of arranging them on their new shelves.

'You will have much to do, restoring the land to its former state,' I gently reminded him, for during our absence the fields around Thornfield had been let or left to lie, and I knew from letters I had written at my husband's behest, while acting as his secretary, that there were difficulties concerning the lead mines which lay in the hills beyond the village and which had been leased to a mining company.

'That is so,' he said. 'And the foxes have taken over. We shall have some good hunting, you may be sure.'

I said nothing, though my heart sank. I dreaded to see Edward riding hard. He had but one hand and though he had learned to control the strongest of horses in ordinary circumstances, the rigours and dangers of the hunt are exceptional and can bring the most capable of riders to grief. Nor was he talking of hunting lowland fields and brooks. At Thornfield the hunt may run uphill, even into the mountains, where there are high cliffs, and mists may come down very suddenly. Yet, of course, I held my peace, remarking only, 'You will have little time to restock a library then, while you are galloping after foxes.'

'There will be time,' he assured me.

Then in came the nurse with my medicine and he said to Mrs. Poole, who was still standing by, 'And when is, luncheon, pray?'

Mrs Rochester

And so we sat by our fireside at Thornfield talking, and I was content and believed soon I would be stronger – for so the doctor had promised – and that these moments marked the beginning of a new, happy life.

Chapter IX

Indeed, it was not long before I was fairly well again and the nurse sent away. The doctor, though, continued to urge caution and care and I was forced to obey his commands. Gone were the days of early rising, of breakfasting with Edward and Jonathan, and going about my normal duties, for now I had to keep to my room until midday. Gone, too, were the happy walks to school with Jonathan, for as there was no suitable school nearby, and his friendship with Mr. Weatherfield's sons was so strong, we had decided that for the meanwhile, he would board at the Weatherfields and continue his lessons there.

This separation was very hard on me, yet a mother knows that a boy must go from home early on in order to learn self-reliance and both must endure it. 'Why,' said Edward cheerfully, when I mentioned how I should miss my boy, 'he is seven years old and will be but thirty miles off. I was sent a hundred miles from home, to school, at that age.'

And so it had to be, and perhaps it was best for me to be less of a mother to the boy for a while. There could be no more afternoons in the gardens, for I must rest during those hours, rising only for dinner. I would, though, still have my evenings with Edward yet I knew, my early departure to my room each evening, ordered by the doctor, grieved him for he was forced to spend the later hours of the evening alone.

A Sunday came when I declared we must all go to church. Jonathan was home that weekend, so he, Edward and I took our carriage through a landscape bright and cold. The hayfields on either side of the road to the village were browning, the village itself, as we drove through, was quiet with a Sunday hush. The cottage chimneys smoked.

As we left our carriage outside the church and walked up to the door, others entering the church gazed at us with interest. I leaned on Edward's arm; Jonathan came behind as we walked up the aisle to take our seats in the high-fronted pew which stood along the side wall of the church at right angles to the altar, opposite the choir stalls on the other side. This was the pew specially retained for the Rochesters, and I was happy that after so long an absence it was reoccupied, and seen to be so. Not since the day when Edward had first tried to marry me had I entered the church. I was surprised to find myself quite calm, for I had not expected to be. But the serenity of the old building, with its air of having been a place of worship for so many hundreds of years, soothed the pain of recollection.

The organ swelled and Mr. Todd entered from the vestry. The congregation, consisting of the more prosperous folk of the neighbourhood stood to sing the opening hymn, 'A safe stronghold our God is still'.

A safe stronghold. Ah, how glad I was to stand there, loved and secure, with my Edward beside me, he singing the hymn in his strong baritone voice – a safe stronghold indeed.

Then came a little flurry in the congregation. I turned
my head; other heads in the rear pews were also turning
to look at a figure standing in the church doorway, an
unaccompanied lady in black. She stood, tall and erect,
the sunlight behind her, apparently unashamed of her
lateness. She took one graceful pace forward, intending,
I suppose, to sit down quietly at the back in the pew
nearest to her. I received the strong impression that this
was the lady who had driven her carriage past me on
the day I visited Thornfield during the summer. I had
only glimpsed her face as she hurtled by, but that pale
oval countenance, the prominent nose and general air
of command had impressed me strongly. And, since she
had moved into Old House, opposite the church, it was
natural that she should attend worship here.

These thoughts lasted only seconds, but as I turned my
gaze from her I observed Edward's face and was startled.
I had unconsciously noted that he had ceased to sing the
hymn some moments before, and as I looked at him I saw
his head, too, was turned in the direction of the church
door and the black-clad lady. His eyes blazed and his
pale face was set and rigid, as if he were trying to master
some strong emotion. Witnessing that countenance I felt
a sudden pang of dread, for that expression belonged to
the old days, his days of anger, secrets, pain.

As if drawn to her, my eyes returned to the lady,
who was now seated in a pew on the aisle near the
door. She was gazing at me – no, past me – I saw.
She looked at Edward. And with such a calm, steady,
yet unyielding gaze!

Putting his hand to his brow, Edward brushed past
me with a muttered apology, descending the two steps
leading down from the family pew. He walked, calm of

face and steadily, from the church, not looking to right or left as he went. I saw the lady in black looking at him. She turned her head when he arrived at the church door, to watch him go out. And then – he was gone.

This entire episode had taken little more than a minute. During it, the congregation had continued to sing the hymn. I moved towards Jonathan, who was standing a little bewildered at the sudden disappearance of his father. I gave him a reassuring smile and raised my voice again in the hymn, while pointing out for him the place in his hymn book. During this time I struggled to maintain a calm demeanour, for some of the congregation must have undoubtedly observed this strange episode and I did not wish the first visit of the Rochesters to their own parish church to occasion gossip and speculation, nor to unsettle my boy. It was hard, for my mind was full of questions, but I endured the rest of the service, though with scant attention. Had it indeed been the arrival in church of the mysterious lady that had led to Edward's sudden disappearance? If so, who was she, and what had she to do with my husband? However, I maintained, I hope, my composure, though I could have wished Mr. Todd's sermon, on Christ's advice to render unto Caesar that which is Caesar's, shorter than it was.

At last came the final hymn and we left the church. Mr. Todd, in the porch, enquired had Mr Rochester felt himself unwell at the commencement of the service? There was no sign of the lady. Seated at the back, as she had been, she would no doubt have had time to leave and return to her home by the time Jonathan and I reached the porch. Old House, I noted, as I got into the carriage, showed signs of repainting. The garden had been tidied and was freshly dug, indicating,

I thought, her intention to remain some time in the neighbourhood.

As we neared the gates of Thornfield I observed, coming off the path which led across the fields to the church, not just the mysterious new tenant of Old House but, with her, Grace Poole. They were in conversation. I saw them turn from the path on to the road past Thornfield as we approached the gates of the house.

I was absorbing this strange sight, and pondering its implications, when we arrived back at the doors of Thornfield. However, when I entered and asked where was Mr. Rochester the maid replied that he had not returned.

Luncheon was ready, but I could not think of eating. My mind was confused. I could understand nothing of what seemed to be a very strange combination of circumstances – Edward's leaving the church and the association of Grace Poole and the new tenant of Old House. As soon as I decently could, I collected my shawl and ran, like any common woman whose husband has not returned home, down the drive and into the road. Glancing back and forth wildly, I could see no sign of Edward, nor of the women. The road was deserted.

Clouds had covered the perfectly blue sky of morning. I roamed to and fro on the road and then found myself at the thorn-field. Leafless, twisted branches under lowering skies; long, straggling grass, brown and faded green – and here, black backs turned to me and talking intently, were the lady of Old House and Grace Poole, going uphill away from me. I gazed at them from the road, in horror. Grace Poole took a long pace over the little stream not a foot wide, which coursed downhill from the mountains, then turned and gave the other woman her hand to help her cross. As she did so I envisaged them both, in one of those surges of the imagination – so alarming – as unwilled – as two black crows in a field, hopping and leaping.

I turned to go back to Thornfield. Carrion crows, carrion crows, came a voice in my head. What do they mean, those carrion crows?

When I returned Edward had still not come back, and I spent a wretched afternoon wondering where he might be and why he had sent no message. I kissed my boy and put him in the coach back to Mr. Weatherfield's, then spent a long, anxious evening of vigil. It was not until after nine that a man came from Millcote, with a brief note from Edward saying only that he had been suddenly called to business in Manchester, where he was partner in a cotton mill and had been forced to leave immediately. He would be back within a few days.

This action amazed me, for never before, during our ten years of marriage, had he gone off precipitately, without saying farewell.

A long lonely week at Thornfield, during which time I was scarcely for one moment free of doubt and dread. All the time questions hammered in my head. What were Grace Poole and the lady of Old House to each other? What was Edward to the lady?

It was impossible to go to Grace Poole for explanations. She was a servant, and we were not, in any case, confidential. Had she been my dear old Mary from Ferndean, things would have been otherwise, but, alas, here they were not; and could not be. During Edward's absence Mrs. Poole behaved entirely as usual, being efficient as ever, correct and polite without warmth. The suspicion that she knew something of the mysterious woman and that this might have a bearing on aught to do with Edward preyed on my mind, but I could do nothing.

During that period, also, there came from up the village a note in an unfamiliar hand. It lay on Edward's desk in the study, unopened, mysterious.

And so began a time when I understood very little of the events surrounding me. Not since my early days at Thornfield had I felt so uncertain of my world and what was to take place in it.

Chapter X

I take you now to a location where I was not, London, for it was thither Edward went after he left the house so precipitately. He arrived on the crowded wharves of the Thames and found the offices of Grover and Sims, shipping agents, where he chartered a vessel, the *Janus*.

That evening he found himself in a noisy, smoke-filled inn near the waterfront, speaking to the robust sun-tanned man who would captain his ship to the West Indies.

'Do not,' said my husband earnestly, 'on any account land at Kingston, in Jamaica. I have had serious warnings from friends whose position grants them access to much confidential information, and they assure me riots and other disturbances are expected there. Put in at Kingston and you risk ship, cargo and even the lives of your crew. That is why I desire you – nay, command you – to avoid Jamaica at all costs.'

The ship's master readily agreed. 'If those are your instructions, Mr. Rochester, I will do exactly as you say.'

And then, his business done, Edward came home.

Chapter XI

Edward returned after a week at night, entering the drawing-room just before dinner. He crossed the room towards me, powerful, strong in limb and shoulder, but with a dark and brooding expression on his face which alarmed me. He dropped a kiss on my brow then went to a chair opposite and fell into it, as if very weary.

'Do you wish anything?' said I, standing up.

'Ring for the maid and sit down, Jane, do,' he said. 'You've no need to wait on me hand and foot yourself.'

I rang the bell and sat down, attempting to be calm. He had been gone for many days, had given no real explanation for his going and now – now, on his return, seemed angry with me for no reason.

When the maid came he told her, 'Bring a hot rum to the study,' then got up and left the room.

At dinner he ate little and said almost nothing, and his manner was if anything gloomier than when he had first entered the house. Distracted with anxiety though I was, I knew I must not persecute him with questions, though when one course had come and gone I asked, as calmly as I could, 'Is anything the matter, Edward? You seem silent. Please tell me if there is anything wrong.'

At first he did not reply. Then, 'You might ask, is anything right?' he burst out. 'For one thing – read this'. And he seized from his breast pocket a letter and handed it to me – yet this was not the note the servant had brought from the village but another piece of correspondence which had been delivered during his absence. This, I knew from the handwriting, was from his ward Adèle, once my charge, who was away at school in Switzerland. I read it. It was couched in very affectionate terms and said in essence that since she was almost eighteen she felt it was time to leave school and come home.

My relationship with Adèle had been, perforce, distant. She had been away at school for long periods and at sixteen had elected to leave and go to Switzerland, to a very good place widely known for its skills in broadening and expanding the minds of its pupils, granting them a greater degree of polish and knowledge of the world than they could find in any comparable institution in this country.

All had been done for Adèle that could have been done, but now I felt it would be almost more than I could bear to have the responsibility for a grown-up young woman placed on my shoulders. What could I do with her? I said, though, only, 'Might it not be better if she stayed until spring, until after our child is born?'

'If that is what you wish,' he said.

'No, Edward. If it is what you wish,' I replied. 'I merely suggest.'

'Then,' he told me, 'I will accept what you call your suggestion, and you may write to her accordingly.'

'She wrote to you,' I pointed out. 'Should you not reply to her yourself?'

'Perhaps I should,' he said, 'but I desire not to. I would

prefer it if you replied.' Then he stood up, saying, 'If you will forgive me, I will go now to the study. There are affairs which require my attention. I will bid you goodnight now, for I may not have the pleasure of seeing you before you retire.'

I was left at the table alone, surprised and wretched. The coldness of his tone chilled me. His manner was that of the old Rochester, enduring a hopeless marriage; with no prospect of future happiness. Sadness swept over me and, weakly, I thought, Oh, how could he have been so loving, so true, at Ferndean and then, no sooner than we are back at Thornfield be once more the old Edward Rochester, bitter, hard, ironic, disillusioned? My feelings overwhelmed me so that, a very brief time after he had gone to his study, I sought the shelter of my bedchamber, where I could be alone and unobserved in my distress.

I hastened from the room. At the foot of the stairs was Mrs. Poole, standing, erect in her black dress, by the newel post. 'I hope dinner was to your satisfaction, Mrs. Rochester,' she said.

'Yes, thank you, Mrs. Poole,' I replied.

'I could not help noticing that neither you nor Mr. Rochester ate well tonight.'

'Mr. Rochester is tired and I am a little unwell,' I responded. 'That is the reason. There was nothing wrong with the dinner, thank you. Goodnight, Mrs. Poole.'

'Goodnight, Mrs. Rochester,' she said.

I felt her eyes watching me as I ascended the stairs and reflected that it is a bitter thing to have an enemy in your own home.

Chapter XII

I could not keep to my bed next morning, for it seemed important for me to talk to Edward and try to resume our old, free communication. I knew – I could not help knowing – that he was troubled and I wished to find out what his anxiety might be and, if it was in my power, assist him.

I rose early, dressed and went down to breakfast. Mrs. Poole was there in her black dress, hands clasped before her as usual. Impassively she told me that my husband had gone out early, asking her to tell me he was with Mr. Sugden, the estate manager, inspecting outlying farms. She asked coldly, 'It is early, madam. Should you be up at this hour?'

It was a dark and blowy day, gloomy, with intermittent rain, which ran like constant tears down the window-panes. I sat in the drawing-room at my little desk, where I wrote to Adèle that her papa and I were agreed she should stay in Switzerland until spring, though we looked forward to seeing her at Christmas. Having done this, I tried to sew, but all the time anxiety gnawed at me. I had still not spoken to Edward and I began to think he was avoiding me. My morning went sadly on.

At midday, a seamstress came from Hay, her task being to adjust the lengths of any curtains in the house which were not at the correct levels. As she knelt on the drawing-room floor, pinning up a hem, she glanced up at me, asking, 'Were Mr. Rochester taken ill in church last Sunday?'

'Yes, he was,' I answered.

'Aye, well he might,' she responded as if my reply satisfied her in some way. I could not fathom what she meant, though there was something angry, even unpleasant, in her tone. But I knew nothing of her or Hay, except that I had seen it to be poor. I ignored what she said and stood back to study the effect of her pinnings. 'That will do, I think,' I said. 'By the by, I do not think there is a school for the children in Hay?'

'There's never been a school in Hay,' she replied.

'Do you not feel the lack of one?' I asked.

'Aye, perhaps,' she said, 'but the people are poor.'

'Let us go upstairs,' I said. 'There is other work to do.'

'Mrs. Poole used to do this,' she told me as we ascended the stairs, I in front.

'She is too busy now,' said I.

Her voice came from behind me. 'A good deal has changed at Thornfield. But some things, and some folk, do not change.'

I waited for Edward throughout the long, dark day. When he returned through the bad weather it was so late I had sent the servants to bed and was sitting by the drawing-room fire by the light of one lamp.

'Jane?' he said. 'I thought you would be abed. You should be resting.'

'I am quite well now,' I told him. 'Let me take your coat. How wet you are.'

And with my own hands I took off his coat and then led him to the dining-room where I had fire and food waiting for him.

'A little cheese will do,' he said, standing by the fire, muddy from his long ride, 'for the bone-weary.'

'Sit and eat,' I instructed. 'Here's soup and cold meats—'

'Jane,' he interrupted, 'I need my bed.'

'You will catch cold if you go to bed hungry and frozen,' I told him. 'To please me, sit and eat.'

Once he had wine and food before him, I sat down opposite, contemplating him while he addressed himself silently to his plate.

When he had taken some food I said to him 'Edward. there is something about which I am curious. Will you satisfy that curiosity?'

'As much as is in my power,' he responded, in a discouraging tone.

'Well then, pray do,' I continued steadily. 'Will you tell me, if you please, what caused you to leave church so hurriedly on Sunday? We have not spoken since then.'

'I was suddenly ill,' he said.

'But you are not ill now.'

'I *thought* myself ill,' he said impatiently. 'It is not unknown to feel oneself ill and then discover one is not. Jane, do not badger me. You have never been the wife to worry a weary man. I hope you are not beginning to be one now. I felt ill – I left the church – but I was mistaken – I was not ill. That is all there is to it. We need say no more.'

'I wondered if your abrupt departure had anything to do with the lady who has taken Old House, the lady who entered the church after we were seated?'

He threw down his knife and fork. 'The lady – What

lady? – Oh, the lady,' he said very rapidly. 'Yes. It is true I thought I recognised her, but that had nothing to do with my leaving. Jane, have you taken leave of your senses? What is all this? I am cold, tired, and was hungry before you set on me, though I now lose appetite. I do not want any more questions.'

'Edward, my dear – I have not set on you. Please do not say that.'

'Very well. You have not,' he said and took up his knife and fork again.

There was a further silence.

'And so, when you left the church, you realised you had recognised the lady as someone you knew,' I prompted gently.

But as I spoke a rage I hated to see suffused Edward's face. Then he mastered himself and stood up. 'I will go to bed,' he declared, and left the room with no embrace, no farewell, no promise for the morning.

And I – I went to my bedroom and lay awake until dawn, grieving at the distance that seemed to be growing between us and wondering what was the cause of it. A bitter, sad night, and not the last I was to experience at Thornfield Hall over the coming months.

Chapter XIII

A grey day dawned and I kept to my room all morning, thoughts swirling in my heavy head. It seemed vain to try to talk to Edward again, and this separation was causing me such distress no other form of action could appeal to me. The house was silent. No sound came from downstairs. No one came or went. From my windows I saw rain sweeping over the lawn, over the walled garden.

Just before luncheon I saw Edward return and hand his horse to the groom outside. Then I heard him coming upstairs to change his drenched clothes. When that was done, he came to my room, embraced me and led me down to luncheon.

As the maid brought in the first course, he said to me, 'Jane, I am deeply sorry I was so hasty last night.'

I replied, 'My dear, I pressed you when I should not have. You were so tired . . .'

But even as we smiled at each other, Mrs. Poole, came into the room, saying, 'A lady has come to see you, sir.'

There was something in her manner which alarmed me. Not so, Edward. He leaned back in his chair and said,

'Mrs. Poole, why do you interrupt us at a meal? Who is this lady? What does she want?'

'She will not say.'

'Then, Mrs. Poole,' he said, 'she must surely wait.'

'Sir,' she said in a warning tone, 'sir – I think you would wish to see her now.'

'The devil!' he exclaimed. 'Why do you think that? I ask again – what is the lady's name?'

She hesitated, then said in a low voice, 'It is Madame Roland.'

I saw his face alter, then he stood up with an oath and, crashing his chair back, walked from the room, leaving me alone at the table.

The words were forced from me. 'Mrs. Poole, what is this? Who is Madame Roland?'

'Madam,' she responded, 'it is better you do not know.'

'Mrs. Poole – what insolence!' I exclaimed, but she turned and left the room. In anger I called after her, 'Mrs. Poole!' but she did not come back.

Without a moment's thought I left the room. I was in the hall, wondering where Edward had gone, when I heard raised voices in the study, though, through the thick oak door I could not distinguish any words, only Edward's raging voice interrupted by the woman's in what seemed to be passionate declarations. I stood some feet from the door, half concealed behind one of the tall pillars of the hall. Could it be that this woman was some creature from Edward's past come to reproach him or make some claim, to cause trouble, disturbance and pain?

Then the study door was flung open. The woman stood in the doorway, turning back to look at Edward within, her face deadly pale, eyes blazing, 'You *will* give me satisfaction, Mr. Rochester,' she cried in a powerful voice. 'I go now, but I will return, as God is my witness.' She swept past me, not noticing me, through the hall and out of the open front door.

The study door slammed shut. Something inside, a chair perhaps, fell to the floor. I stood for a moment, then crossed the hall, walking automatically towards the drawing-room. Mrs. Poole was standing at the door, which she, expressionlessly, silently opened for me. As I passed, I gazed into her eyes. They were triumphant.

Inside the room I sank into a chair, my heart beating wildly. I felt dizzy and ill and, 'My child,' I thought, 'my coming child. I am ill. My child may be harmed.'

Who was this woman? Why was she in Hay? Had she come there by chance – or deliberately, in order to persecute my husband? What relations had she had with him – and what could she want now? She had a French name, yet, when she cried out, her accent had been that of an Englishwoman. Had she come from France? Had she known Edward during the years when Céline Varens had been his mistress?

I was wholly bewildered. Our life together had been clear, perfect, and now some ugly phantom had arisen to oppress us. From the occasion of Madame Roland's first appearance, in church, all had changed between Edward and myself. His brusqueness to me, his anger, dated from that moment. And his desire to avoid me and my questioning.

And yet, I reflected distressfully, perhaps this was not a woman from the distant past. Perhaps – a dreadful thought – she was some woman Edward had met in Manchester, when he had been there on business. It was there he had found Mrs. Poole and given her employment. And the two women knew each other, for I had seen them together. Was that why Mrs. Poole was here, at Thornfield? Because she knew the secret of Edward's relations with this woman?

My mind filled with the most hideous suspicions, suspicions that only a few months previously I should never have believed I could entertain, I lay in my chair, waves of sickness going through me. How could I mistrust my husband, so suddenly, after years of perfect faith? I could not – I must not. Yet what was I to think? All was very far from well. And he would explain nothing to me – nothing.

Even as I agonised, the door opened suddenly and Edward was there, dressed for riding. 'I must leave for Manchester again,' he declared. 'I am sorry. After that, I may have to go to London.' There was pain in his face, and love for me – that I knew.

I ran to him. 'I will pack for you.'

But, 'It is done,' he said. 'Mrs. Poole has done it. Jane, my dearest I must go.' And he pressed me to him, in a kind of agony, it seemed to me, then held me from him and his fierce eyes were glistening with tears. 'I would not willingly leave you, Jane,' he said, 'but I must – I must. Be well, my darling, be careful of our child – wait for me.' And he was gone.

Through the drenched windows I watched him leave the house and mount his big grey horse, held for him by the groom. I watched him ride away, across the lawn, down to the road, in the rain.

I could make nothing of the day's strange events. Even if the black-clad woman were an old lover of my husband's or some connection of Céline Varens, that Parisienne so-called 'opera dancer' (a description which I understood better now than I had at eighteen, when Edward had imparted Adèle's history to me), even if she were his present lover, what difference could it make? It had been plain that, even while angry, and sometimes cold, yet he loved me. And that, perhaps, I reflected, was all that should concern me. If he loved me, we could together resolve all other difficulties, if he loved me no harm could come to me, to him – to either of us.

Chapter XIV

Next day I rose determined, for I knew, though my husband was gone, though I was still anxious and fearful, that I had duties to perform for him, for Thornfield and perhaps above all for myself. I would visit Mr. Todd, even though in doing so I would be obliged to pass Old House. Yet that, I was resolved, would not deter me in my mission.

I descended from the carriage opposite Old House, which was shut up and quiet, and discovered Mr. Todd at the vicarage, enjoying a late and ample breakfast. He took me to see his garden and his fruit trees. We stood by the bee-hives round which bees, sated on the apples and plums lying beneath the trees, buzzed lazily, though the air was cool. He asked me about Edward's disappearance from the church on Sunday. I told him Edward had felt unwell.

'I came,' I told him, 'because I hear there is no school in the village. I wished to discuss with you the matter of beginning one. When we were at Ferndean, I created a school which still thrives, and I would wish to do so here, for Hay, I see, is a poor place, and I believe conditions among the lead-miners in the hills may be worse. To teach the children some reading and writing, and something of correct conduct, would be a marvellous thing.'

'With the greatest respect, Mrs. Rochester,' he said, 'I have never been convinced of the wisdom of educating humble folk whose paths are destined to remain humble, and to whom education is unnecessary. Hay is wretched not because the people are deprived of schooling but because they have no work, and this lack of work is caused by circumstances over which we have no control. Once the villagers were wont to weave cloth in their own homes, but now the new factories in the industrial towns can weave faster and more cheaply. Therefore, Hay's trade is dead. What I do not think we wish to do, in this unfortunate situation, is stir up a ferment of thought in weak and inexperienced individuals. There is always danger in that, do you not agree?'

I confess I was not surprised by this response. I confess also to a stratagem – I knew I must not proceed without informing Mr. Todd of my intention, knew also that he would oppose it. This visit and my declaration that I supported the idea of a school was the opening salvo in my campaign.

'But if one were to found a school,' I asked, 'is there a building in Hay which might be used for the purpose?'

He shook his head, 'Alas, no. Hay is a sorry place, a cluster of houses, several inns – too many – and that is about the sum of it. A suitable building would have to be built and then comes the old question, how would the money be found?'

'Perhaps by means of a subscription raised among the better people of the neighbourhood.'

He shook his head. 'I wish I could assure you of

their support, but alas, they are not as generous as they might be. The church roof is in great need of attention, and yet money for that even worthy cause is slow in coming, alas.'

'That is most unfortunate,' I told him, 'but tell me, does the new lady who has come to the neighbourhood, Madame Roland, offer you any support?'

'She has been generous,' he admitted.

'How excellent of her,' I said. 'What do you know of her, Mr. Todd?'

'Not a great deal,' he told me. 'Her name is Madame Justine Roland. She is English but was married to a Frenchman, and was a resident of Paris until the death of her husband a year ago.'

Paris, thought I. 'What brings her to this neighbourhood, do you know?' I enquired.

'A desire for a peaceful retreat in which to live quietly and mourn her dead husband,' he said. 'She told me she has no longer any connections in England, but had been told much of this neighbourhood by a close friend, who once lived at Millcote.'

'It must be pleasant for you to have Old House occupied at last, and by such an agreeable person,' I observed, and soon took my leave, reflecting that now at last I knew a little of Madame Roland's history, if indeed what she had told Mr. Todd was the truth. When I passed her house it was still silent and no one appeared to be stirring, either inside or out.

I stopped the carriage outside Hay, and sent it back to Thornfield without me, deciding to walk home through the village in order to obtain a more precise impression of the place and its inhabitants.

When I had awoken that morning, though afraid and

doubting of all, I had nevertheless resolved that, if I were able, the poor of the locality should henceforth get that assistance and good government from the neighbourhood's chief house which had for so long been wanting. And so I descended at the bend in the road leading into the village and walked first through bare fields until I found on the outskirts of the village two fairly commodious houses, no doubt dating from the days of prosperity when wool was spun and woven by the cottagers. But both were now dilapidated, the doors nailed up, the windows boarded.

Then came the first small houses. There were some twenty-five in all, straggling up the village street. At one, surrounded by a neglected garden, a woman at the door, evidently about to throw out a bucket of water, saw me, gaped, then went inside quickly, closing her door. I walked on. Two men standing leaning against the wall of a set of five cottages, which led directly on to the street, turned away with no greeting, avoiding my eye. A knot of men with tankards of beer disappeared into the ale-house. As I went up the street, dry now, but full of pot-holes containing water, scenes of this kind were repeated again and again. The village emptied before me, as if a signal, unheard, was going out as I advanced. Two children were called in from playing in the street even as I approached. They ran inside and slammed the cottage door behind them. Had it not been for the plumes of smoke from chimneys, the figures I could see through the open doors of a silent ale-house as I passed, a dog turning over a rag in the gutter, I might have been going through a place deserted by all its inhabitants. And thus I passed through Hay and out into the fields beyond.

As I walked back to Thornfield I felt a chill which had nothing to do with the wind blowing about me. I could not account for what had happened. Did they fear me, suspecting I meant them harm? Or were they keeping some secret, such as will sometimes arise in isolated, neglected places such as Hay? I had gone some quarter of a mile along the narrow road up and was walking between hayfields, bare now under autumn sun, when a voice hailed me from a distance. 'Mrs. Rochester!'

Turning, I espied behind me on the road the figure of a man, who called out again, 'Mrs. Rochester!' An elderly man, leaning on a stick, was effortfully coming towards me. As he advanced, I went back to meet him. He was bent and grey and plainly poor, though his clothing was neat and clean.

He was breathless when I reached him. 'You go fast, for such a little woman,' he told me, with some humour. This was the first friendly voice I had heard coming out of Hay. 'Well, you've young legs,' he continued.

'Do you want to speak to me?' I asked. 'You know my name – but who, pray, are you?'

'You'd best not take a lofty tone with me, Mrs. Rochester,' he said, his tone blunt but not unamiable.

'Even so,' I said, 'you might let me know your name.'

'Why – do you not recognise me, Arthur Crooke, the old butler, from before your time at Thornfield, when you were Miss Eyre? We met, do you remember, ten years ago at the inn I ran then, when you had first seen the ruins of Thornfield. It was I told you what had occurred.'

I was startled. Of course this was Crooke, ten years older. I recalled now questioning him desperately about the whereabouts of Edward Rochester. So great had been my agitation at that time that perhaps it was unsurprising I had not at first recognised him.

'I remember you now,' I said, and asked him how he did.

'I've little money and less health,' he said shortly.

'Let me ask Mr. Rochester to look to your condition,' I said.

But even as I spoke, he became agitated. 'Please do not do that, I beg you, madam,' he said in a tone of great urgency.

'But why not?' I asked in astonishment. 'You are an old servant of the family. He would not wish to see you in want.'

But he became yet more disturbed and implored me, 'No, madam, no.'

'I do not understand.'

He spoke rapidly. 'I saw you pass through Hay. I could not speak to you then for fear of the villagers. So I crept out by a back way and have caught up with you here to ask you for help. Not knowing you, they do not trust you, but I do, madam. I have heard of how you nursed Mr. Rochester back to health and of your goodness to the folk at Ferndean. I believe you are one who would always see justice done.'

We stood on that empty road in the wind, no soul near us and no sound but the curlew's cry. 'Tell me what you want, Crooke,' I said.

'It is the lady and Grace Poole,' he averred. 'Will you command them to leave me alone?'

I was surprised – wondered, even, if the old man were losing his wits. 'What can you mean?' I asked. 'Are they disturbing you in some way?'

'Yes, indeed they are,' he said emphatically. 'It began

two weeks ago, when you and Mr. Rochester came to Thornfield. Since then those two ladies have given me no peace. The first morning both came and knocked on my cottage door, Mrs. Poole and the new lady from Old House, who dresses like a widow. They came with gifts, to relieve my want, they said, but soon the conversation turned to events which happened long ago. And better forgotten, to my way of thinking, as I told them.'

'But they would not allow me to be silent. They would not cease to speak of those events nor leave, as I wished they would. Finally I was obliged to tell them I could not – did not wish to – speak of the past and they left. But alas, on the following day they returned in the evening after dark, avid as before. They threatened me, madam,' he appealed. 'Mr. Rochester is my landlord and what money I get comes from him. Mrs. Poole told me she had great influence with him and could use that influence to lose me my home and my allowance from the family if I did not comply and tell her and the widow what they wanted. I cannot tell you how afraid I was, to hear from those two ladies, with their cruel faces lit up by the flickering candle, that if I did not obey them I was like to be turned out.'

I could hardly believe what I heard. That Grace Poole had claimed to be able, through my husband, to ruin this old man seemed to me horrible and outrageous beyond words. But why were these two women – the other, undoubtedly, being Madame Roland – in an alliance, and what was their purpose?

The answer must lie in the nature of the information they tried to prise from old Crooke and this was what I wanted, yet dreaded to hear. And so, disguising my trepidation, I asked him what they had wished to know.

His eyes sought the ground. He muttered, 'They wished

to hear the accounts men give of the fire and the death of the late Mrs. Rochester,' then burst out, 'Madam, I was afraid – I could not resist, so I told them, and thought – there, that is done, it is over. But next day the widow came back, alone, with more questions, many of which I could not answer, for they concerned matters I could not know – and then she came alone, a third time, this morning early, Mrs. Rochester,' he said passionately, 'desiring me, yet again, to remember what I saw on the night of the fire, and what others saw. Madam, I have told her all I, and the others, know, and it is very painful and disturbing to rehearse again that terrible event. But she will not be content. It is as if there is something yet to be known, and this information she desperately craves and she will not give up until she has got it. She is like a woman possessed.'

The old fellow was plainly very much alarmed. And I no less so, I believe.

What mystery could there be concerning the events at Thornfield over a decade ago? Mrs. Poole had been there – heaven knows, she had been there. My head spun, yet I was forced to rally myself for the old man's sake.

I put a hand on his shoulder. 'I will speak to Mrs. Poole, find out what is occurring and why you are being worried in this way. I will speak to Mr. Rochester, also, and get his guarantee as to your safety. Go home now, and rest. You are upset.'

He thanked me, turned and left. I stood for a while, gazing out over the fields and up to the foothills of the mountains, where long fringes of shadow extended down their slopes. The wind was chill and I began to hurry back to Thornfield, my mind in turmoil. I was not helped by the knowledge that for so many years I had taught myself not to think much on those old days there, nor of the fire which had destroyed the house. Old days, long ago, yet suddenly I knew they were coming closer, just as those long shadows reaching down over the hills came, saying to me, no sun without shadows, Jane, no sun without shadows. And, brood as I might, I could still find no explanation for the questioning of old Arthur Crooke by the woman from Old House and Mrs. Poole.

I made my way slowly back to Thornfield, knowing sadly the house to be empty and that it would be many days before Edward returned to me.

As I came through the open door, I observed Mrs. Poole and Madame Roland in the hall, talking like conspirators and, again like conspirators, they broke apart when they saw me. The woman Roland even had the audacity to advance towards me, in mock politeness, as if she had merely come to call. She could not know that I overheard her arguing with Edward, and confronted me brazenly.

I did not greet her or hold out my hand, but assumed a firm demeanour, though in actuality I concealed some inward uncertainty. I said, 'I have just seen an old servant from Thornfield, Arthur Crooke. He is very upset that you have been visiting him frequently and questioning him against his will. And I believe you, Mrs. Poole, have been threatening him with the loss of his cottage and his income – by what right, I do not know.'

Grace Poole, during this, had been standing in the shadows, by the pillar. I said, 'Come forward, Mrs. Poole. I am anxious to discover why you have been badgering that poor old man. I think we will go into the drawing-room. There, perhaps, you will both explain yourselves to me.'

And with that I led the way into the drawing-room and

they followed. Once inside I closed the door. 'Will you sit, Madame Roland?' I invited coldly.

'No, Mrs. Rochester, thank you,' she responded, and her mien and tone were very stately. 'I would prefer to stand.' And stand she did, tall and erect, entirely composed and with a challenging look. 'You wish to know why I have been visiting Arthur Crooke in his cottage, asking him questions about the fire at Thornfield and the death of the late Mrs. Rochester?'

As I have said, I cannot hear that woman, Bertha Mason, given the title of Mrs. Rochester, without a shudder. It wounds me like a blow.

'Bertha Mason, you mean,' I said.

'No, Mrs. Rochester is who I mean,' she told me.

'I am Mrs. Rochester.'

'You say that proudly,' she observed. 'Perhaps that is understandable in view of your beginnings. Yes – I see you are proud of your title, Mrs. Rochester of Thornfield. We shall see how proud you are when you have heard what I have to say.'

Stung by her insolence, I replied, 'I do not know what you mean. I know only that, though you are able to frighten a poor old man, you cannot frighten me.'

'I am glad you are so brave. I think you had better sit down and listen to me.'

Angered by her daring to speak to me so in my own drawing-room, I contemplated telling her forthwith I had no desire to hear what she had to relate, that she must leave. But Grace Poole, who had been standing quietly near the door, raised her voice, saying, 'You would do well to listen, Mrs. Rochester. There is much you do not understand.'

I hesitated. Madame Roland was arrogant, Grace Poole,

my housekeeper, had spoken to me as an equal – moreover, as a servant she had no place in this interview. Yet I was surrounded by mysteries Edward was not here to explain and, wisely or unwisely, I heeded her and decided to hear more from Madame Roland.

'Leave the room Mrs. Poole,' I ordered and this she did. Then I turned to Madame Roland. 'I will hear you,' I told her, 'if you will speak civilly and explain your actions.'

'You do well' she said, with a cynical air. 'After all, where is your husband now? Vanished, at the first sign of trouble.'

'If this is the tone you propose to adopt, Madame Roland,' said I, 'you will have to leave.'

'Do not be so proud – and listen to me,' she demanded. 'Now then, know first what evidently your husband has not chosen to tell you. I am Bertha Mason's sister.'

I gazed at her, unable to believe what I heard. This could not be true. I had heard of no sister to Bertha Mason, only a brother. But as I searched my memory for recollections of the madwoman, I saw that there was resemblance between that raving, dishevelled creature and the woman who stood before me. There was the same massy black hair, though Bertha's had been matted and tangled and Madame Roland's was smooth. There were the great black eyes, though Madame Roland's burned with a fire at least reasonable, where Bertha's had rolled, fearsomely, in her insanity. There was the same dark complexion, the same strength of body – though Madame Roland's strength was contained, while Bertha's had been uncontrolled, expressed in desperate writhings and violent assaults on others. Nevertheless, comparing the two women's appearance, what Madame Roland said might be true.

'You had better sit down,' she advised me, without sympathy. 'You are expecting a child; I hear you have been ill. We shall both sit, and you will hear me out.'

And I obeyed her.

'You will know, at least,' she said, 'that when your husband arrived in the West Indies, where my family lived, he was a penniless younger son and his marriage to my sister made him, through her dowry, prosperous. It was only later, when his older brother died, that he became Rochester of Thornfield.' The expression of contempt as she said these words was chilling. She continued, 'What I imagine you will not know is that before the marriage your husband agreed that Bertha's dowry was to be repaid to her family at her death, if she died childless. Had she had children, of course, her dowry would have gone to them. That is not an unusual provision. Bertha is dead, but the money has not been repaid.'

'You have come to claim money?' I said.

'That is part of it,' she told me. 'You must know that when that unfortunate marriage took place and the dowry was paid, the Masons were a prosperous family with rich plantations in Jamaica. But soon after, with the abolition of slavery, the plantation owners, my family among them, found themselves much reduced, in some cases ruined. My parents are aged and still in the West Indies. They are in want of money. My brother, whom you saw when Rochester attempted that travesty of a marriage to you, is in Jamaica with them. He has written to your husband, more than once, explaining the family's need for the return of the dowry, but Rochester has not condescended to reply. My brother is unwell and cannot travel, so it fell to me, since I live no further than Paris, to approach your husband.

He has told me he cannot and will not repay the dowry.'

She gazed scornfully about her. 'I'm afraid you must accept the fact that this grand rebuilding, all your paint and papers and furniture, have been paid for by money brought to him by my poor sister. You look at me with the contempt of a creditor facing an importunate debtor but let me tell you, it is you who owe the debt. But that is the least of it. I am here to discover the truth about my sister's death. You will not find this strange. You are not a bad woman, I feel. You will understand that I loved my sister.' She paused. 'Have you never asked yourself what really occurred on the night of the fire at Thornfield?'

'I know what occurred,' I said faintly, for in my mind's eye I saw, yet again, that last desperate scene, as, the servants rescued, my husband tried to save Bertha from the roof, whither she had fled.

'No, Mrs. Rochester,' Madame Roland said emphatically, 'no one knows what occurred that night, no one but Edward Rochester. He and Bertha were the only people left in the house. It is to discover what really took place that night that I have come here, talked to Mrs. Poole, and questioned the old man. You see, there are aspects of Bertha's death which were confusing at the time. The only account we, her family, had of the events came from Edward himself, written under dictation when he was still blinded and gravely injured. We believed him, of course – how not?

'And then other reports began to reach us. Rochester was wed, and to the very lady he had tried to marry fraudulently while my sister was alive! – Rochester's health was recovered – Rochester was father of a healthy boy – and, finally, Rochester was rebuilding Thornfield!

And all that remained to us, Bertha's family, were unanswered questions, and an unrepaid dowry. What do you think we felt, Mrs. Rochester? Do you think we come too soon, after ten years, demanding the truth? You know now who I am and why I am here. Do you not wonder – are you not curious – why your husband has chosen to tell you none of this?'

'You talk of truth,' said I. 'It is not truth you come for. You come to get vengeance.'

'What you call vengeance, some would call justice,' she returned angrily. 'Do you think it pleases me to come here, to talk to the man who drove my sister mad, brought her here to this cold and hostile place and incarcerated her in an attic – and then, for aught I know, killed her?'

I stood up. 'Mrs. Roland – you are vile! You must leave.'

But she ran on, unstoppable. 'What an opportune death,' she cried, 'that of a mad and wealthy wife, when all the time he wanted to marry his bastard's governess, had indeed tried to do so though the wife was still living. Oh,' she said, 'he has charm, Rochester, he is fascinating, attractive – but a villain nevertheless. What of his child, Adèle still unacknowledged?' She came up close to me. 'What, in the end, of you, my dear, if he decides he wants you no longer. Look – look – at the man you married.'

I was sick, dizzy, blackness before my eyes. I must have found a chair; I think I heard the door close. Moments later, when I looked up, Madame Roland had gone and Mrs. Poole was at my side.

'Madam,' she said, 'shall I help you to your room?' But I could not bear the thought of her touch and said, 'No. I will go alone,' and managed to do so.

I lay for hours like one struck down, my mind fogged,

my limbs seeming too heavy to move. I understood that for my own sake I should be thinking about what Madame Roland had told me, but my body and indeed my mind resisted, perhaps knowing that for the sake of my coming child I should do nothing. Alas, I thought, for the woman who must meet such emergencies when she is with child.

Before I knew it, darkness had come. Though still scarcely in control of mind or body, I rose and went into Edward's dressing-room through the connecting door and then into his bedroom. The lamp I carried illuminated a spartan room, where all was proper, yet there was little of decoration or comfortable touches. I had not imagined, when planning the house, that Edward would use this room for so long. There was his empty bed, the cover stretched tautly over it, there were the pillows, undented where his dear head should have been. I put the lamp on the floor and sat down upon that empty bed, mourning his absence.

I felt helpless. Perhaps I should not have listened to Madame Roland's fearful allegations while Edward was away. But then, I had no idea of what would be their nature until she spoke. And, with Edward gone, how could I refute them? I could not understand why he had told me nothing of all this. Plainly he had recognised Madame Roland in church, either from her past or from the resemblance to the sister he had married. Madame Roland dwelt in the neighbourhood. She had written to him; she had come to the house – and still he had told me nothing.

Where, I wondered sadly, had his old confidence in me gone? Where now was that reliance on my judgement of which he so often spoke? He had extolled me for my help to him not just as wife, but as companion, friend, partner, though of course the lesser one, in his affairs.

And now, at this time of great difficulty, he was silent. Of Madame Roland's charges I thought little; her claim in the matter of the dowry was dubious; her suspicions about her sister's death absurd. It was chiefly Edward's silence that troubled me. And now he was gone, gone away without explanation. In my robe and nightgown I clutched my arms about me and rocked to and fro in anguish, my hair tumbled about my shoulders.

Meanwhile a wind had come up. It struck the windows; the lamp flickered. Glancing sideways, in the dim light, I saw in a small mirror set on the far wall the very figure of a madwoman. At this I stood up quickly and reproached myself bitterly for giving way in this manner. What use could I be to my husband in his affliction, I asked myself? What use to myself? I must be calm, retire, rest, if I could not sleep, and plan for the future, decide what action, if any, I might take to assist Edward.

I took up the lamp and left the room. As I passed through Edward's dressing-room, I paused. The air smelt faintly of the soap he used. There was his wardrobe; there his boot-jacks; there the walnut table with ewer and basin, the tortoise-shell-backed hair brushes, with his initials set in silver. He always kept a pistol in one of two shallow drawers of this table in case of burglars entering the house. Had he, I wondered, taken it with him on his journey, indicating that he was going to a place where there might be something to fear? Such a thought would not have entered my head only a few months earlier. That it did so now was the measure of my anxiety. And so I opened the drawer.

The pistol, to my relief, still lay there, but beside it was another object, small and gleaming in the light of my upheld lamp. It was a miniature, framed in finely engraved gold, portraying a woman, young and very beautiful. Her fair hair was piled softly on her head in such a way that curls framed her delicately made face. Her eyes, brilliant and hazel in colour, were set beneath beautifully arched brows. She was smiling, a cool smile, knowing and gay, with a kind of worldliness in it.

I had no need to ask who this woman was. I knew the face, knew it well. It was almost identical to the face of Adèle, but this was not she. This woman's hair was artfully arranged in a way which spoke of sophistication, tendrils clustered beside the long white neck, which bore a costly necklace of pearls. She was not a girl; she was a woman. It could only have been a portrait of Céline Varens, Adèle's mother.

I had never seen this picture before. It had not been in this drawer while we had been at Ferndean. I took it up and shone the lamp I held on to it. Light fell on that beautiful face, and I wondered, in anguish, what this could mean and, alas, in my jealous heart I imagined my husband in the long watches of the night, perforce lonely, brooding over the portrait of his former mistress. It could not be, it could not, I told myself, but it was no use – the worm of jealously grew ever greater in my unhappy breast.

I had received little comfort in my early life and, being motherless, no love. I think those who have been so deprived can never have true confidence in the love of others, never believe that, one day, love given may not be taken away. It is an affliction to be borne, and borne privately, a want of faith in others which must be struggled with – but now, in the darkness of that night, I was wounded at my weakest point.

My heart filled with pain and despair. She was beautiful, Céline, so beautiful. She had betrayed and mocked

Edward, and when she abandoned her eight-year-old daughter it was he who had rescued the child from destitution – he had brought her to England and provided for her ever since. All this I knew full well. But Céline had been beautiful, a love of his younger years, taken up, admittedly, when he had been forced to recognise he was permanently tied to a madwoman but – nevertheless, Céline had been the early love, the love of a whole man, young in a beautiful city. It would not be strange if now he brooded over that dead love. Did he perhaps think of her beauty and compare her with me, small and undistinguished as I was?

My limbs were leaden, the child within me seemed, at that moment – may heaven forgive me – like a burden I carried unwillingly and could not put down. I laid the portrait back in the drawer and returned to my room, Céline's face ever before my eyes. My resolution, to calm myself and try to think steadily about the situation in which Edward and I found ourselves, was quite gone. I passed the night in great agony of mind.

Chapter XV

I lay sleepless till dawn, with the wind banging on the window-panes and howling around the house like a soul in pain. Then at dawn I rose, determined of only one thing, to bring Edward back to my side, for I could not, in my frailty, endure any more time alone, in ignorance of facts which only he could supply and suffering tortures of doubt concerning his love for me. Madame Roland's cruel contempt, the discovery of the miniature of Céline Varens in the drawer in his dressing-room, everything conspired to damage my confidence and faith in myself – even, heaven help me, in him.

My love for Edward and his for me had transformed my very existence. The threat of any withdrawal or diminution of that love filled me with a fear greater than that of loss of life itself. I knew that without Edward's love and support I would be plunged into torment, utterly bereaved. It was an incontrovertible fact that I could not sustain life without him. I could no longer endure this agony alone.

I wrote to his partner, Mr. Jessop, in Manchester, enclosing a message to be passed urgently to him. In it I said, 'The lady from Old House, Madame Roland, has been to me with many calumnies about you. I am anxious and unwell. Please, my dearest, come to me soon.'

That day I had appointed to go to Mr. Weatherfield at Ferndean to see my boy, and though I felt unwell and the weather was poor, I must go, for Jonathan expected me. I had begun to collect together the little gifts I was to take with me when Dolly, the maid, came to me with the information that I could not set out at once for one of the carriage horses had cast a shoe. To shorten the delay, Jeremy had harnessed up the other horse and taken the carriage down to the village smithy. Once the second horse was shod, he would speedily harness it and come back to the house for me.

'If the carriage is in Hay,' said I, 'I will go down and meet it, and we will start the journey from there.' For in spite of the weather I felt stifled and nervous in the house. I had the impression that the great mansion was bearing down on me and that I was unable to sustain its weight.

'Oh no, madam,' Dolly called out in alarm, 'don't do that. Do not go to the village alone.' Then her hand went to her mouth, as if she wished she had not spoken so.

She was a good girl, from Lower Hay, lacking the dullness and lack of hope which seemed to me characteristic of that place. 'Why do you say that?' I asked her.

'I shouldn't have,' she said in confusion. Yet, once again she burst out, 'No, Mrs. Rochester, madam – you must not go to the village. It would be dangerous for you.'

'Dangerous? What can you mean?'

The poor girl was confused and blushing. She twisted her hands. 'Those folk – the folk of Hay – are very ignorant,' she mumbled. 'Madam, they fear Mr. Rochester

– and you too, for you are married to him. They are saying things – such things. Madam, the mood is very ugly in Hay. I ask pardon for speaking thus.'

And then in came Mrs. Poole for her morning orders and, overhearing these last words, gazed at Dolly sternly, then at me. She asked, 'What are you saying, Dolly?'

The girl's confusion grew deeper. 'Mrs. Poole I . . .I . . .'

'Oh, be off with you,' said Mrs Poole impatiently. 'I will talk to you later.' And Dolly went. 'I'm sorry, Mrs. Rochester, if the silly girl has been troubling you,' said Mrs. Poole stiffly. 'I'm doing my best to train her, but the local people are unused to good service. I will be stern with her.'

'Mrs. Poole,' I said, 'she tells me there is hostility to Mr. Rochester in Hay, and I believe you may have something to do with it, you and Madame Roland, with your gossip and tales and your persecution of Arthur Crooke. Let me tell you this. I do not intend to be kept out of Hay by these stupidities. Nor do I intend to forget your part in all this. There will be consequences, let me assure you. Meantime, please have the goodness to fetch my cloak. I am going down to Hay.'

'Madam—' she said.

'Get my cloak,' I told her.

She bowed her head so that I could not read her expression. 'Very good, madam,' she said in a low voice, and went she off to do as I had bidden.

I took up my packages and left the house. The wind was tearing at the trees; the last remaining leaves whirled through the air. On the road to Hay, I felt forced along by the wind pushing at my back. So, thought I, the malevolence and evil talk of those two bad women has stirred up the village against Edward. This explained, of course, why, as I had walked through the day before, all doors had been slammed against me.

There could be no question now that Mrs. Poole must leave the house. I would persuade Edward on his return that his charity towards her had been misguided.

The blacksmith's forge lay at the far end of the village street so that to reach it I should have to walk the length of Hay. From where I stood I could see our carriage outside the blacksmith's. As I began to walk towards it one of a group of three working men, plodding uphill, evidently towards the lead mines, noted me below and pointed me out to the others. All three turned, lamps in hand, to watch expressionlessly as I walked by. A woman on her knees outside a cottage, plucking a cabbage from her kitchen garden no more than ten feet from me, stared at me, on her face an expression of what looked like apprehension, even fear. As I got further into the village matters grew worse, much worse. I heard a door slam behind me, ahead a woman dragged a crying child indoors. The street appeared deserted. Then, from a narrow gap between two cottages, two men appeared and barred my way. Both were young, ill-shaven and grimy, their waistcoats and trousers ragged and dirty. They looked at me ferociously, like savage dogs. The street was otherwise quite empty.

'May I pass?' said I, attempting to appear calm.

'We don't want you here,' said one, the taller – and I thought with alarm of the child I carried.

'I am on my way to the blacksmith's. You have no right to bar my path,' I told him.

'Right or no right, we do not want you here,' he said.

'Not you, nor your husband, nor any Rochester,' said the other. 'I warn you – turn back, lady.'

There was a pause. I was hardly able to believe they

were prepared to lay hands on a woman, and a woman, moreover, whose husband was their landlord, yet that, I saw, must be their intention.

'I do not understand,' I said. 'I think you owe me an explanation. What are your names?'

'I will give you no name, but I will give you an explanation,' the taller man said. 'Your husband is an evil man – wherever he goes, he brings harm. Some round here fear him, saying he is in league with the devil, others think him a plain villain, an exploiter and a wife-murderer. And you, so small and meek-seeming as you are – you are nothing but an accomplice to him in his wickedness. You own the houses, the land and mine, all that there is about here, and for this reason many fear you; but you do not own us all. We do not want you here, and some of us are ready to tell you so, no matter what the punishment.'

'And punishment there will be,' I assured him hotly. 'I will find out who you are. How dare you speak thus of my husband?'

'Just go,' said the second man, his eyes hardening.

But I could not decide what to do. I was deeply frightened, yet how could I allow myself to be chased from the village?

Mercifully, just then a voice from the other end of the street called, 'Mrs. Rochester!'

It was Jeremy, who stood outside the forge at the end of the street, holding the newly shod horse. He paused, then, handing the horse's bridle to the blacksmith, began to walk towards me. Meanwhile, I and the two men stayed where we were, as if frozen.

Halfway between us and the forge, Jeremy called out, 'What's going on here?'

The tall man looked at him as he came. 'We're inviting

your mistress to go home, return to her big house and leave us to our squalor,' he called back contemptuously.

'Don't be stupid, man,' called Jeremy, still coming on.

The tall man turned back to me. 'Stupid we may be, and ignorant we may be, but we're not mad and wicked like Edward Rochester.'

I opened my mouth to speak, but Jeremy had reached us now.

'Be quiet, man, or you'll get into trouble,' he told the other. 'Let the lady pass – she's nothing to do with all this.'

With that he walked round the two men, held out his arm to me, I took it and we walked away. I felt eyes, many eyes, on my back as we went down the deserted street to the forge, and my legs seemed weak and barely able to carry me.

The blacksmith was outside the smithy as we arrived, an expression of anxiety on his face. 'There's a stool in there, Mrs. Rochester,' he said promptly. 'We'll harness the coach up now and you can be off. My wife will fetch you some water.'

He helped me to a stool at the side of the smithy, his wife gave me water in a horn cup and, attempting to disguise the alarm I was still feeling after being so roughly used, I drank.

Not long after, Jeremy had the second horse back in the traces and he helped me into the carriage. 'I hope you are better now, madam,' he said. 'This is a nasty place. Some villages go bad, like people, and I fear this is one of them. Do you still wish to go to Ferndean, or will you go home instead?'

My boy was waiting for me at Ferndean and with that in mind I said, 'To Ferndean,' and we set off. I was much relieved to put Hay behind us and glad to be travelling towards that quiet landscape, those fields and orchards where Edward, I and Jonathan had been, it seemed to me, happiest. Yet, as we went, I could not forget the angry faces of those two brutes who had menaced me, nor those of the two evil women who had stirred up so much trouble against us.

When we reached the rectory my dear little Jonathan ran out, all smiles, to greet me, followed by the kindly Weatherfields and their sons. The boys jointly opened the gifts I had brought for Jonathan.

'But I would sooner live at Thornfield with you and Papa,' my boy said wistfully over lunch. There was that in my face as he spoke – and I think she may have seen other signs of disquiet – to make Mrs. Weatherfield take me to one side later and, shortly before my alas all-too-early departure, enquire, 'My dear, is all well with you at Thornfield?' To which I replied, 'I fear it is not. There are difficulties, but I hope they will be of short duration. In the meantime I owe you a great debt for taking such good care of Jonathan.'

I wished I could have told her more, for at her concerned enquiry I was suddenly aware how heavy was the burden of anxiety I bore alone, without the help and consolation of one human being whom I could count a true friend. Yet I could not reveal to anyone the affairs of my husband and family, though I knew that tears had come to my eyes, and kind Mrs. Weatherfield had noted them, though she said nothing. It was weakness, I knew, yet so little kindness had I received over the last weeks (and so much, I could not help thinking, of the reverse).

'Well, Jane,' said Mrs. Weatherfield, 'I shall pray for heaven to protect you. And be assured, we shall take as good care of Jonathan as of our own sons.' And we embraced.

I bade Jonathan farewell, telling him I would come again soon, and departed that place where for ten years all had been love and happiness, with, I confess, the feeling of being cast out of Eden.

How I wished during the journey back to Thornfield that I might find Edward at home on my return, but I knew it was most unlikely my letter had yet reached him. So I re-entered a silent, empty house, ate a little supper and went, exhausted, to bed.

Eventually I shut my eyes in sleep, only to be woken with a start not half an hour later. I heard the madwoman's laugh, Bertha Mason's laugh, echoing through the house. I lay in horror in the pitch darkness of the room in a kind of waking dream, still hearing the maniacal laugh of that woman, ten years dead, ringing round. Then my mind went again to the beautiful face, to the lovely, knowing eyes in the miniature of Céline. Tired, worn, sobbing weakly, I lay in a kind of stupor. That laugh came again. Oh Edward, Edward, I cried silently, come home to me soon.

Chapter XVI

S uch nights, however, end and are succeeded by morning and the day's tasks. I summoned up my resolution and rose early next day, determined to go about my normal duties, for I knew that the tale of what had occurred the day before in the village would have reached the house and I wished it to be seen that I was unmoved and in full charge of my household.

When Mrs. Poole came for orders just as if I had not been angry with her the day before, I sent her back to her room, indignant at her insolence. I then called Mr. Sugden, the estate manager, and spoke to him at some length about the restoration of the garden. He had been in charge of Thornfield during its years of decline and I knew him, for he had come twice a year to report to my husband, and I believed him a trustworthy man.

I outlined my wishes and plans for the garden and ordered the hire of a man and a boy to begin the work of digging, rebuilding the walls and marking out beds. I then said, 'The village is very stirred up against Mr. Rochester. Will you tell me why?'

The abruptness of this question took him back. 'Mrs. Rochester,' he said, 'I know there is bad feeling. But please understand it is not my place to say anything. The people there are very ignorant – that I will say.'

'There are ugly rumours flying.'

'That there are. Mr. Rochester will be able to deal with everything on his return, I expect.'

'I am sure he will,' I told him.

Now, I had risen after that dreadful night – when my imagination had brought back to me that demon Bertha Mason and the beautiful, mocking face of Céline Varens – with full determination to chase these devils away with useful action. Yet, in truth, after talking to Sugden, there was little left for me to do. At Ferndean we should have been preserving for the winter but here at Thornfield there was nothing to preserve, for nothing had been grown. Nor could I work at gardening, for such was the state of the garden that much rough work, of which I was incapable, must be done before I could begin. At Ferndean I might have played with my son; or gone to the kitchen to create with my own hands a tasty dish for Edward – but the lady of Thornfield could not go into her own kitchen, and alas, the lady of Thornfield's husband was absent. In short, I had anxieties aplenty, and no occupation.

Therefore, to throw off melancholy, I put on my cloak, gloves and hat and took my way, from the back of the house, across the fields of the home farm in the direction of the mountains, waking over walled field – poor ones, it must be said, fit only for hay or oats. The activity consoled me somewhat. Ahead lay the mountains, their slopes coloured by grass and patches of bright heather; overhead was a huge pale-blue sky full of moving white clouds. Then over the brow of a hill some quarter of a mile from where I stood I saw a sea of moving sheep, some figures running, and dogs, and then the figure of

Sugden on his big brown mare. They were bringing the sheep down for winter, for slaughtering or for pasturing in lower fields, away from the fierce weather to come.

I stood watching this spectacle for some time, as Sugden and his men and dogs gathered up more than a hundred sheep and drove them, in a long, living stream, along the top of the hill and down one side of it. Keen-eyed, at one point he spotted me and lifted an arm in friendly greeting.

A little calmer and more cheerful for my walk, I turned for home, hoping against hope that on my return Edward would be there. Yet I had to recognise that he might have left Manchester for London and having no London address for him. I was reliant on Mr. Jessop's forwarding of my message. How long it might take my letter to reach him in London I did not know. I knew nothing now of my husband's movements, not where he had gone, nor why. I had never known so little of his concerns. He had never told me so little. Nevertheless, I returned to Thornfield more optimistic than I had set out. What was marred could be mended, I hoped.

On my return I was greeted with the news that a visitor, Lady Norton, awaited me. This lady had formerly been Blanche Ingram, the beauty whom I had once believed to be Edward's chosen bride. An invitation to her wedding to Lord Norton, whose estate and home, Raybeck Hall, lay some fifteen miles from Thornfield, had come one day to Ferndean, but Edward had chosen not to go, pleading his ill health and incapacity. So I had not seen that haughty beauty Blanche Ingram, now Lady Norton, since I was first at Thornfield, as governess to Adèle – and she had thoroughly snubbed me then. In short, we had not been friends and I was doubtful that we ever should be.

A call by Lady Norton was what I least desired at this troubling time and had I had any choice in the matter I should certainly have preferred to receive her with Edward in the quiet of Ferndean rather than now, alone, at Thornfield. This was a challenge, though one I felt I must do my best to meet, giving her no hint of my anxieties, not allowing her to patronise me on account of my former position.

I entered the drawing-room, where she was seated and she arose, hand outstretched, to greet me. She was tall and dressed in high fashion; the years had done nothing to erode her beauty. She said in her low pleasant voice, 'Mrs. Rochester, how delightful to see you again after so many years. I hope you will not mind my calling unexpectedly. I had business in Millcote and, thinking you must now be fairly well installed, I thought I would allow myself the pleasure of a visit. You look well – have you been out walking?' For her eyes had evidently taken in my plain dress.

'Yes,' I said. 'I have been watching them gather up the sheep from the hills.'

'The countryside about here is not short of such opportunities,' she remarked.

'Will you have some tea?' I offered.

She accepted and then said, 'I am so glad to see the Rochesters back at Thornfield. Indeed, we all are. They told me Mr. Rochester is away from home at present.'

'He has business affairs in Manchester to attend to. Do you spend much time in the country, or are you more in London?' I asked.

'Oh, half and half, I should say,' she responded. 'I like to be in town. I find it stimulating. You must persuade Mr. Rochester to bring you. I should be pleased to recommend you to friends who sometimes let their houses there.'

'I shall be content here for some time, I expect,' said I.

'I expect you will,' replied Blanche Norton. 'And how is your little boy? Well, I hope.'

'He is. Have you children, Lady Norton?'

'Alas, so far we have not been blessed.' She looked about her, without evident pleasure. 'This is charming,' she said. 'Mr. Rochester must be most pleased to have returned.'

'I believe he is,' said I.

'He will, of course, have sad memories. That dreadful fire – we feared for his life. How splendid, what a tribute to his fortitude, that he has managed such a magnificent recovery. Your husband is a man of extraordinary capabilities, my dear.'

I noted that as we spoke her manner, fashionably charming, had become a little hard.

'Will he hunt, do you suppose, now he is back?'

'He speaks of it. I confess I am not so enthusiastic. It is after all a dangerous affair.'

'You must not try to trammel the free spirit of Mr. Rochester,' she said with a cold smile, adding, 'How welcome his return – ten years' absence from a neighbourhood is a long time for the land and for a locality without the stabilising force of a landlord close at hand.'

'Yes. It has been a long time,' I said dully. Blanche Norton had lost nothing of her old air of command. Indeed, it had increased with the years. She was overwhelming now.

'Mr. Rochester will no doubt get all in order now he is back,' she said evenly. I suspected she, a woman who did nothing without a purpose, had heard there was trouble

117

in Hay and come to discuss it, since the troubles of one landlord often affect his neighbours.

'I am sure of it,' I responded. 'And for myself I plan to start a small school at Hay.'

She leaned back in her chair. 'My dear!' she exclaimed. 'What need?' Her next sentence confirmed my view that rumours were flying. 'What is required at Hay is the regular presence of the landlord and a sense that he is in control and says what is to be done, and not done. Of course, there will always be difficulties in places where there are mines and men getting employment unconnected with the land. It leads to a certain attitude . . .' Her voice trailed off then strengthened again. 'No, my dear, I must tell you I do not think your plan a good one. The working folk do not need unnecessary learning. I know of many cases where such things have stirred up trouble in the neighbourhood – machine-breaking and the like. What is required in the countryside today is not more book-learning, it is a firm hand. Besides, my dear, you will soon have other matters, more interesting ones, to concern you. Now, tell me, will you dine with us on Thursday? We have coming Sir George Lynn, Colonel and Mrs. Dent and one or two others. I hope you will agree to join us.'

And, reluctantly, I was forced to accept the invitation. She stood up to go and as we parted asked, 'And when do you think Mr. Rochester will be back?'

I stammered, 'I have sent him a message – I am not sure.'

She nodded, but was unable to conceal some satisfaction at my discomfiture. 'He will be back soon, then. And so – we expect the pleasure of your company on Thursday.'

In the drawing-room doorway she paused, looking out into the hall. 'No – I cannot believe my eyes. My dear!' she exclaimed, and moved swiftly forward.

She blocked my own view so that I could not see whom she addressed. But as she moved into the hall a figure, in a travelling-cape, wearing a smart fur hat, holding a muff and with a valise at her feet, was revealed to me. Adèle! Adèle to whom I had written telling her to remain in Switzerland. She was tall and lithe, her pale hair was charmingly arranged under the fur hat, and her lovely face bore a calm smile. Yet, as I approached in welcome and her eyes turned to mine, I saw that though her lips smiled those almond eyes did not. They were cold, cold as topaz. Then those eyes swept over me and I believe she noted instantly I expected a child.

I chose not to ask her whether she had received my letter, but led her into the drawing-room saying, 'You have just come from Switzerland? You must be tired. Will you have some tea? Or will you go and rest?' Blanche had followed us, unwilling to depart before she had seen Adèle's homecoming.

Adèle dropped her mantle on the floor and seated herself comfortably in a chair, with a sigh. Looking about her, she said, 'Oh, how nice. And how lovely it is to be back in my old home, dear old Thornfield. But, Step-mama, I must tell you of the wonderful curtains made by the weavers of Lyon. I am sure if you saw their work you would pull down all the curtains in the house and replace them.'

'There is nothing wrong with a good English decorative style, I think,' Blanche said. She turned to me, 'These young things, they have their ideas.'

'N'est-ce pas?' laughed Adèle, and with a charming

gesture, added in French, 'The old must give place to the new – am I not right?'

'Oh,' smiled Blanche Norton, 'I see we shall have to look to ourselves, with Miss Rochester, the revolutionary of the decorative arts, among us.' Then she asked Adèle, 'Have you plans, my dear, now you are home?'

'I have had enough of plans,' said Adèle. 'For so long I have been subject to routines imposed by others – lessons, church, exercise, then exercise, church, lessons. I think I deserve a little time without plans.'

'I am sure you do,' Blanche assured her, while I understood from this last statement that Adèle believed herself home for good, which, I confess, was not welcome news to me.

I wondered how this young woman would employ herself all day. She was now the age, eighteen, that I had been when I set out into the world to earn my living and in pursuit of this aim had gained a position at Thornfield Hall as her governess. But, thought I, as tea was brought into the room, Adèle would have no fixed employment such as that, which was perhaps the better for her, but what else could we find for her to do? I could not imagine in her a useful assistant in duties concerning the people of Hay – more particularly, in the school I planned to found. As a child she had been vain and pleasure-loving and the years had not altered that. No more improbable figure could be imagined than Adèle visiting the sickbeds of poor villagers, or teaching the rough children of the locality to chant their ABCs.

As soon as the table was set and the tea placed, Adèle captured the teapot. 'I must learn how to be a proper Englishwoman,' she said merrily, 'and teach myself to preside over the tea table. How glad I am to be home. And how is my amiable guardian, my lovely father, my beloved Rochester?' which name she pronounced in the French way with a rolling 'r' – Rrrochestair. I noted that she had, gracefully, inserted the word 'father' in her description of him. She poured the tea and handed it to Blanche Norton, who, judging by her manner, seemed well pleased with this new member of our household.

'I have been trying to persuade Mrs. Rochester to come to London,' said she.

'Oh, how delightful. That, if anything, is above all what I desire, to see London, the museums, galleries – above all, the theatres.'

'And the shops, no doubt,' added Blanche.

'Oh, them above all,' agreed Adèle, and she and Blanche burst out laughing.

'Well,' said Blanche, when the laughter had died, 'well – my dears, I must leave you or I shall be late for my guests at dinner.' She stood, we all stood, and, repeating her invitation to dine at Raybeck Hall, this time including Adèle in the invitation, she departed.

Once she had gone, Adèle sobered. 'How pleasant it is to be back,' she said, leaning back in her chair, a piece of cake in her hand. 'But where is Rochester?'

'He's away on business,' I told her. 'Did you not receive my letter at the school?'

'What letter? No,' she said, biting into the cake and putting it back on her plate again with a grimace. 'I must have a word with Cook,' she declared.

'So you received no letter saying your father thought it better if you were to stay on until spring?' I asked.

'No,' she said. 'But, Step-mama, why should I stay? I'm eighteen now. It's time I began life away from school.

Did you urge him to keep me there until your child is born?'

'The decision was his,' I told her.

'Well, never mind. I'm here now,' she announced.

'What a charming English welcome – "Did you not receive my letter telling you not to come?" But I am here, Step-mama, and that is a fact, whether it pleases you or not,' and with that she got up and left the room. I heard her calling for help with her baggage and ordering it to be taken upstairs. She had not asked me which room she should take, but I thought I knew she would take the largest, the best.

I have said that, over the past ten years, Adèle and I had seldom lived together. When at school she had spent many of her holidays with friends. Since she had been in Switzerland she had returned to England twice, but on one occasion had stayed with my cousin Diana and her husband since there was insufficient room for her at Ferndean. Each spring Edward had gone to to visit her at school in Switzerland. Our encounters had been so few since her childhool it could have been said that Adèle and I did not know each other at all.

There was also a difficulty as to how, precisely, Adèle was to be described. When she lived at Thornfield as a child, the world had believed she was my husband's daughter. He had never stated this precisely, though he had told me once, years ago at Thornfield, 'perhaps she may be'. But there is a vast chasm between 'perhaps she may be' and 'is' in matters of this kind. Meanwhile, she was known as his ward. She had not scrupled to name Edward as her father before Blanche Norton, nor me as 'Step-mama' but, without my husband's absolute word on the subject, the question was not settled. If Adèle had returned to England for good, the matter must be resolved formally, so that everyone knew in what light she should be regarded.

I own it – I did not welcome her return. I did not like her claim to be my husband's daughter; I could not imagine how she would employ herself at Thornfield.

She did not come down to dinner and I sat alone in the dining-room, hoping against hope Edward would return that evening and begin to resolve the difficulties besetting us. But he did not come.

Chapter XVII

My sleep that night was penetrated by nightmares. When I woke the following morning I lay in a kind of stupor, recalling visions of fire licking roof-tiles, the madwoman poised on the parapet with her dishevelled hair, teeth bared, flames around her. In that state I rose, disturbed by the knowledge I was dwelling in a house which was an exact copy of that in which all these horrors had taken place. Above me was a replica of the top storey where the madwoman had been kept; above that – the roof from which she had plunged to her death.

Edward had been gone four days and I knew not how much longer he would be away. I decided I must be resolute and concern myself with what I could usefully do in his absence, for though my mind was ill at ease I knew I was stronger in body. I went early to the garden, where men were beginning the work on rebuilding the wall nearest the house and the gardener's assistant was digging out the paths. The gardener himself was on a ladder cutting back the wild tangled branches of the fruit trees. I moved to the far side of the garden and looked through the broken wall at the expanse of long, wild grass and at the thorn trees, all leaves gone now, their branches spiky and skeletal. I shivered and then, as if to defy the fearful image, thought I would see something more of the world of Thornfield Hall in which I found myself.

Mr. Sugden had come up to see how work on the garden was going, and I asked him to take me up to the lead mines, for this was what I had resolved earlier. He was very shocked. 'Mrs. Rochester,' he exclaimed, 'I cannot. Mr. Rochester would never want you to go there.'

'Why? Are the lead-miners and their families tigers, that I should be afraid to go among them? I understand they are employees of a company, yet they and their families are part of my care.'

'I do not think so, madam, with respect.'

'If not mine, then whose?' I asked him. 'Will the company which leases the land care for them? Come, Mr. Sugden. We both know there is bad feeling against the Rochesters in Hay and the mines are part of Hay; there are many dwellings there, and the people may be in want. I must see for myself.'

'I would much prefer not to, Mrs. Rochester,' he said soberly.

'Then you must tell me why not.'

'The people there are poor, profoundly ignorant. Their lives are brutish in the extreme. It is no fit place for you, Mrs. Rochester. Please believe me.'

But I insisted, for those mines were Edward's, and would be Jonathan's, and though the Blanche Nortons of this world are reared to believe they are born to be supplied and others born to supply them, I was not so educated. And I suspected matters at those mines, high up in the hills, might be very bad – and indeed they were.

I am an uncertain rider but Jeremy found me a quiet mount and we plodded to the verges of Hay, then took the rough track uphill towards the mines. On either side was hillside, where a few sheep grazed. As we ascended, the landscape became barer, a desert of stone and tufted grass in patches. Behind were the great bleak shapes of the mountains, overhung with cloud, snow on their heights. In many places the ground was pitted with vast excavations where the company which leased the land had dug pits in order to discover side-seams leading off from the main vein of lead.

The sound of a steady thumping came from all around, growing louder as we climbed. Ahead of me on their rocky track, Sugden called back, 'The sound is that of the steam pump at the bottom of the pits, pumping out the water. Usually in these parts the work stops during the winter months, for conditions are too hard, but profits are low at present, so they will keep working.'

'That must be bad for the miners,' said I.

'No worse than it will be later when they have no work and no pay,' he responded dourly.

Now we had reached the miners' dwellings. These straggled beside the track, or a little way off, in no pattern or order. Some were of wood, mere huts, others of stone, with one room or two. Chickens scratched on the bare ground in rough enclosures; there was a pig in a stone pen. A dirty brook ran down the hillside nearby.

There must have been, scattered across the hillside, some thirty or forty homes. Outside were the people, mostly women and children. If Hay was poor, these folk were poorer. Half the children had no proper shoes; some were barefoot, in spite of the cold. These children stared blankly as we progressed. Thin women, shawls over their heads, gazed at us, with guarded expressions on their faces.

'The wages here are low,' Sugden muttered. 'In the mills and factories, and among the canal-diggers and such, there's often good money, but these folk get much the same low rate as farm labourers and they can grow little here to feed themselves, on this poor soil. The great thing, Mrs. Rochester', he added, 'is to avoid Mangan, the manager. He thinks I've no business here.' Then he spotted a man on crutches, apparently about to take a bucket down to the stream. He called, 'Hey, Watkin!'

The man limped over slowly and stood by Sugden's horse. 'This man is out, due to an accident,' Sugden explained to me. He said to Watkin, who stood, pitifully thin, with his old greatcoat whipping about him in the bitter wind, 'Here's Mrs. Rochester from the big house, wanting to see how you're going on here. I don't want to talk to Mangan, though'.

'Oh, Mangan – him,' said the other despondently.

'Leg healing?' enquired Sugden. He turned to me. 'Mangan says I've no place here – he's the company's man, of course, and wants no interference from the landlord's agent. He sends for me fast enough, though, when there's an accident.' He turned back to the man. 'So, Watkin, is your leg mending?'

'It improves, by a miracle,' Watkin replied. 'He'll shut down the mine, though, before I'm ready for work again, Mangan will. On account of the weather.'

'The company will, I expect,' agreed Sugden.

'And then the hard times begin.'

'Well, you'll have a friend here in Mrs. Rochester,' Sugden told him. 'She wants to assist you. Look here, Watkin, you're a man who can read, write and figure. What you must do is make a list of all here, each family, with how many are working and how many children and their ages. Then you must give it to me and I will hand it to Mrs. Rochester and she will try to do her best for all of you.' He added, with emphasis, 'But do not tell Mangan, for I cannot afford to come up against the company at first. Once the deed is done and Mrs. Rochester is in charge, all will be well. Why should they object then,' he said, turning to me, 'when you will be making up the miners' pay? Had you considered that, madam?'

'I had not until now,' I told him. 'But I can't make it my business to quarrel with the employers, for that is beyond my sphere.'

Sugden nodded, satisfied. I looked down at the other man's wasted face. 'Mr. Watkin,' I said, 'will you, can you, do as Mr. Sugden suggests – make a list?'

'Speak up, man. Answer the lady,' Sugden told him impatiently. 'Here's a chance none of you can afford to refuse. Do your part, then, make the list. Look, here's a pencil and some paper. Will you do it?' He took a stub of pencil and a notebook from his breast pocket tore out some pages and passed them down to Watkin. 'I'll be back in two days. Not a word to Mangan.' Then to me he said, 'Come, Mrs. Rochester,' and, giving his horse a kick in the flank, he turned the animal round and set off down the hill.

I followed him down the steep and rocky path, past those dismal houses and their benumbed inhabitants, the majority, if not all, of whom were, it seemed to me, too cold and undernourished, too robbed of any hope, perhaps even to feel any emotion as we passed. My heart was weary at this sight for I believe no beings should be permitted to exist thus.

We were silent until we were down the hill and on the road back to Thornfield.

Then, 'Well, Mr. Sugden,' said I, 'thank you. You have been most helpful.'

'I hope Mr. Rochester will not blame me for taking you to that ugly place.'

Back at Thornfield I thanked him again for his help and told him I hoped my husband would agree to my making some efforts to improve conditions among the mining folk. 'It is wrong, surely, for men and women to live in such wretched conditions,' I said.

He looked at me soberly. 'You are very good, madam,' he said. 'If you wish my wife to help you I am sure she would be pleased to do so. She has often said . . .' he faltered a little ' . . . said that something might be done.'

'Good. That is excellent. I should welcome her assistance. However, the whole matter is of course for Mr. Rochester to decide,' I said, and we parted cordially.

I re-entered the house, still a little shaken by the sights I had witnessed at the lead mine. They told me Adèle had gone out for a walk. I went upstairs to change from my riding-dress and then noticed, as I tidied my hair in the glass, that the simple objects on my dressing-table – my brushes, a silver box of hair-pins, a flask of lavender-water – were disarranged. I opened a drawer. The box in which I kept my few items of jewellery had been moved, I thought, and I looked further and discovered more signs of careful search, though nothing was missing. I have that sense of order imposed on those brought up narrowly under strict regimes, or I might not have noticed the tiny displacements, for all that had been examined had been most carefully replaced. I had little doubt, alas, about the identity of the searcher. It must have been Adèle, though her motive was obscure to me. However, those who are curious about the possessions of others need no motive but their own curiosity.

I was angered, for such deeds, furtive and intrusive, are abhorrent and then, by a curious inspiration, went swiftly to Edward's dressing-room and looked in the drawer where I had discovered the miniature of Céline Varens. It was gone.

Returning to my own chamber, I sat down on the chair by the window, much perturbed. I could not accuse Adèle directly for she would undoubtedly deny the charge and there was no proof there had been a search, or that, if there had been, she was responsible. Such an accusation would transform me into the wicked step-mother she would so dearly like me to prove myself. And as to the miniature – to point out its removal would only establish that I was no better than she. I, too, had made a search in a place where I had no business to look.

Meanwhile, I wondered, where was she? The maid told me she had gone by the footpath to the church and so I thought I would follow her. In any event, I planned to call on Mr. Todd, with a view to discussing with him what measures might be taken to ameliorate the conditions of the mining folk.

I took the footpath also, for it led directly across fields from Thornfield a mere half-mile, and would not tax me unduly. The footpath led through the churchyard and as I entered it I observed a group of five people all staring in the direction of the church wall. Beside the wall was Adèle, kneeling on the ground, bent over, seeming to be in paroxysms of grief.

As I stood, amazed, I observed Mr. Todd hurrying along the path from the direction of the vicarage with a concerned air. Catching sight of me where I stood on the path, he came up to me. 'Mrs. Rochester. How delightful to see you. I have been called by my housekeeper, who told me there is a lady in the churchyard, much upset.'

'I believe it is my step-daughter, recently returned from abroad,' I said. 'I shall go to her.'

'Allow me to come with you,' he said. 'Perhaps I can be of assistance.'

We crossed the churchyard together. By the wall Adèle knelt, bent over a grave which was headed by a small stone. She was weeping. Mr. Todd went to her, spoke gently to her and raised her, still sobbing, to her feet. I looked at the headstone – a plain oval stone, rounded at the top, bearing the simple words 'Bertha Rochester, wife of Edward Fairfax Rochester of Thornfield Hall', with beneath them the dates.

This was the madwoman's final resting-place. For the first time I felt a little pity for that wretched creature, married off to a foreigner by an unscrupulous family who had concealed their hereditary taint, then, far from friends, descending into insanity, incarcerated at Thornfield – then the fire and her terrible death. When I had visited Thornfield while it was being rebuilt, I had wondered where she lay buried. This was a cruel way to find the place, with Adèle weeping beside it.

I could not understand why Adèle, having arrived back at Thornfield, had chosen to visit that grave so promptly, and express such strong emotion so publicly. She had not known the madwoman, who had been kept closely confined while Adèle was a child, and had no reason to mourn her so extravagantly. We led her, sobbing and leaning on Mr. Todd's arm, towards the vicarage, followed by the interested gaze of the spectators.

On the road outside the church, just as we were about

to turn into the vicarage drive, Madame Roland flew from her garden, grasped Adèle firmly by the upper arm, then turned to me and Mr. Todd saying, 'I see this lady is in distress. Let me take her inside and do what I can.'

Mr. Todd, a man whose first instinct was ever to avoid any complications in his life not previously assessed as being positively to his advantage, responded instantly, 'How very kind, Madame Roland. A lady's house may well provide more comfort than my own,' and began to guide Adèle across the road to Old House.

Madame Roland had acted so quickly that before I could protest Adèle was being supported into the house, where a trim maid waited. She was laid down on a sofa in the drawing-room and Madame Roland bent over her solicitously. From an upper room in the house, I realised, the lady would have had a complete view of that corner of the churchyard where Bertha Mason's grave was situated. Her arrival at her gate just as we were about to take Adèle into the vicarage was possibly, therefore, no accident.

The maid was instructed to fetch smelling-salts and prepare a tisane. 'Such things are most calming,' Madame Roland coolly informed me as, stunned by her audacity, I stood, reluctant, just inside the room.

Mr. Todd, meanwhile, began to withdraw, uttering many expressions of good will. As he did so, there came a furious knocking at the front door. Instants later, the parlour door filled with a form, weary and travel-stained – Edward's. His face was strained, his lips set firm.

'What is happening?' he demanded angrily. 'Why has Adèle been carried here? What is wrong with her?' All these questions were addressed to me, in a tone of cold rage.

133

Mr. Todd said uneasily, 'I was about to take my leave, sir.'

'Then please do so, Mr. Todd,' my husband said brusquely. And, with muttered greetings, compliments and hopes for the young lady's recovery, Mr. Todd eased himself past me and Edward, who had moved a pace or so into the room. Unacknowledged the clergyman then seemed to disappear.

'Get up, Adèle,' ordered my husband.

'Oh, Papa . . .' she said.

'Get up,' he repeated, and when she showed no signs of moving from her sofa he took several rapid strides towards her and, grasping her by the shoulder, raised her to her feet. Adèle shocked, made no resistance, but once erect stared at him in alarm.

'It is interesting to see a demonstration of the ruthlessness for which you are so famous, Mr. Rochester,' Madame Roland said coldly. Her maid began to enter the room with a tray, but she waved her back. 'I will ring for you.'

'My ward appears perfectly well and I do not wish her to remain any longer in your house,' responded Edward. 'You may call that ruthless if you wish.'

'She calls you Papa, but you call her your ward,' Madame Roland said. 'Which is it?'

Without a word Edward began to lead Adèle past me and towards the door. Madame Roland crossed the room quickly to intercept them. 'Since you are here,' she said, 'I have something to say to you.'

'I have nothing to say to you. Let us pass,' he commanded.

'Not until you have heard me.'

'Do not oblige me to put you out of my way,' he replied forcefully.

'Hear me.'

'No,' he said and, advancing still with Adèle on his arm, he made as if to walk, so to speak, through Madame Roland as she stood, still blocking the doorway. He was close to her now.

I moved forward, imploring, 'Madame Roland—'

'Rochester,' she hissed directly into his face, 'be still. Now listen to me, then I will let you go.'

'No one can prevent me from going where I wish to go. Move aside.'

'You killed my sister. I can prove it,' she said.

He halted. All three of us, Adèle, Edward and I, stood staring at that handsome face, twisted and black with bitterness.

'None but you,' she continued, 'knows what happened on the night of my sister's death – or so you thought. For up to now it has been your account – only yours – which has provided the explanation of what took place on that awful night. You have said that Bertha released herself from her room, set fire to the house, that you, discovering the fire, went upstairs, helped the servants down, then went up again, to release your wife from her cell. Then, you have said, you found her on the roof, whither she had escaped through the window.

'That was a strange story to tell, Rochester – that your wife had released herself from her place of confinement, set fire to the house, returned and locked herself in again. And that, locked in, she was unable, once the fire had taken hold, to release herself again. Nor apparently, could Mrs. Poole, also inside that locked room – it would seem neither of them had the key. Who had the key, Rochester? Who had the key?'

I gazed at her in horror. Edward, his face ghastly pale,

advanced, still grasping Adèle by one arm, and shouldered Madame Roland out of the way.

'You locked her in. You were prepared to burn down your house in order to kill my sister.'

As Edward pushed past her she stumbled backwards, almost losing her footing, then fell against the far wall. Before she had recovered herself Edward was back. He picked me up and carried me from the house, crying to Adèle who stood, bewildered, at the garden gate, 'Adèle! Go to Mr. Todd's and wait. I will send the carriage.'

In seconds Edward, carrying me, was in the road. He set me before him on his horse's back and we were off down the road, to Thornfield.

Chapter XVIII

E dward insisted on putting me to bed. The doctor was called, and on his advice the nurse was brought back.

'There is no need,' I protested from my bed as Edward and I sat hand in hand that afternoon, but he bent over me, chiding gently, 'I have full reports now of all your naughty doings and dealings while I was away: gardening, visits to Ferndean, even, heaven help us, riding uphill to the lead mines, where you might have been subjected to any insult by the miners or their womenfolk – who are nearly as rough as they are. The doctor instructed you to rest; I informed him that you would. I turn my back and you are off like a bird. Jane,' he reproached me, 'my Jane, are you not ashamed of yourself?'

'I am quite well,' I said, but oh, how happy I was, how soothed by my husband's concern. I was forced to admit it – I was now very fatigued and weak.

'Dear,' I said to him, 'I am sorry to have called you back, but I was so worried and frightened – events here have become so troubling that I knew only you could help.'

'Called me back?' said he. 'I did not know.'

'I wrote to Mr. Jessop in Manchester, asking him to give you a letter.'

'Which did not reach me. I must have been in London by then and so knew nothing of it. My business done, I came back as quickly as possible. Almost home, I saw on the road a figure, much like Adèle, being supported into Old House, and you, my dearest, whose person I would recognise from twice as far away, with the group. Thus I found you, for some reason, entering that abominable woman's house. Well, Adèle has told me something of the business, and perhaps we should say no more, particularly at this time.'

'But Edward,' said I, 'one of the reasons for my appeal to you to return was the dreadful charges brought by Madame Roland, which she has now had the audacity to put to you herself. She says she is Bertha Mason's sister. And that there was a doubt in the matter of' – my voice grew lower and lower, for I spoke of a subject seldom mentioned between us – 'of her death.'

Meanwhile he regarded me steadily, something like a smile on his lips. His consoling grasp tightened on my hand.

'You heard her yourself,' I said. I think my voice broke as I appealed, 'Edward – something must be done.'

He leaned over to kiss my brow. 'Now, Jane,' he said, 'comfort yourself. There is no need for alarm. The woman is deranged. Small wonder, for there is madness in that family, as all know, and I most of all, having bought my knowledge of it so dearly. But I will not – *will not* – allow her to disturb my own little wife. Come, Jane, you are over-tired. Be calm. I will deal with everything. But tell me first, why is Mrs. Poole upstairs, in apparent exile?'

'She must be sent away,' I said passionately. 'She is

in a conspiracy with that woman, Madame Roland. I believe she is feeding her with stories about the fire, and its results.'

'I will speak to her. But she is loyal, I believe, and told me some weeks back that Madame Roland had approached her for information about the night of the fire. I suggested she pretend to comply in order to find out what the woman was discovering, or thought she was discovering, and what she planned to do.'

'Why did you not tell me, Edward?' I asked. 'Why, when I reproached her, did not she?'

He smiled tenderly. 'It was decided you were not to know, my dearest. For the doctor told me you must keep calm and quiet. I thought to spare you, and Mrs. Poole had instructions to do the same. But how was I to know that as soon as I was out of sight you would begin a course of fierce activity? That you would be out and about, worrying yourself and fretting and letting Madame Roland disturb you with her tales? Jane – you endanger yourself and our child. If I did not love you so much I should be a little unhappy with you, but how, I ask the heavens' – and he cast his eyes up humorously to the ceiling – 'how could I ever be displeased with my dear over-conscientious lovely Jane?' He smiled again.

'And now I'm forced to go, for I have strict instructions from the doctor that you must not be wearied. Here are some books I have brought you fresh from London. And, because you are such a dreadful little Puritan, with such a dreadful little Puritan conscience, tomorrow I will allow you to begin listing what books we must get for our library, because we must begin to stock it this winter and continue to build it until the end of our days. And that,' he said with mock firmness, 'is what I will allow you to do – but that is all. All other matters will be attended to by myself, your helpmeet and husband.' He stood up. 'Edward Fairfax Rochester, at your service.' With that he kissed me, made me a great formal bow, and left the room, turning in the doorway to admonish me, 'Rest. I will be with you later.' And he was gone.

I leaned back on my pillows, a tide of comfort and well-being sweeping over me. My husband had returned. I was no longer alone. The difficulties and agonies which had beset me during his absence were gone, any that remained would, in his strong presence, disappear. You little fool, Jane, I told myself, how could you have allowed yourself to be disturbed by the accusations of Madame Roland – a madwoman sprung from mad stock?

I was tired now, worn out by the fatigues I had imposed on myself during the past few days. Although I knew there were difficulties ahead, which must be met, they would be dealt with by one stronger and more capable than myself – my husband.

The next days passed peacefully. Edward visited me in my room, and Adèle briefly, radiant with the excitement of being at Thornfield, with him. They had been out riding, she said, and the dressmaker had been summoned to make her new dresses compatible with her new status as a grown-up young lady. She was, she told me, wholly, completely happy. She did not mention the scene in the churchyard, and I chose not to question her, though I resolved to ask her, at some point, the reason for that extraordinary scene.

I was pronounced too frail to dine at the Nortons'. 'You will not object, my love, I am sure, if I take Adèle?' Edward requested. 'She is excited by the prospect, and has bespoken so many new dresses for the evenings that she is even now bending over the seamstress to urge her on. She demands to show off her new finery. And it is time she saw something of the world. At all events, I cannot answer for the consequences if she is prevented from wearing what she calls her "rose silk". She is passionate about it – with such a passion. She has the soul of a Parisienne.'

I could do nothing but assent. They visited me in my room before departing for Raybeck Hall. Edward so strongly handsome in his tail-coat, Adèle, on his arm, so charming. Her pale hair was piled high on her head, enhancing the lines of her elegant neck. The 'rose silk' set off a slender waist and graceful figure. Whether her character were good or bad, Adèle was undeniably a beauty.

Edward came over to kiss me. 'How I detest these events,' he whispered. 'Only you know how much. But duty must be done.' He straightened up. 'Come, my dear. Cinderella – you *shall* go to the ball.'

In the middle of the room, he bowed and Adèle sank down in a deep curtsey, her skirts spreading around her like the petals of a flower. The pearl necklace she wore about her slender neck was from the store of family jewellery, I saw. This handsome treasury of jewels, collected over the centuries, had been at the bank when the fire took place, and thus was saved from harm.

Adèle saw my eyes on the necklace as she arose from her curtsey and put one slender hand self-consciously to her throat. 'Papa has made me a present,' she said. 'Is he not the kindest Papa in the world?'

'Indeed he is,' I agreed.

She had changed little from the eight-year-old who had been my charge, with her babble of 'toilettes' and 'cadeaux'.

Later, I heard their voices in the hall, their entering the carriage, the sound of horses moving off, and the slamming of the front door. I suppose that many of us, when others go to some festivity and we are left alone, are overcome by a kind of sadness and so, I own, it was with me. I tried to rally myself but only half succeeded. I tried to read, but did poorly at it.

It was past midnight when I heard Edward and Adèle come back. Later, I heard the sounds of them creeping upstairs, some whispers in the gallery, then the rustle of Adèle's skirts as she went quietly along to her room, the sound of Edward's door opening as he entered his bedchamber. The door closed.

The house became still and silent, yet I could not sleep. I lay sadly awake, reproving myself, telling myself I had all a woman could want and yet, still, I was melancholy. I have ever been active and I suppose by then confinement to my room was affecting my spirits. I concluded that when the doctor came in the morning I would urge him to let me up, back into the world again, and so, finally, I slept.

Chapter XIX

The doctor came at ten. He agreed I might rise that day and by eleven o'clock I was up and dressed, surprising Edward in his study. He came to me, arms outstretched. 'Jane – my Jane.' And from the couch beneath the window, where Adèle lay extended, holding a book, 'Are you better now, Step-mama?'

'I am indeed and allowed up.'

'On condition that you keep to the house and its near environs,' Edward told me.

'Indeed no,' I said with a smile. 'The doctor tells me I may ride a little, a very little. His opinion is that some fresh air and exercise will be beneficial. And, my dear, will you permit me to visit Mrs. Sugden, so that we can discuss plans for the amelioration of the mine labourers' conditions? I will do nothing strenuous, I promise.'

Edward looked grave. 'I am not sure that your health will be improved by that. And there are, moreover, considerations concerning the relationship between the workers and their employer to be borne in mind.'

'I will of course do nothing without your consent, Edward.'

'Very well,' he said. 'See Mrs. Sugden if you must, but

commit yourself to nothing. We do well to act cautiously in such matters.'

'You will gain a reputation for saintliness, Step-mama,' Adèle said gaily, 'if you will be delivering coals and blankets to the miners' wives all the time.'

'There is nothing extraordinary about the exercise of charity in the locality by those who are, for whatever reason, placed in a more fortunate position,' I exclaimed. 'It is not unusual.'

'There are those who say it is by such exercises we avoid turbulence in society,' observed Edward.

'That is good, then,' said she, 'if it is a means to avoid revolutionary excess.'

'For myself,' said I, 'it will be enough if I can prevent excessive want. Tell me, how went your party last night?'

Adèle burst into raptures about the dinner party – the twenty guests, the décor, the candles and the ladies' dresses, which she described in minute detail. 'And then we danced,' she exclaimed, 'in the picture gallery, where Lady Norton had set a pianoforte expressly for that purpose. Sophie Lynn and I played, each taking turns so the other might dance. I was a success – *un succès fou, n'est-ce pas, Papa?*'

'You seemed to be, when I came to watch. Lady Norton titled you "fairy",' he said with some amusement. 'But now, my dears, I must ask you to go elsewhere to talk further of last night's entertainment, for I have weighty business here connected with my visits to Manchester and London.'

'What is that?' I asked.

'It is too heavy for you, Jane.' He paused. 'Perhaps too heavy for me, I sometimes think.'

'May I not help you?'

He shook his head. 'I do not think the doctor would approve. Now, begone, ladies – begone, Jane, begone, Fairy. I must to work.'

Adèle and I repaired to the drawing-room. It must be remembered how little time she and I had spent together since her childhood. We were virtual strangers, yet here we were together, sharing a home and likely to share it for some considerable time, until Adèle, I supposed, married. I was very uncertain of how matters would go between us.

'Well then, we have received our discharge,' I said, as I sat down and took up some sewing. 'We must now decide how to employ ourselves today. Have you any particular desires?'

Adèle stood at the window, looking out towards the garden wall. She sighed, 'There's little to do here. The weather is very poor.'

'It will be so for some months. I fear we must make the best of it.'

'I am not sure my resources are equal to that,' she replied. 'I wonder that yours are. I wonder you do not ask Papa to take you to London. But then, of course, you are not well.' Her voice expressed some discontent for, as far as she was concerned, I suppose, my frailty was the barrier between herself and the pleasures and stimulus of London life.

'Lady Norton travels to London next week,' she informed me disconsolately. 'I had thought perhaps she would suggest I went with them, since I believe she has some affection for me and the Nortons have no children of their own. I fancy it would be beneficial to me to see something of the world. But Lady Norton said nothing, and when I suggested to

Papa he might hint about it on my behalf he said he could not. Why is that, do you think?'

'I have no idea. He does not like to ask favours.'

She looked at me hard. 'Perhaps you might write and suggest the plan to Lady Norton. You have an interest in the plan, for you do not want me here.'

'Of course I want you here,' said I. 'Why should you think I do not? My only concern is that you should amuse yourself and use your time profitably.'

'Around the hovels of the lead-miners?' she mocked. 'No, Jane – you do not want me here. Had you desired me to live with you and Papa, you would not have kept me away at school. Did it not occur to you I would have preferred to be at home with Papa?'

'I selected the schools with the greatest care. I dreaded to think you might experience the sadness of my own early years. I do not think you suffered.'

'There was nothing wrong at the schools,' she declared, 'other than that they *were* schools. Why did I have to be sent away?'

'Your father—'

'My father. No – you,' she declared passionately, '*you* decided. You wanted my Papa all to yourself. That is why I was sent away from him.'

'Adèle,' said I, 'your father, at first was very ill. He was blind, maimed and, I must tell you, was in such a state of despair he did not care whether he lived or died. He needed all my care. He desired all my care. It was not I who sent you away but he; and I did not dispute the decision for at that time it was a grave necessity or, perhaps, you would have found yourself without any father at all – he might have died. You must understand that.'

146

'And after that, it seems the necessity became desirable. I could have come back when he was better but no, by then you had Jonathan – your child. There was no room for me.'

This argument, and it was no less than that, was not an encouraging start to our relationship. It seemed Adèle felt very bitterly about her years of education away from home. Yet it was true that at first she could not have stayed in a home so uncomfortable and anxious, with a sick, blind man and his young wife, desperate only for his welfare.

What she did not know – and I could scarcely tell her – was that I had supported, even encouraged, Edward's desire to keep her away at school. I felt very deeply that she must be armed for an uncertain future – with attainments developed to their uttermost. For Adèle was not acknowledged as Rochester's daughter, and how was this young woman without name or fortune to maintain herself, if not by her own talents? For though she called Edward 'Papa', he did not call her 'Daughter'. Others might name her 'Miss Rochester' – they had no other title to give her – yet she had no real right to bear that name when only half acknowledged by her father. Her future was unsure. I had not the heart to point out these harsh truths to her, though. Perhaps she understood her situation; perhaps she did not. At all events, the matter was for Edward to decide.

'You did not want me. There was no room for me here,' she said again.

I felt her pain, for how often had I felt the same agony of rejection, from childhood on, and known there was no place, no security for me, anywhere. I bent my head. 'I am sorry, if you thought that,' I said.

'You should be. You should be sorry,' she was exclaiming, just as Edward came into the room. Even as the door opened she ceased to speak, and within seconds her manner had changed completely; the very position of her body became easier and more fluid, her angry expression disappeared and was replaced immediately by one of sweetness and submission. For this I was grateful, as I did not wish Edward to be disturbed in his home by arguing females. There is nothing worse for any man, whoever he may be, than long-running subterranean womanly warfare inside his own walls. Yet with a chill I saw confirmed my supposition that during the years in which I had seen little of her Adèle had become a consummate little actress and arch-dissembler.

Edward did not sit down. He said, 'Well, Jane, I've done with the worst of my papers and should like a stroll, if you will take one with me.'

I stood up to get my cloak and Adèle followed me. 'Mrs. Poole,' she said, 'fetch our cloaks, if you please. We are going for a walk.'

Edward, I believe, wished to be alone with me and did not intend Adèle to come with us. But there seemed no choice but to submit to her presence and so we went, all three, out into the grounds. We looked into the garden, where work proceeded; then Adèle expressed herself as eager for a brisk walk up the thorn field and into the open country. 'To blow the cobwebs away,' she said gaily.

I was hesitant about this. I did not feel strong enough as yet and feared that, if Edward agreed to her suggestion, the result would be my returning to the house and their going on together, which was, I believe, what she intended. Happily, Edward rejected the idea, telling her, 'You may take your march, but Jane is not well enough.'

However, she would not leave us, and after turning and going back to look at the elms about the house we returned.

Over lunch I attempted to raise the question of Adèle's future, for the prospect of having her about the house, unoccupied, for some indefinite length of time was hard to contemplate. I said, 'Adèle, it will be very dull for you here. Is there some course of study you would like to pursue? We might get a music teacher for you.'

Her response was unenthusiastic. 'Oh. I have had enough of lessons,' she said, and Edward added, 'It is probably time for Adèle to be at home, learning some of the domestic arts. She must discover how to manage a house, and who better, Jane, than you to instruct her?'

'I shall so enjoy that,' she smiled. 'Perhaps this afternoon we should pay some calls.' She meant us, I think, to call at Raybeck Hall, in order to renew her campaign to persuade Lady Norton to take her to London.

Before I could respond, though, Edward answered, saying, in some irritation, 'Call on whom, pray? I hate to see women running all over the neighbourhood, back and forth, calling on each other. Of all the futile and profitless occupations the world can offer this custom of roving the countryside, banging at each other's doors, is the most useless. I will not have my household disturbed by this to-ing and fro-ing, nor my horses worn out carrying my womenfolk to gossip in other people's houses. Let women occupy themselves at home and keep to their own firesides – that is best.'

'Conversation is not gossip, Papa,' Adèle murmured.

'There is a fine, if not indistinguishable, line between one and the other where ladies are concerned,' he assured her. It was plain he had made up his mind and would not change it.

Adèle cast down her eyes. 'Oh, Papa – but I expect you are right.'

Edward left the table, saying he had more work to do. I thought I had better begin to follow his suggestion that I instruct Adèle in the domestic arts. 'Will you come down to the Sugdens' with me, Adèle? Mrs. Sugden, you see, is in charge of the home-farm dairy, which I have not yet seen.'

'Pooh,' said Adèle, 'cows – and cheese.' Her glance struck the window on which there were raindrops. 'It is raining again. Is Papa genuinely opposed to calling on the neighbours?'

'The question barely arose at Ferndean, we lived so quietly. I believe at first some ladies called, but Edward was ill and demanded all my care. And I later avoided that kind of society, having no great taste for it myself.'

'You were not brought up to it, I suppose,' she said coolly and drifted a weary eye round the salon and then on to the prospect from the windows.

I stood up. 'I will go to the dairy, Adèle. I would prefer it if you came with me, but if you will not, I shall not force you to do so.'

'You could not,' she said. 'I am not your pupil now.'

I said no more, but stood up and left the room, in no happy frame of mind.

And so, leaving her behind, I went to the Sugdens' – they lived in a house on Rochester land a little out of Hay – and was shown round Mrs. Sugden's clean dairy. I made fresh orders for deliveries of milk, butter and cheese and Mrs. Sugden offered tea, which I insisted we took in the kitchen, where we might be comfortable. I raised the topic of conditions in Hay.

'The lead-miners have the worst of it,' she told me, 'but all will require fuel and bedding to get them through the winter. It is sad the weaving is unprofitable since the big wool mills opened up in the towns. And, madam, with the estate having been left alone so long, there has been little work there, either. The strong, or those in most despair, have drifted off. There will be great want in Hay, this winter.'

'The women may require wool and flannel for the making of clothes, I would think.'

She laughed. 'No, madam, for alas, they cannot sew. They could weave, for that was for their trade, but they cannot sew.'

'Perhaps that could be remedied,' I said. 'But meanwhile I understand there is feeling against the Rochesters in the village.'

She was a sensible and direct woman, but my question embarrassed her. 'There's all too often something festering below the surface in country neighbourhoods,' she said. 'Together you and Mr. Rochester will set it right, I'm sure.'

On my return to Thornfield, I went upstairs to rest, and I considered again the necessity for a school at Hay, where boys and girls could learn to read and write and the girls might learn sewing, cooking and other domestic skills.

When I came down to dinner I found Adèle again curled up on the study window-seat, while Edward worked at his papers. I told him dinner was ready, but he said he would have none, and Adèle and I ate alone, saying little. Sometimes I would find her eyes on me, brooding, but she told me nothing of her thoughts.

Chapter XX

Winter was setting in. At Ferndean, time, summer and winter alike, had passed swiftly in a mixture of activity and repose, but I began to find the short, drab days at Thornfield wearisome, the nights sad and long, the more so when Edward was away from me.

One evening, late, I went, in wrapper and night-gown, to his room, to talk and laugh with him, as we had once used to try to re-establish our old natural, friendly communion. Outside his bedroom door, as ever, lay vast Pilot, my old Pilot, but he did not move aside as I approached the door and even, as I leaned over him to put my hand to the doorknob, growled at me. 'Now, Pilot!' I said in astonishment and he growled again. 'Pilot,' I exclaimed, 'move!' But he would not stir from Edward's threshold.

Edward opened the door, in his robe, pen in hand. 'What's to do?' he asked, laughing at me as I stood behind the great dog, who had now risen to his feet.

'Pilot has decided not to let me in,' I explained.

'That is because you are too infrequent a visitor,' he told me, drawing me into the room. It was lit by one lamp. I sat down by the fire, he opposite, the dog between us, on the rug. He said, 'It will be agreeable to have one of our old conversations for I am dull and lonely.' He yawned. 'Excuse me. Tell me the truth. Do you regret this move to Thornfield?'

'I sometimes regret Ferndean.'

'We were closer at Ferndean,' he mused. 'Here, I seem beset by problems. I have no time – I am distracted, Jane. I know my mood is sometimes – not good.'

'Oh Edward,' I said, crossing to him, 'let me help you.'

I was standing in front of him. He took my hand, murmuring, 'If you could, if only you could. Sometimes, Jane, I wish to go away, as far as I can from here.'

'Then if you wish it, let us leave, at least for a while.'

'How can we do that?' he said. 'You are specifically instructed to stay quiet. And would you leave Jonathan?'

'Jonathan could come with us wherever we went, and if we cannot leave now, for my health's sake, surely we can make our plans.'

'Sadly, the thought of waiting many months to make a journey and then setting forth with an entourage appeals little,' he said, grimly. Seeing my unhappy expression, he relented, saying, 'Well perhaps – perhaps – in future. And to turn to the present and pleasant thing I have got you a horse, a pretty but plump mare. Her name is Ruby. Sugden brings her tomorrow.'

I kissed him. 'Edward – you are too good, too good.'

'Nonsense,' he said. 'You must have your exercise but you must promise me you will take short rides, and only when the weather is good. Now sit down, calm yourself, talk to me and enliven me for I know I am a bear. A bear,' he repeated and his head sank on to his breast.

And so I did. I tried to speak to him of many things, but his mood had become gloomy; his replies were terse and without animation. For my own part, I felt the ease and confidence between us less than it had been, and I knew well, talk as I might, the moment must soon come when I would have to return to my own room and our conversation would end, the union of the moment cease. Nor could I forget those matters which confronted us but which were not to be discussed; I saw this from Edward's manner: he required distraction from care, not the raising of unpleasant and disturbing topics.

So I spoke of Jonathan's progress with Mr. Weatherfield, the plans for his next visit home, the garden, the library; but I could not help enumerating silently those issues before us still ignored and unresolved. Adèle's future was unsettled, the folk of Hay at odds with Thornfield Hall. Above all, Madame Roland was still in Hay and no one looking at that cold, angry face, the face of an avenging angel, could believe she did not threaten us. She would do all the harm and spread all the scandal she could.

Before my eyes hovered the image of the miniature of Céline which Edward had kept in the drawer containing his gun, and which had now vanished. Perhaps, because of these concerns, my manner was less calm, less easy, than it might have been.

Wishing to relieve the inevitable melancholy of dark winter days I asked, 'Would you enjoy it if I invited my cousins Diana and Mary on a visit?' for I knew he liked both of them and their husbands and Diana's husband, Captain Fitzjames, in particular.

But he shook his head. ' Forgive me – I am in no mood for company.'

'Perhaps you are tired. You have been busy in your study all day. It will take time, no doubt, to make sure all is as it should be at Thornfield.' And as I stood to leave him, I thought I heard him say, his head still bowed on his breast, 'Time. Yes. It will take time.'

I kissed him but he scarcely responded to my kiss and I returned to my room gravely concerned. I had been constrained to visit him; he would not come to me; his endearments had been forced. He was unhappy, my poor husband, and I, now, little less so.

Once again, as after I had discovered Céline's picture in his drawer, I was forced to wonder if Edward's affection for me was less than it had been, and found myself looking into the void, that cold and empty universe, I would be left to inhabit if he no longer loved me.

Yet next day dawned bright and the world seemed somehow restored to me. Over breakfast, Edward said, 'Well, Jane, there is a treat in store for you.' He stood up and went into the hall, whence he returned with a scarf which he, laughing, placed ceremoniously over my eyes. And then he led me to the stables, while Adèle, behind us, chattered excitedly.

Once in the stable-yard, Edward led me to a certain spot where he unveiled me – and there, before me, was Jeremy, holding a brown cob mare, my Ruby, plump and, I thought, as close to smiling as a horse can be. She wore a lady's saddle of fine leather. I am nervous in general of horses, but from the first moment I set eyes on my Ruby I loved her. I ran to her, saying to Edward, 'Thank you – oh, thank you.'

'Small enough for my little wife,' said Edward, 'and sweet-natured enough, too.'

Nothing would do for me, or him, but a ride straight away. I ran upstairs to change. Edward, meanwhile, mounted his big grey and when I came down we set off through the stables, over the paddock and past the trees to where the ground began to rise gently upwards. We rode slowly, for I am no horsewoman, over a rough stone-walled field.

'Edward, I cannot thank you enough. You have given me my freedom.'

'Nevertheless, Jane, you must be careful,' he said

The sky was overcast, the wind somewhat boisterous, but together we had a splendid ride along the hillside, taking our midday meal of bread and cheese in a farm kitchen and then we mounted up again and rode on, close and loving.

Towards the middle of the afternoon we found ourselves close to Raybeck Hall. 'Dare we conclude our ride by a visit to the Nortons?' wondered my husband.

'Oh Edward,' I reproached him, 'dishevelled as I am? I am in no fit state.'

He contemplated me and said, 'No. You are bright-eyed and smiling, and your cheeks bear a tender flush and – oh, my Jane, you have never looked prettier.' He seemed almost sad as he gazed at me.

We went on for a few paces. 'Well, then,' said I, and to cheer him only, for I had no great wish to call on Blanche Norton, 'I am so encouraged by your flattery that I agree. Let us go to Raybeck.'

'I would not object to having a few words with Sir Stanley,' Edward admitted. 'There is the small matter of a boundary in question and I would rather settle it soon, in a friendly manner, than start the lawyers working on it.'

Before long we were taking the path through the Nortons' lowland fields, where their fat cows still grazed, in spite of the lateness of the year.

Raybeck Hall was an old manor, built, I would guess, in the time of William and Mary. The windows were mullioned, the walls ivy-clad; the house looked down over a well-kept garden to a river. However, as we made our way down the drive and reached the front of the house, with its delightful prospect, enlivened even at this drab time of year by rare shrubs and trees, our attention was violently distracted, not, alas, by the charm of the house, but by another sight. Our own carriage stood outside the house, Jeremy, our coachman, beside it.

'What in God's name is our carriage doing here?' Edward demanded furiously. Then he raced towards it, his horse kicking gravel up behind him. When I caught up he was shouting questions at Jeremy, who regarded him with a startled air.

'How come you here?' cried my husband. 'How long have the horses been standing?'

'Miss Adèle is inside, sir, visiting Lady Norton,' Jeremy explained. 'We have been here these two hours.'

'Are you mad?' he cried.

I intervened. 'Edward, this is not Jeremy's fault.'

'Wherefore not? He had no instructions to bring the carriage out.'

Now Blanche Norton, smiling, came down the steps of the house towards us. 'Mr. Rochester,' she greeted him. 'And Mrs. Rochester. How pleasant of you to call. I have had the pleasure of Adèle's company all afternoon, but she did not tell me to expect you.'

Then Adèle appeared in her new plum-coloured dress, very lovely but with a manner betraying, I thought, a little trepidation. She came down the steps to greet us.

Edward mastered himself to a degree. 'I am sure you have had a delightful afternoon,' he said to Blanche, 'but now we have come to fetch Adèle home.'

'Do step in for a little while,' she said.

'No, Blanche, thank you. We will not. Adèle, will you come home?'

'Papa,' she began, but the look he gave her was so intimidating she ceased instantly to appeal to him and said, hastily, 'Very well, I will collect my things.'

But he cut off her words saying, 'A servant can bring them. You will get into the carriage, please.'

This she did. Blanche, showing no sign of confusion about this awkward scene, instructed the butler to fetch Miss Adèle's cloak and gloves.

'Since the carriage is here, my dear,' Edward said, 'We might as well enter it.' He then ordered Jeremy to hitch our two riding horses to the back of the carriage and handed me in. Adèle, already inside, was biting her lip and tears, not of grief, I think, but of rage and shame, were in her eyes.

As Edward handed me into the carriage and I sat down, he still being outside, she said to me in a fierce undertone, 'I am humiliated. To order me from the house and into the carriage – it is too much.'

In the same low voice I said to her, 'Disguise your feelings, Adèle.'

As swiftly as any actress, she banished from her face the expression of chagrin and smiled brilliantly. She bent towards me and said, as if imparting something of pleasure and interest, 'Well – I will conceal my feelings. Thank you for your worldly advice, Miss Butter-would-not-melt-in-your-mouth.' And then she leaned from the carriage to where Edward and Blanche stood and said to her hostess, 'I thank you so much for a pleasant afternoon. I hope London will be as gay and entertaining as you anticipate.'

'I am sure it will be. Next time you must come with us,' Blanche replied.

Settling back in her seat again, Adèle, still smiling charmingly, said in a low, vicious tone, 'Next time. Next time. Why not this time? Your fault, Jane.'

I looked at her with dismay and could not reply for a moment. Then I said quietly, 'In your view, I think, Adèle, everything is my fault.'

Edward then mounted the carriage and sat down beside me.

'Well, I am sorry your visit was so brief,' Blanche Norton said through the carriage window.

Edward bowed slightly and ordered Jeremy to drive on.

As soon as we started to move Adèle said pleadingly, 'Oh, Papa – I am full of remorse. I should not have ordered the carriage without asking you. But I was so lonely and miserable when you and Step-mama went off riding and I did not understand that I might not do so. Will you forgive me? I will not do it again.' She leaned forward and laid her hand on his knee. 'Do say I am forgiven.'

'Oh, very well,' he said impatiently. 'I cannot claim to have told you not to take the carriage. I am more angry with Jeremy than with you, for he should have known better.'

And so it seemed Adèle was to be forgiven and Jeremy blamed, which I thought unfair, for how was he to refuse the request for the carriage from the daughter of the house when he had no instructions to do otherwise? Moreover, I was certain that, while Jeremy had done no more than what he thought must be his duty, Adèle had guessed she should not have asked for the carriage but was nevertheless determined to go to the Nortons' in order to make one last effort to induce Blanche Norton to invite her to go to London with them. However, I thought it best to hold my peace. Alas that I did, for I might have been able to prevent the consequences of Adèle's foolish deed.

So Adèle was forgiven, her seizure of the carriage seen as a prank and, over dinner, a solemn promise was given by Edward, that she should be taken to London next spring.

'Let us hope you will be well enough by then to come with us,' Adèle said, in the drawing-room later, Edward having gone to his study. But her eyes as she spoke were very strange and cold. There was that in her gaze which chilled me. I believed she wished not that I should be in London with her, but the opposite – that and worse. There is no woman who, knowing her confinement lies only a few months ahead, does not sometimes fear for her own life. I do not know if this is what she meant – that I might not survive the birth of my child – but I looked into those lovely eyes and was afraid – for her as well as for myself.

'Adèle,' I said gently, 'you must understand that I am married to your father, and where he goes, I go. I am sorry that because of my condition we cannot go to London now, though I must point out that for ten years we have been quite content to stay at home, not travelling, rarely visiting, happy in our own company and living in our own quiet way. However, you are young, and wish to travel and see life, and that is quite natural. But you cannot always do what you wish to do and have what you wish to have.'

She stood up angrily and made as if to leave the room. 'No,' I told her, 'sit down and listen to me.' Which command she obeyed, though her face was mutinous.

'I will not permit you to go on like this, ever unkind,

angry and perverse,' I told her. 'I repeat, I will not allow
it. You must change – you must – or I shall be obliged to
ask your father to send you away. He may not wish to
do so, but, if I insist, he will, I assure you. I do not want
matters to come to this pass, Adèle, but I warn you, if
they do, you will have to leave here.'

During this speech she sat on, her head bowed, her eyes
fixed on the carpet, an angry expression on what I could
see of her face.

I was fatigued after the ride; I had rallied myself in order
to make this, as I saw it, necessary statement, and now I
felt exhausted. 'Do you understand me?' I asked but she
did not reply.

I stood up, and left the room, going upstairs to bed,
thinking sadly of the happiness of the day Edward and
I had spent together before we reached Raybeck Hall,
and how our old communion had been restored – until
the day had ended badly, so very badly.

Chapter XXI

Next morning was frosty, with a threat of snow. I rose early, breakfasted alone and went out to the stables. Edward's horse was gone and I was surprised to find Ruby out in the yard and saddled. The other horses were in their stalls, but for one which was being groomed by Jeremy's boy, who looked at me warily. There was no sign of Jeremy.

'I came to ask where Mr. Rochester had gone this morning,' said I.

'He left for Millcote early,' the boy said. 'When I came down he had saddled up and gone.'

I was surprised, for there had been no previous talk of Millcote. However, it lay only six miles off, so whatever his business Edward would return that day.

I glanced at Ruby, standing there with my saddle on her back. 'Did he order Ruby to be saddled before he left?' I asked.

'She was thus when I rose this morning,' he told me.

'So she has been standing saddled in the yard for over an hour? How strange. Where is Jeremy?'

The lad told me, 'I can't say, madam. He's most like on the road to Ferndean. He said he would go back to see his parents.'

'Gone to Ferndean?' I questioned.

'Aye,' said the lad, looking at me strangely. 'He were that sad, though, nigh on crying, when he left. It were a pitiful sight, missus, after Mr. Rochester turned him off so roughly.'

I could scarcely believe what I heard. 'Has Mr. Rochester dismissed Jeremy?'

'Aye,' he told me, as if surprised I did not know. 'Mr. Rochester come down to the stables very late, near midnight, roused Jeremy and told him to pack up and go that very minute. He blamed him for bringing Miss Adèle in the carriage yesterday said he could trust him no longer; he must go. He would listen to no pleas or arguments – Jeremy must go. He gave him his wages and would not let him wait even till dawn.

'He were very confused, Jeremy, but he stood up to the master, saying he and his family had worked for Mr. Rochester for more than ten years and he had done nothing but obey Miss Adèle's wishes and that he and his family had always been true. Yet, he said if the master wanted him gone then he would depart and make no trouble. Jeremy ended by pleading with the master – but he told him again to go, most roughly, and then turned away and left. So Jeremy put his things together and he said he would go back to his mother and father.

'And then out came Mrs. Poole, saying Mr. Rochester had roused her to come out and tell Jeremy his orders were to go and go immediately, not waiting for morning. And so he went, sad, dark and cold as it was. I hope he got home safe,' said the lad, 'or found somewhere warm and dry to bide till daylight came.'

I could not understand why Edward had acted thus. Jeremy, faithful, sensible and loyal had been employed by us all his grown life. I reasoned that this deed of Edward's could be no more than a passionate act and was confident that, on his return, the smallest of intercessions from me would cause him to change his mind and take Jeremy back.

Meanwhile, I thought that, since Ruby was saddled, I would take my ride in the direction of Ferndean, for if Jeremy, as the stable-lad surmised, had spent the night in some cottage or barn on the way to Ferndean, he might still be on his way there and, he being on foot, I might catch him up, give him a little money and reassure him that as soon as his master was home I would make representations on his behalf.

I therefore dressed for riding and, mounted up, took Ruby out on to the road and set off in the direction of Ferndean. With hindsight I see how lucky it was that I took to the road in pursuit of Jeremy, not to the fields and hills, for otherwise I might have lost my life.

I was only a mile from Thornfield, with fields on either side, when Ruby began to quiver and toss her head. Suddenly she kicked her back legs up, once, twice, then again. As I struggled to keep my seat she broke into an uneven canter, her ragged gait making it almost impossible for an inexperienced and nervous rider such as I, taken by surprise, to remain in the saddle. Then she leaped forward in a wild gallop, veering from one side of the road to the other. I had no chance of keeping my seat, for I felt the saddle slipping forward as if the girths had suddenly slackened. I was pitching towards the ground. Mercifully, the lady's saddle is one the rider can slip from easily; mercifully some instinct of self-preservation showed me, in a flash, just ahead, a grassy verge beside the road. I eased my foot from the stirrup, and threw myself sideways on to the grass.

The fall drove the breath out of me, and I lay, dazed, gasping for breath and half swooning, hearing the clatter of Ruby's hooves as she galloped on. I could not tell if I were injured, but in my head rang the thought that the fall might have harmed my coming child.

I heard feet running and a man's voice crying, 'She's here. I've found her!'

There were two voices; huge hands raised me up, tended me and wrapped me in a coat of rough wool. Eventually I was placed on a cart and borne slowly back to Thornfield.

I had been very fortunate. Two men who were rebuilding a dry-stone wall, uphill but not far from the road, had witnessed all and run to help me. As we approached Thornfield the threatened snow began to fall, and I am persuaded that Ruby had thrown me in open country, where there was no one to find me, I might have perished.

And so I was carried in to Thornfield and my rescuers rewarded. I was put silently to bed by Mrs. Poole. Even in my dazed state I remember remarking the strange quiet of the house. The next I knew was the doctor leaning over my bed and beyond him, through the window, I saw a curtain of thick white snowflakes softly descending, masking out the light so I could not tell what time of the day it was.

The doctor examined me and expressed delight that I was not worse hurt than I was, though I was sorely bruised. He gave it as his opinion, as I, too surely knew, that I had been more than fortunate in falling so soft and being found and helped so soon. As far as my continuing health and that of my child were concerned, he said, the next few days would tell all. He gave me a draught and said he would give instructions for a light meal to be brought to me. Then he took his leave, fearing to be caught in the snow.

I fell asleep in that noiseless world created by snow and awoke to darkness, my lamp burned out, and the bedroom fire burned almost to extinction. Outside the windows, where the curtains had not been drawn, it was black, though there were two or three inches of snow heaped on the window-ledge. It was deadly quiet. No sound came from outside, no wind, no hoot of owl or cry of fox. And inside, the house was as if deserted: the noise of a coal sliding in the grate was like a pistol-shot.

I recollected that the doctor had said he would send someone to attend me, but no one had come to put coal on the fire or draw my curtains. It was as if I were quite alone in the house. Yet surely Edward must be back from Millcote by now.

Then I stiffened. In that profound silence I heard voices downstairs. The hour was late. I felt fear. I knew I must not rise, for the doctor had warned me not to, yet how could I be there, alone, apparently abandoned, hearing strange sounds below and do nothing?

So I rose – with difficulty for the bruises from my fall were exceedingly painful – and went quietly on my bare feet across my cold room and into the corridor. There were, indeed, voices, below in the hall. Once at the top of the stairs I could hear what was being said. The first voice I heard was that of Grace Poole: 'She must not be told. I have sent him packing again.'

Then, to my horror, the low voice of Madame Roland: 'But what will you do about the other business?'

'She is a fool – a fool,' came Grace Poole's reply, in a contemptuous hiss.

'What is happening?' I called, my voice seeming very weak to me.

'My God!' came Grace Poole's cry. 'Is that you, Jane Eyre?' Standing at the head of the stairs, I saw, in the darkness below, a lamp held high by one of two black-clad figures. I began to descend.

'Do not come down,' called Grace Poole.

'I will,' I said, and slowly and tremblingly, clutching the banisters, went down, step by painful step. Then Grace Poole was at my side on the stair, assisting me. At the touch of that loathed hand I stumbled; and would have fallen, had I not gripped the banister more tightly.

'Do not touch me,' I ordered. And I continued my slow descent without her help.

'You should not be up,' she told me when I reached the bottom.

'Perhaps I should,' I said, 'for I see you have let Madame Roland into the house when you thought no one would know. Where is my husband?'

There was no reply for a moment. Then Grace Poole said, 'He returned from Millcote, then rode off again.'

I felt wretched at hearing this. I was alone in the house, it seemed, with these two evil women, my enemies. I presumed Adèle was also there, upstairs, asleep, but what help would she give me if the need arose?

'Where did my husband go, Mrs. Poole?' I demanded, but 'Ask no further questions,' she replied and put her face close to mine – I felt those bottomless black eyes burning. 'You are ill. You must go back to bed.'

A nightmare seemed to descend on me. My voice broke

as I said, 'Mrs. Poole, where is my husband? Tell me – is he safe? Where is he?'

There was a long and terrifying silence. Then Madame Roland said, her voice low and calm, 'You have no choice. Tell her.'

Grace Poole then said, 'Madam, you are cold. Go upstairs where there is a fire.'

'I will not be commanded by you. You must tell me now – where is Mr. Rochester?'

She said, 'After you were carried home, Miss Adèle left, without saying where she was going. Due to the anxiety about your accident we did not discover her absence until Mr. Rochester came home in the afternoon. Once it became plain she had left, of her own will, Mr. Rochester went after her to bring her back.'

'In this snow, without rest? Do you know where she went?' There was a further pause. I stood in the dark hall, very cold and bewildered. 'What is the hour?' I asked.

'Midnight,' said Grace Poole.

'And why are you here, in the house, at midnight?' I asked Madame Roland.

'To offer help,' she said.

'Help? What help could you give, at this hour? You have crept in, knowing my husband is away, to conspire with Grace Poole against him – and you call that help. You must leave, both of you, now.'

'No, Mrs. Rochester,' said Grace. 'You must go back to bed.' There was something menacing in her tone.

I could think of nothing but ridding myself of that threat. 'Go!' I cried. 'I order you to go. Wherever you two are is trouble, misery, plotting, pain. I want no more of you in my house, in my life. You must go. Now Adèle is gone, and Edward is gone and I am sure you, both of you, are somehow the cause of it. Go!'

'Into the snow?' asked Grace Poole, as if incredulous.

'Into anything. What do I care? What consideration do you deserve, either of you?'

Madame Roland fixed me with her eyes, 'Mrs. Rochester, you are ill—'

But 'Fool!' Grace Poole hissed at me. 'You are a fool!'

'I have ordered you to leave!' I cried.

'Contain yourself. You tread on ground dangerous to yourself,' said Madame Roland in a tone of contempt.

I could not bear that this woman should speak to me so. 'Will you go, or shall I have to get servants to deal with you?'

'There are no servants,' Mrs. Poole told me.

'What? My husband—'

'Be quiet,' said Madame Roland in a tone of deep anger. 'I have warned you – I have done all but beg. Now, hear this – your servants are gone – your husband is gone. You make wild charges, you threaten to hurl me into the snow. Mrs. Rochester, you are in danger. Your health is poor – go back to bed and be quiet and cause no further disturbance.'

I was dizzy. I felt weak and defeated. I had no one to call on. My words stumbled from me, 'Edward will deal with you. Edward will punish you, you evil woman.'

'You do not know where he is,' she told me in a low, vicious tone. 'We do, and you must be told. He is on his way to London following Adèle.'

'She has gone to London?'

Madame Roland gave an exclamation of rage and despair. 'Mrs Poole has tried to spare you. God knows, even I have tried, in the face of all insults. Very well –

know now – Adèle left a note. She has gone to London, to see her mother. Rochester has gone after her.'

'Her mother? Céline Varens?' I cried. 'Céline Varens is dead.' Yet as I cried out I knew she spoke the truth; I saw that lovely face in the miniature in my husband's drawer, and thought of its disappearance.

'No – Céline is alive,' said Madame Roland.

As she spoke I gripped the newel post to keep from falling. Her voice flowed, remorselessly, over me. 'Had you not deliberately kept yourself from the world, at Ferndean, closing your eyes to the past, protecting your own little paradise on earth with such care, you would have heard her name before. She is the most famous tragedienne in France, the most celebrated actress of her generation. Now she is in London, with her company, and Adèle has rejected this cold unfriendly house to be with her.

'Mrs. Rochester, I have known Céline Varens for many years. It may be that you would scorn her morals in your English way, but I say to you, she is a good woman and brave, very brave. After the duel Mr. Rochester fought over her, with her lover, the vicomte, her fortunes declined sadly. She formed an unfortunate union with a singer who deserted her in Italy. She fell into destitution – was friendless, without money and ill when she returned to Paris. She could not care for Adèle – she could not care for herself. Adèle might have starved had Rochester not taken her. Céline might have died without the pity of the good sisters of Saint-Sulpice. Yet from grave illness and wretched poverty she rose up, and now the world is at her feet.

'Adèle has gone to her now – and your husband, too.' There was triumph in her voice as she spoke.

Mrs Poole put a cold hand on my shoulder and said, 'Now – will you go back to bed and cease to interfere? Your presence cost us all dear at Thornfield a decade ago, Jane Eyre, and will cost us dear again unless we are careful. You are innocent – yes – and mean no harm, but the price of your innocence and purity is high.'

I did not heed her words; they meant nothing to me. I was in despair. The image of Céline would not leave my mind. For how long, I asked myself, had Edward known she was in London? Had he seen her there? For how long had he known she was not dead? And now he was riding through heavy snow to be with her. My head whirled. I felt a huge emptiness.

Grace Poole's voice came coldly and implacably through this confusion. 'You are bereft of servants, and of your husband, but you may have your way in one respect. I will not stay here any longer. You have always hated me, Jane Eyre, and today you have made your hatred too plain. I called you fool, and now you are beginning to see the depths of your folly. Madame Roland and I will go to Old House. She will shelter me while I make my plans. No hardship, no poverty, no difficulty, could be worse than remaining here.'

Together, still holding the lamp, they crossed the hall, leaving me in darkness.

In the entrance Grace Poole turned. 'You find yourself alone. The maids have left, for their families decided they would rather starve than have them work for the Rochesters, and once they had gone the other servants would not stay. You know the neighbourhood believes Mr. Rochester killed his first wife. A man who has killed once may kill again. Think on that.'

I heard them pull back the heavy bolts of the front door.

Cold air flooded in from the expanse of white which was the lawn and the road beyond. The branches of the leafless trees bore a burden of snow.

'Think on that, Jane Eyre.'

And they were gone, through the open door. As I stood transfixed I saw them, arm in arm, two black figures against the snow, helping each other across the white waste.

Chapter XXII

Mechanically, I crossed the hall and closed the door. Chilled to the bone, I found my cloak and threw it on over my bedgown. I went into the drawing-room and sat down by the cold grate, full of ashes, alone in that great, cold, echoing house.

The anguish of that long night is with me still. Try as I might, I could not drag my thoughts away from Céline Varens. Had Edward truly gone in pursuit of Adèle, or was it her mother he sought? My mind was in confusion; I could not tell true from false, real from unreal. The clock struck one, then two, then three . . .

And then, the doctor's potion still working within me, no doubt, I dozed for a moment or two and it was as if I were returned to that night when, a girl of eighteen, I left Thornfield; I saw myself creeping off to 'dreary flight and homeless wandering'. I heard Edward's voice after the mock marriage had been revealed for what it was: 'You understand what I want of you? Just this promise – "I will be yours, Mr. Rochester."' And I had denied him. I could not live with him as his mistress. Then he had said – and oh, with what pain – "You condemn me to be wretched, and to die accursed." But though one part of me had desired to yield, I had not.

Then I heard his voice again as I had heard it after I had been separated from him for so long and it called, 'Jane! Jane!' and I saw myself journeying to Thornfield to find him and finding only a ruin, and then going on to Ferndean to find that dear man maimed, so ill, so lonely, that he cared not if he lived. I recalled our mutual joy at the discovery that we still loved. In that brief half-dream by the empty grate on that fearful night, I remembered happiness.

I woke with a start and knew the fearful circumstances I was in, and yet knew again that happiness which had come to us after much sacrifice and suffering. 'Fool' and 'innocent' Mrs. Poole had called me, and she named me 'Jane Eyre' as if the name itself were a term of contempt. That fool, that innocent, that Jane Eyre, had survived, somehow, the crushing blow at Thornfield so long ago, had left for integrity's sake, had struggled and found her love again – and perhaps, I thought, in her folly and innocence, she could do so again. The truth was, I could not live without knowing Edward loved me. I could not live with this uncertainty eating away at my trust in him. He was half my soul; without him life had no meaning. During the course of my marriage my part had been to comfort, to create order and content. Now, to save that marriage, I must take action.

I re-lit the lamps, and the fire. There was no help for it. I could not stay alone at Thornfield. I would follow Edward to London.

Great difficulties faced me. The weather was bad and might become worse. I was sore and bruised from my fall. I had no coachman and would need to find another, with, it seemed, the whole village against me. And yet, I thought, I will try.

Worse than all that was one thought I could hardly bear, that the rough journey in such weather might cause me to miscarry my child. Yet, I told myself, when you were Jane Eyre you were forced into desperate straits, risking all, even your life, as you wandered friendless and alone. Now you must risk all again, even this. Even this.

Dawn was breaking when I passed through great, empty, frozen Thornfield Hall, went upstairs and packed a small bag with the bare necessities for my journey. If the village would not help me I would have to go through the snow to the vicarage, where Mr. Todd would, I hoped, lend me his carriage and coachman.

In the kitchen I found and drank a little milk, to sustain me, and ate a crumb or two of bread, though I had no appetite. Though the fire was out, though I knew the air in that room must be piercingly cold – there was frost inside the window-panes – I thought I felt a little hot.

Nevertheless I went into the hall, picked up my bag and opened the front door. I would walk to the vicarage by the footpath across the fields, through the snow.

A cold wind had got up since the previous night, and I looked in trepidation at the expanse of snow before me, knowing that behind the trees at the end of the lawn lay the road and behind that the way across the fields to the church and vicarage. I would have to traverse a distance of little more than half a mile, no distance at all on a fair day, but a hard challenge to me as I was, in weather such as this. And I had an inkling I was not well, chill at times, warmer at others. Yet, well or ill, I would not and could not stay in this empty house, bereft of my husband and beset by anxieties of every kind.

There is a point, I believe, at which a woman can and will throw away the normal constraints of her sex, and act with the resolution expected of a man. For me, that Jane who had once been an orphan, thrown on her own devices, in a world which showed little sign of friendship to her, that time had come.

I would go from Thornfield, I would go to London, if I must, find Edward and then, if I was spared, find some means to begin to resolve all the mysteries and horrors which beset us. I would do it, or die in the attempt. And though it may seem, from what then ensued, that I was not forced at that time to put this resolve to the final test, this moment was for me a turning-point.

As I stepped on to the snowy threshold, bag in hand, the wind seized my cloak. Then, in the silence, I heard the whinny of a horse. I thought little of it, knowing the remaining horses in the stables were without food or water, a state which I would have to ask Mr. Todd to remedy. And then, from the side of the house where the drive ran I heard a voice: 'Jane – hulloa! Jane!'

Advancing from the portico, I turned to look. A tall, becloaked figure, with an old shovel-hat on his head, hunched over upon a weary horse, raised a hand to me. He slid from the horse and came towards me, showing me a thin face, yellow-brown. As he took off the hat I saw above that gaunt and aquiline face short hair, very pale, as if bleached by strong sun. It was my cousin, St. John Rivers. I had thought he was in India, where he had gone long ago as a missionary.

He came towards me through the snow and embraced me. As he released me he looked about him wryly at the expanse of snow, saying, 'England provides a cold welcome to a returning son.' Then, his hands still on my shoulders, he said, 'Jane, you do not look well. I was so glad to see my dear little friend when I spotted you in the entrance; but then I wondered, where goes she, with a small bag, alone so early on such a day?' He looked up at the imposing house and said, 'So this is Thornfield, rebuilt. What a great sight it is.'

'It is so good to see you, St. John,' I said. 'You must come in, though it is but a cold, sad welcome I can give you.'

'I will, and gladly. Is there a man to take my horse? The old chap has served me well through all this snow, but he is done up, now.'

'There is no one. I will lead you to the stables,' I said.

The stable-yard was a sad sight, untidy, with a bucket overturned, a heap of dirty straw and many other signs of disorder. It was as if the stable-lad had abandoned his work and gone off – as I suppose he had. The two carriage-horses were in their stalls, peering out but – which astonished me – also in a third stall, peering over, was Ruby. I wondered where she had been found and who had brought her home. I went over to her and stroked her nose. She nuzzled at me.

'Where are the men, Jane?" enquired St. John.

'One's dismissed; the other has run off,' I told him. 'Indeed, all the servants are gone.'

St. John looked at me curiously, but asked no further questions. 'I'll see to the horses, then,' he said, and, rapidly unsaddling his own horse and throwing the saddle in a corner of the yard, he bent to the pump, which mercifully was not frozen, and started drawing water. 'Go inside. Jane,' he said. 'You must not get too cold. Is Mr. Rochester at home?'

'He is gone to London,' said I, and heard my voice coming out very small and weak, almost like a child's.

St. John straightened up and gazed at me in consternation. 'Then, who is with you?'

'No one.'

'All alone – at such a time?' he said, which told me one of my cousins, Diana or Mary, had told him I was to have a child. There was concern and pity in his tone as he spoke, but then it changed and became brisker. 'Well, I do not understand all this,' he said, 'but I see I can be of use.' And he turned again to the pump. 'Go inside, Jane. This cold and sharp wind may harm you.'

'And you, St. John,' I said. 'You must be used to hotter climes. What brings you back?' At the same time I began to carry his saddle into the tack-room beneath the servants' quarters.

'Put it down, Jane,' he commanded.

'The exercise will warm me,' I told him.

'Obstinate woman,' he muttered, carrying water to the stables. When he returned with the empty bucket he said, 'I'm invalided out. I'll be well enough for work here, but never again in a fierce climate. But this,' he said, back at the pump 'will set me up wonderfully.'

I led his horse to an empty stall and shut him in and, as I did so, wondered a little at St. John's free manner – new to me, for he had ever been a stiff and sober man, with a sense of right and wrong, but leaning more towards justice than mercy. His ten years in India had changed him, I saw.

At last we were done with the horses and St. John led me inside, sat me down in the drawing-room, cleared and remade the fire and instructed me not to move until he had found some food. While he went off to search the larder I sat still as a frozen bird on a twig. All I knew was that I must go to London to find Edward. But how?

St. John came back with bread and cheese, and set the kettle over the fire on a tripod he had found. As we waited for it to boil, he said self-mockingly, 'You will note my life abroad has made me practical, adaptable and capable.'

'And most comforting and reassuring,' I told him. 'But have you been very ill?'

'I was, I imagine, very ill. But I am well now and greatly content. I was called to the missionary field. I followed that call and now, it seems, Providence has dictated I withdraw from that area. I shall seek a parish here now, where I may continue my work. For the time being, I am at liberty, which is why I come here for a visit.'

The years had treated St. John kindly, in many ways. The classical beauty he once possessed, more of a statue than of a man, had been changed but not destroyed by time and the vicissitudes of climate. There was in that steady blue eye a kindlier light; that once-smooth brow now bore some lines – I gained the impression they had been drawn by endurance and the necessity to tolerate, forgive and understand. The old, pure beauty had grown older, had suffered, yes, but in his new gauntness, in the marks time had set on him, one saw the fruits of experience met, and bravely met. St. John had been tried in the fire; had learned of victory and defeat, had confronted weakness, not least his own, and had emerged from that fire tested, stronger, more humane. This was the man whom, young and ardent for his faith, yet withal unyielding and condemnatory, I had once found it impossible to marry.

He bent his keen yet patient eyes upon me. 'May I take the liberty of a cousin and ask some searching questions?

I learn Diana and Mary have not heard from you for some time. They assumed that your removal, and the state of your health, might be occupying you and thought little of it, save that they eagerly awaited news of you. However, now I am here I find you alone in an empty house and about to abandon it on foot. With your permission I will ask questions, and if you find them unpleasant I rely on you to check me.'

I was busying myself with making tea, lifting the boiling kettle from its trivet, pouring the water into the teapot. My eyes were on those activities, not on my cousin's, as I replied, 'I cannot pretend all is well here.' But I could not go on. Tears filled my eyes. I put the lid on the teapot and, head averted, somewhat to conceal them, returned to my chair.

'Jane, Jane,' he murmured, 'do not distress yourself. I am here – you know I will do all in my power to help you. How is Jonathan? And Mr. Rochester?'

'Jonathan is at Ferndean, staying with the clergyman there, Mr. Weatherfield, and Edward – Edward is well.'

'He is away on business, I presume. Now, tell me, when I caught you leaving your house with your valise, where were you going?' And I explained the servants had all gone off, owing to the village's hostility, and that I had intended to go to Mr. Todd and beg the use of his carriage to take me to London. That was what I told St. John and no more. I believe he suspected that this was not the whole tale, but he did not press me further, only spoke of his experiences abroad, of the deserts and plains of India, of the mountains, of the people and his work to convert them.

The heat of the fire was making me drowsy and St. John, concerned, came and felt my hot brow with a cool hand.

'Jane, you have a fever,' he said in alarm. 'You must go to bed. Which is your room? I will light the fire and you must go up as soon as it is warm.'

I had no choice but to comply, for I was, indeed, now ill. St. John, patient and tender as a woman, lit the fire in my bedroom, warmed the bed, carried me upstairs to retire and, later, brought me a soothing drink. Then he asked for instructions on how to get to the church, saying he would appeal to Mr. Todd for assistance. 'My horse is weary, though,' he said. 'May I ride your mare?'

'No,' I said in alarm, 'do not ride Ruby, for yesterday she bolted and threw me.'

He was shocked. 'No wonder you are ill. Well, I will take my own horse. He's good for another mile or so. Now, you must rest. I shall be back within the hour.'

And so he left me and, through fatigue and illness and the ease of knowing St. John was with me, and strong in support, I fell asleep. The next I knew I was summoned for dinner – that is to say, I professed myself much better and arose, not wanting St. John to sit alone at table, and found Mr. Todd's housekeeper, Mrs. Willows, in charge and a young woman and her brother, relatives of Mrs. Willows and fully vouched for by her, already installed, she upstairs, he in Jeremy's old quarters in the stable-yard.

'You have worked miracles,' said I to St. John as I sat down at a well-laid table. 'I will never be able to thank you enough.'

'I thank God I came in time to stop you from struggling through the snow to Mr. Todd's,' replied St. John. 'Todd is no zealot, that's plain to see, but he proved staunch in this emergency, which is to his credit.' He broke off at that point and I guessed Mr. Todd had told him something of what had been happening at Thornfield. Mr. Todd probably knew, also, that Grace Poole was residing at Old House. What else St. John had been told I could not tell, but perhaps it was a great deal for, though not an energetic clergyman, Mr. Todd knew all that happened in the neighbourhood.

My situation was difficult. Loyalty to Edward, that loyalty a wife owes to her husband, was paramount. And, though St. John's manner towards me had been all along frank and free, as though that long-ago proposal of marriage had never been made, I felt that memory to be another constraint on speaking too candidly. Yet he and Mr. Todd must have spoken of events at Thornfield, so I thought it foolish to pretend naught was amiss. Moreover, I owed St. John some candour, for had he not come with help when it was most sorely needed?

'Mr. Todd may have told you of some difficulties we have had,' said I. 'You will know now that the servants leaving is the least of it.'

'I confess I am at a loss to understand precisely what is happening,' he told me gravely. 'Mr. Todd tells me the late Mrs. Rochester's sister is making grave allegations publicly against your husband. You must forgive me, Jane, if I am blunt but I speak as your friend and also, it must be said, as your only male relative and natural protector – after your husband, of course.

'It seems you are living in a cloud of rumour and doubt, and unspoken suspicions and allegations made but not answered. Such things are more damaging than any truth – to you, in particular, I believe, for knowing you as I do I am certain yours is a nature which requires straight paths and the open light of day to satisfy it. You have ever been happier facing a truth, however hard, than doubts, uncertainty and obscurity.'

'It is all the fault of that dreadful, wicked woman Madame Roland and her accomplice, Grace Poole,' I declared.

'Perhaps,' he answered. 'But, Jane, may I be direct? You have ever been ready to meet your challenges, confront things as they are. This is one of the reasons you are so dear to us, me, and Diana and Mary. You must remember that, because you are our cousin, and so dear, we will never fail you. You are not alone, Jane.'

I gazed at him, my heart so full of gratitude I could scarcely reply. 'St. John . . .' I stammered.

'Will you hear me out, though, Jane, for I must come to the point. Madame Roland is damaging your name, and more particularly Mr. Rochester's. I gather there is also a difficulty with a sum of money, a dowry, not returned. That is not so important, though the world, I have to say, does not look kindly on such oversights. But more serious by far is the gossip she is spreading hinting that Mr. Rochester contrived his first wife's death.'

It was profoundly shocking for me to hear those words spoken aloud by my cousin, whose life had been straightforward, guided always by duty. 'St. John,' I appealed, 'please do not speak of this matter. These things have been said by a dreadful woman, whose family history is full of corruption and madness. Edward, by an early and imprudent marriage, became part of all this. His life was warped and almost ruined by his involvement with the Masons. He should have been freed by Bertha Mason's death, yet still that family haunts him.'

'Please believe, Jane, that I do not wish to upset you by speaking of these matters. But Madame Roland will not keep silent. The poison will spread. I believe Mr. Rochester must silence her once and for all, if necessary by taking an action against her to clear his name, for, if he does not, I am afraid it will be believed there is some particle of truth in her story.

'Alas, there are those whose chief pleasure lies in always believing the worst. Mr. Rochester may consider the matter best dealt with by ignoring it, treating it with contempt. Such a view is not unreasonable but my own opinion is that it may be time for stronger action. This rumour may not die down. It may need stamping on with some vigour. I speak for your sake, Jane, for you are involved, and so, indirectly, is your son. I am telling you this, my dear, for you should know I intend to speak to this effect to your husband on his return.'

I feared it was probable this would anger Edward and said, 'I wish you would not, St. John, for I am not sure Edward will thank you for your intervention.'

'Interference, you mean, little diplomatist,' he said with a smile. 'Well, I know that in Mr. Rochester's shoes I should not welcome comment from a man whom I had never met, who returned after ten years away, claiming to be your cousin, and who immediately took the opportunity to tell him his business in an affair of such delicacy. No, I should not appreciate such an intervention, nor do I relish the prospect of making it. But, Jane – if I do not speak, who will?'

I gazed at him wordlessly. The prospect of this confrontation made me almost afraid. I could all too easily imagine Edward's anger, either cold and contemptuous or openly expressed. And yet I could not help wondering if the course suggested by St. John, an open challenge to Madame Roland, ending doubtless in her humiliation, might not prove effective. Once defeated she would be forced to leave the neighbourhood, would probably return to France, silenced for ever. It was Edward's way – the way of the Rochesters of old, no doubt – to treat with contempt the gossip and speculation of others about him.

The Rochesters had always been their own men, resolute and hardy, taking a pride in their indifference to what others might say of them. 'They say – let them say' might have been their family motto. And so my husband had treated Madame Roland's words with contempt. And such a man, too, will know well what action to take when impugned by another man, but not so well how to deal with a woman.

'Do not worry too much, Jane,' St. John said, seeing my thoughtful face. 'You must eat now. You have scarcely touched this good food Mrs. Willows has provided for us. Eat – and will you play for me after dinner?'

'Gladly,' said I, and duly, as St. John made himself comfortable by the drawing-room fire, I played for him the tunes I remembered he loved.

It was long since I had played and doing so gave me great joy. I had just completed the final bars of that dear old country song 'Barbara Allen', which St. John had, from his chair, sung with me, and all was peace and tranquillity when, seated still at the piano I heard a scratching noise from the window nearby. I ignored it but it came again.

This time my cousin, too, heard it. 'What's that?' he cried, leaping from his chair, and going to the window. He peered out. I followed him and saw, outside in the darkness, a figure I recognised and a face, pale, fearful and desperate, a little dirty, which I knew well.

'Jeremy!' I cried, and to St. John said, 'It is Jeremy, our coachman.'

'Do you wish to let him in?' questioned St. John.

'Yes, of course,' said I, going to the drawing-room door.

St. John followed me, warning, 'He may have been drinking.'

'If so, that is the first time. Jeremy does not drink.'

St. John may have doubted this confident assertion, but he followed me to the front door. Jeremy was standing some distance away, as if ready to flee, when St. John opened it. Seeing us both, he evidently took a decision and hesitantly came towards us, a finger to his lips. When he stood below us on the steps I saw him to be in a very bad way, shaking with cold, his clothes unbrushed, his hair dishevelled.

'Madam,' he said, 'may I please speak to you? – But no one must hear.' He looked doubtfully at St. John. 'It must be private, madam – I beg you.'

'I am Mr. Rivers, Mrs. Rochester's cousin,' said St. John. 'What have you to say?'

'Be kind to him,' I said. 'He has worked for us from boyhood on. His parents are our old servants from Ferndean. Jeremy, come in.'

He shook his head. 'I dare not. The master has dismissed me. Then, when I came back with Ruby, Mrs. Poole sent me off and said I would be found and arrested if I dared come back again.'

'The master is away, and what he did I am sure he did hastily. He may reconsider. And Mrs. Poole is gone. Come inside.'

Jeremy, hesitantly, did come in, still shaking with cold.

St. John was still doubtful and confronted the desolate figure in the hall. 'Speak up, man,' he ordered.

'Come, Jeremy,' said I, 'you must eat,' and I compelled him into the warmth of the kitchen. I bade him sit down and I gave him bread and cheese and hot milk; he began to look more easy.

'So you found Ruby and brought her back?' said I encouragingly. 'And that after you were dismissed.'

'I could not leave her straying,' he told me. 'I was ten miles from Thornfield when she came galloping past me on the road. I was bound for Ferndean, having spent the night in a barn after I was turned out, for it was too dark and cold to travel. I was up early and on my way when I saw her race past, unsaddled, but with her bridle swinging down. But by that time she was a little calmer, I suppose, and when I called after her, knowing my voice she slowed and then came back to me. Seeing no saddle on her, madam, but only a bridle, I was alarmed for you so I led her back along the road towards Thornfield, looking for you as I went.

'There was no sign of you, but some miles along I found a lady's saddle in the road. When I picked it up I was sorely afraid, for it was yours, madam, and the girths were broken.

'And so I reached Thornfield. I was obliged to stop outside, for, though I had the horse and dearly wanted news that you were safe, I was turned off and Mr. Rochester was in a great rage when he discharged me. I feared to approach the house, yet how could I go back to my parents with the tale that I thought you had been thrown from your horse but had done nothing to discover if you had got home safe and well?'

'I was coming after you when Ruby bolted,' I told him.

'I did hope that, madam, anxious as I was. I did hope you had come after me.'

St. John was now, I think, convinced that Jeremy was an

honest man. Nevertheless, he asked, 'If you were turned off, who, that morning early, saddled Mrs. Rochester's horse? Mrs. Rochester will not mind my saying she is no great horsewoman, but this accident would not have happened if the saddle had been properly attended to.'

'That's just it, sir,' he said. 'The matter grows worse. Of course, I should have saddled if I had been here, but I had left the stables in the early hours of the morning, so I do not know who did it. But while I was waiting with Ruby just outside the drive at Thornfield, contemplating the wrath of Mr. Rochester if I returned to the house and whether he would forgive me – for, if you will allow me to say so, madam, though hasty, Mr. Rochester is just – I looked more closely at the saddle. Madam,' he told me gravely, 'the girths of the saddle had been half sliced through. The signs are plain, on both.'

'That cannot be,' I said, but at the same moment St. John said, 'Where is it? You had better show me.'

'I cannot be sure, sir. I brought the saddle to the back of the house, and Mrs. Poole sent me packing. She told me you had been brought back safe, but she would not listen to my story. She told me to take the horse and hand her to the lad and then be off before Mr. Rochester came back and found me still here.

'I left the saddle in the tack-room and set off again for Ferndean, but before I had gone far I thought I must inform you, madam, of the cut girths. But there is worse to tell. On Ruby's back, where the saddle rested, is a wound, an inch or so long, as if something, perhaps a nail, had been placed there under the saddle. Of course, as soon as the rider, yourself, madam, placed her weight on the saddle the pressure of the nail began to cause the horse pain until in the end she bolted. And with the girths half cut through, the saddle would sooner or later start to slip – and the rider be thrown. It was maliciously done, madam.

'I crept up to the house and concealed myself, hoping to be able to find you alone in the drawing-room after dinner to tell you – warn you, indeed.' Earnestly he said, with a nervous glance at St. John, 'You know me well, madam. I am not an excitable man, nor given to extravagant ideas. But events here at Thornfield become stranger by the day.'

I reflected that the previous night I had overheard Mrs. Poole whispering to Madame Roland, 'She will not be told; I have sent him packing again,' and knew it was of Jeremy and his tale of the severed girths that she had spoken.

At St. John's instigation we went straight to the tack-room. I would not be left behind, though that was what he urged. There we discovered the young man brought by Mrs. Willows still at work by the light of a lamp. He looked up, startled, at our arrival.

'We've come to examine the lady's saddle – Mrs. Rochester's,' St. John announced without ceremony. The lad said he had cleaned it and put it with the others but told us, 'The girths are snapped, both of them, and need mending, but I believe they were cut half through, and that was why they broke. I hope no one will blame me.'

'Indeed we shall not', St. John assured him. He and I looked at the saddle. Jeremy was right. The girths had been neatly sliced through and then they had torn asunder: the marks were plain to see.

Next, we went to see Ruby in her stall. The mark on her back was there as Jeremy had described.

St. John was convinced now and deeply shocked. He said, 'The facts are plain. There has been an attempt to harm you, if not kill you, Jane. And the answer lies with whoever saddled the horse.'

I could say nothing. I was too shaken, knowing that somewhere in the world was an individual who hated me so much as to wish to kill me.

With a sigh, St. John turned to Jeremy. 'You had better share your old quarters with the new man for tonight. Come with me into the house and I will get extra bedding and aught else you need. Turned off you may be, but you cannot leave at this hour. Come, Jane, let us go in.'

I went with him. He led me into the drawing-room, retrieved my shawl, put it round me and sat me down by the fire. Then he went off with Jeremy to get what he required.

I was so preoccupied by what we had just learned that I heard, but did not hear, the sounds of a carriage approaching the house. It was not until St. John, his business with Jeremy done, returned to the drawing-room, saying, 'Jane, someone is here,' that I understood what I had heard and by that time came the sound of an angry voice outside the house, then the stamp of feet coming through the hall and a figure appeared in the drawing-room doorway. There stood Edward, muffled in a heavy travelling-cloak, his face furious. Adèle stood timidly behind him.

He took in St. John's presence and said to me with cold anger, 'Ah – I see you have been arranging matters for yourself, Jane, in my absence. In the stableyard I find Jeremy, whom I dismissed, going up to his old quarters, bearing fresh blankets, in case the night is too chilly for him, no doubt. And here by my fireside at midnight is a gentleman with whom I am not, I think, acquainted. I see,' he added, with a glance at the piano, which stood open with some music upon it, 'that you enjoyed some music earlier. I hope you find my wife's playing agreeable to you, sir,' he said to St. John. He advanced into the room.

'I have always found my cousin's playing agreeable, sir,' replied St. John. 'May I introduce myself? My name is St. John Rivers. Mr. Rochester, there are matters about which you must hear immediately—'

'Must? Must?' Edward said angrily. 'Do not presume to tell me what I must hear. You are in my house, Mr. Rivers; you may not command me. I should like the opportunity to speak to my wife alone. Adèle, you will go to bed. You, sir, will oblige me by doing the same. Where is Mrs. Poole?'

Mrs. Willows appeared in the doorway. Edward swung round. 'Who is this woman?'

I stood up. 'Mrs. Poole has left the house, Edward,' I said. 'There is much that you should be told. Perhaps you will let me inform you.'

He said, 'I have returned from a hard journey, having recovered Adèle on the road to London, she having been rendered desperate enough to leave the house. Here, servants are apparently coming and going at will and this gentleman, a stranger, is enjoying my hospitality without my knowledge. Yes, Jane, I should very much like you to inform me.'

St. John said, 'Mr. Rochester. There are very good reasons for what is taking place here. I mean no discourtesy, but I must urge you for your own sake to moderate your tone until you know all.'

'Thank you for your advice. Since I see there is no ridding myself of you, Mr. Rivers, Jane, you and I will go upstairs.'

He gave me a look of command and I unresistingly followed him from the room. Outside in the hall he took my arm in a firm grip and led me upstairs. I own, now, that I was apprehensive. My husband had never after our marriage behaved to me with anything other than tenderness and courtesy – but now I saw a different man, a man almost to dread. Yet I knew, in the sane part of my being, he was still Edward, whom I loved and had married, and that this fierce mood would pass as soon as I had spoken to him.

We entered my chamber and he ordered, 'Sit down, Jane.' I sat on a small, low chair by the window, waiting, while he commenced to pace the room, in silence, like a caged beast, going up and down from window to door and door to window, never once glancing at me. His behaviour alarmed me. I felt here was a man not in command of his intelligence or nerves.

In my heart I blamed Adèle for this, for had she not run away, giving, it seemed from his earlier comments, as the reason that she had been made unhappy at Thornfield - and by me, the implication must have been – Edward would not then have left the house, nor returned in his present mood.

Nor could I put from my mind Céline Varens – again I wondered how long he had known she was in London. Had he seen her there and, more important still, for how long had he known she was not dead?

The silence deepened. There was no sound but that of Edward's pacing. Then, 'Jane,' he said abruptly, 'Jane – have you nothing to say to me?'

'What do you wish me to speak of?' I returned in a calm voice.

'You are recovered from your fall, I hope?'

'Thank you, I am.'

He walked to the window and looked out into the

blackness. 'No sign of a thaw. The journey back was perilous. I had half a mind to stop on the road, but I could not bear to be away longer, though I feared a horse would break a leg.' He uttered an oath. 'Come, Jane, speak to me. This silence of yours is unbearable.'

'I should like to know if you blame me for Adèle's running off.'

'Blame you? Good heavens, no. She is your step-ward, only ten years younger than you. You began as her governess and now you are her guardian's wife. A reasonable man might hope your relations would be easy, but would be a fool to expect it.'

'So you believe I gave her offence, and forced her to run away from here?' I asked.

'No, Jane, no,' he said with impatience in his tone. 'No, I believe nothing of the kind. Does that satisfy you? Are you placated now? Will you consent now to tell me what has been going on in this house since I left only yesterday. Who is that man?'

'The gentleman is my cousin, the brother of Diana and Mary. As you know he has been long away, as a missionary in India. He came this morning and, I believe, rendered me a very great service. Edward – there is much to tell and I ask you to hear me sympathetically.'

And so I told him all – or nearly all – of my recovering from my fall to find only Madame Roland and Grace Poole in the house, of their leaving, of my attempt, thwarted by St. John's providential arrival, to go to Mr. Todd's to get help. But of Madame Roland's revelations about Céline I said nothing. Then I ended by relating the story of Jeremy's return and of what he had said concerning Ruby's broken girths, the nail placed beneath her saddle. As I spoke, Edward's face grew grave; pity replaced anger in his countenance; he sank to the floor beside me, took my hand and said, 'Oh, Jane, Jane.' When I had concluded he said in a broken voice, 'Oh my little dear, what you have suffered.'

But I could go on no longer without speaking of Céline and, placing my hand on his head said gently, 'Grace Poole and Madame Roland told me Adèle had gone to London to find her mother, Céline Varens.' I felt him stiffen at my mention of the name, and as I continued to speak I heard him breathe in sharply. 'Edward, I knew nothing of Mademoiselle Varens's being in London. Indeed, I believed she had died some years ago. It was disturbing to hear from those two wicked women that she was alive and in London. Edward—' I appealed, but broke off. Then, suddenly, he rose to his feet. He looked down at me, his face rigid, his eyes like ice on mine.

'Do you reproach me, by implication, with withholding information about Céline Varens? Do you imagine for one moment that I would insult my wife with news of such a woman? Would you have had me, just after the birth of Jonathan – for that was when I first heard she was not dead – come to your bedside, as you lay there with our new-born son, and hand you the letter from a friend in Paris, containing the story of her being upon the stage? It would have been unbearable news for me to tell and you to hear at such a time. No, Jane, I locked within my heart the information that Céline was alive. I bore it as a burden. As details of her increasing fame came to me, I kept that, also, from you. What would you have had me do, pollute our lives with the knowledge that that woman was still in the world to haunt us?'

I understood, then, his motive in keeping silence. He would have seen it as incumbent on a gentleman to keep such matters from his wife, though for my part I believe I would rather have known the truth.

Now, I said what I should not have said. 'Edward, Céline is Adèle's mother. You have just spoken of her as your ward but you owe it to yourself and to her to acknowledge her as your daughter, if that is who she is. Céline is living. Céline knows the truth and may tell it, and then the world will know.'

I should not have spoken thus and I confess now that what prompted my apparently sage words was a jealous heart. At that moment I think I cared not at all for Adèle nor for her parentage – no more than for Pilot's. I cared that Céline, who I was convinced retained her beauty, was being fêted throughout London and that I did not know whether Edward had loved her once, though I thought he had, and whether, in his heart of hearts, he loved her still. That is what I cared about. What I desired was that Edward should repudiate the woman, his former mistress, say he abominated the very thought of her and assure me he never had a child by her. What Edward desired at that moment was that his loving, patient Jane would afford him some peace and rest in the midst of his difficulties (the gravity of which, I can say, she little knew, as he had told her little). And as I received from Edward no reassurance, so did he receive no peace or consolation from me, only a challenge to say publicly what Adèle's parentage was. There was no understanding on either side of this clash of unspoken desires and therefore the outcome could only be unhappy.

Edward said roughly, 'I've no time for canting talk from you, Jane. It must be the influence of that holy man of God, your cousin, which has overtaken you. I kept the news of Céline from you for good reasons, which I've had the grace to explain and for yet another, which I haven't – which is that I knew once you learned of Céline's continuing existence you would worry yourself perpetually that I loved her still. No acts, no reassurances of mine would have convinced you. A year – five – ten – a hundred years of love between us would have been as nothing – you would have given me no peace over my past days with Céline, nor over her present life. Do not tell me I am wrong, Jane, for I know women. Believe,' he said again, and there was harshness in his tone, 'I know women.'

The injustice, his cold voice, struck me like a sudden, heavy blow. Indeed, I think, rather than hear those words, delivered in that tone, I would have preferred him to have struck me. I recall nothing after that but sinking my head on my breast and murmuring, 'Edward, your unkindness will kill me.'

He started, as if called suddenly to himself, but then said hotly, 'I will say no more, but do not expect me to remain in a house where I am shown no trust or loyalty. I am exhausted, Jane. You do not know what I have to do, to bear. I can sustain these trials. I have sustained such things before and can now again, believe me. But I can do nothing in this atmosphere. Disorder has come to this house; misery, discomfort and suspicion prevail; and you, who should be – whose duty demands that you should be – my chief comfort and resource, are against me. Very well, do as you please, but I will stay in this house no longer.' And he turned rapidly and left me.

Then I was at the door, crying out to him, 'Do not go, Edward. Do not go.' But he went rapidly along the gallery and down the stairs.

Fatally, at the foot of the stairs was St. John, who may have heard Edward's raised voice, may have left the drawing-room to satisfy himself that all was well. Though he acted with the best of intentions, the result was unfortunate.

In the hall, Edward stopped and confronted him. 'Still loitering, Rivers? Well, do not allow me to disturb you – stay, make free of my house and offer as much comfort as you like to my wife. I am leaving.' And he crossed the hall with a rapid stride, opened the great doors and went out into the frozen white waste beyond, now lit by cold moonlight.

I ran after him, downstairs, across the hall, eager to seize him, plead with him, reason with him, make him, by any means I could, remain with me.

In the doorway St. John caught my arm, pulling me up short. 'Stay, Jane—' he began, but I would not.

I ran through the snow, round the house to the stables, the wind cutting at me like a knife, my feet slipping on the frozen surface. He could not leave me, he must not go – I was afraid for myself, also for him. There was danger for a tired and angry man who set wildly off on such a night as this. His horse might fall on the ice, more snow might come, causing him to miss his way.

The stable-yard was patched with frozen snow. In the centre of it Edward was saddling the big grey, which he had brought back tethered behind the carriage. Further off stood Pilot, a great shape in the clear, frozen air, so sensitive to his master's mood that he dared not approach him.

'Edward!' I cried.

He took no notice of me but bent to fasten the girths; then he straightened up and took the bridle in his hand. 'Go back, Jane,' he told me. 'I am leaving. It is better so.'

'How can you say that? How can it be better to leave me?'

The horse was ready, frozen breath clouding from its mouth. Edward mounted swiftly. His horse's hooves clattered on the stone. He rode towards me.

I barred his path. 'No, Edward, Stay!'

The grey came on. 'Go back!' Edward cried.

'I will not.'

'But you will!'

He manoeuvred the horse round me; the beast's huge shoulder brushed mine, jolting me. I stumbled, barely recovered and saw him pass under the stable-yard archway and turn. I was left in the yard, under a cold half-moon, listening to the sound of reteating hooves crunching the snowy gravel in front of the house. I moved mechanically from the yard and past the house. Standing at the top of the drive I watched Edward on the big horse, man and mount black against the snow, with the huge dark shape of Pilot behind, until they reached the road.

I do not know how long I stood there. I recall St. John finding me, putting an arm round my shoulder and supporting me, unresisting, into the house. He rebuilt the drawing-room fire, he wrapped me in shawls, he sat with me all that long night as I, uncomprehending, mourned. I talked, but I do not recall what I said. Certainly I told him of Adèle's parentage, of Céline.

He gave me what comfort he could, which was small. 'He is evidently under some great strain. Be patient; wait. He will think better of what he does, while he is away,' he said.

'He may go abroad,' I grieved, 'as he did before, when Bertha Mason was in the house.'

'You are not a madwoman he is bound to against his will. He is a husband, who loves you and you – you are Jane,' said my cousin.

As dawn came, greyly filling the window-frames, I could not in my anguish check myself and burst out bitterly, 'Oh St. John – if only you had not been here when he came. Your presence angered him, I know. If you had not come, I should have gone to Mr. Todd's, followed Edward, caught him up on the London road and been reunited with him. It would not have ended like this.'

Later, I bitterly regretted my ungenerous speech. St. John, though, made no response to my lamentations, saying merely, 'Yes, Jane, I know. But he will return, I am sure of it.'

Chapter XXIII

The following account is based not on my own experiences after that day but on what Edward told me later of his movements and feelings after he left Thornfield on that awful night. Another account came from Blanche Norton – who had, of course, been in London at that time – when she visited Thornfield recently. She sat with me in the drawing-room, flushed with pleasure at her memories. She had enjoyed that period in her life, a success for her, and did not understand, I think, the discomfort given to me by her words. Her sensitivity to the feelings of others is small, and she has never been one to resist giving a wound to another, on the caprice of the moment.

Edward has described to me his ride that night through the cold and empty landscape, the few houses he passed, farmhouses chiefly, shut up and dark. Pilot plodded after, through the snow, mile upon weary mile. When dawn came a great red sun rose over a vista of fields, frosty and snow-laden. He had come twenty-five miles, into the lowlands. Already he had been obliged to pick up Pilot, sadly spent and with bloodied paws full of ice, hoisting him awkwardly on to his horse; Edward himself continued on foot. The horse, not fresh at the start of the journey, was now ready to fall. He arrived at a small town, ordered Pilot down and the weary man, still leading his horse and with the great dog limping behind, plodded past silent houses until they came to an inn, where he woke the landlord. There Edward rested, half asleep by the fire, until day came, when he bought a carriage and pair, gave orders for his horse to be fed and rested and taken back to Thornfield, and set out once more. Further south there was no snow, only grey skies and a freezing fog. He went on through cold and mist. During this long, slow journey, he said, he was in a haze of fatigue, only penetrated agonisingly by surges of restless and torturing emotion.

It was in this condition that he reached London early the next morning, when the busy, smoky town had been up and doing for some hours. He made his way across the city to the docks, pulled up his carriage and, travel-worn and weary, with the big dog still loping beside him, went down to a thronged wharf.

There he visited the shipping office of Grover and Sims; then he drove to the centre of town and called at his tailor's, shirtmaker's and bootmaker's. Afterwards he betook himself to Belgrave Square, where the Nortons had their town house.

'He came in most affably,' Blanche Norton told me at Thornfield. 'He was impeccable in manner and costume, his company as charming and stimulating as ever. One would never have suspected he had such grave anxieties, although, had one known, one might have noted a certain gauntness, detected beneath his easy manner some sort of reckless despair – that mood, my dear,' she told me sympathetically, 'which prevailed with him during the time when the former Mrs. Rochester was still alive, before you arrived at Thornfield and turned the old

Edward Rochester into the happy man he became. He stayed with us, of course – we would allow nothing else. The reason for his unexpected visit to London he gave as urgent matters of business. I asked no questions, of course, but my husband knew Edward had plunged deep into trade with the West Indies, that the *Janus* was at sea, bound there laden with cargo. However, this matter was not discussed between us. The only hint of trouble we had was his taciturnity on the subject of his trading ventures, about which, had we but known it, he was profoundly anxious.

'He said little, too, about events at Thornfield, telling us only that your cousin, a clergyman, was staying with you, which was perfectly reassuring to us. There were no other indications on Edward's part that there were troubles at Thornfield, or that his state of mind was anything but easy. Soon after his arrival, he sent a message to Adèle, asking her to come south to us. We were pleased, of course, to welcome her.'

For the first few days of Edward's visit, Blanche said, she made sure he enjoyed all the pleasures of town – the Nortons are well connected and know everyone in that small circle which constitutes London society. There were visits to plays, and there were dinners and evening parties. Each morning Blanche rode out in the park with her interesting guest. It was some time since Rochester had been in London; ten years earlier the tale of a mad wife burned and of his own injuries in trying to save her had circulated. Then, less interestingly, I suppose, there had been the story of his marriage to a nobody, formerly the governess of his ward – or was she his daughter?

Now, here was Rochester, once more perfectly garbed, perfectly mannered, maimed but not unhandsome, attractive by reason of his energy and strength. The magnetism of his personality exerted itself on any man or woman on whom he chose to bestow it. In the polite salons of London he had all the attraction of a man whose appearance in the world was impeccable, but who carried with him the fascinations of an interesting past. Though the conservative might eschew the company of Edward Fairfax Rochester of Thornfield, many of the more adventurous of the powerful London hostesses took him up, particularly when Blanche, never discreet, revealed the history of his previous liaison with the season's favourite, Madame Céline Varens. She, the bright star in that season's theatrical firmament, was invited everywhere. It was a fortunate hostess who could persuade her to give a recital at an evening party for the entertainment of her guests.

And that is how they met, in Lady Jago's red and gold music-room, a long room of mirrors and gilt chairs, with a low wooden dais at one end, where, by the light of two great, shining chandeliers, the most celebrated musicians of Europe had performed.

On this particular evening – the evening on which Céline and Rochester were to meet for the first time after so many years – the actress stood on the dais, speaking, in her beautiful voice, the simple words of a poem. Lily-pale, with her golden hair piled on her shapely head, she was clad in a dress of red brocade, without jewellery except for the two pearls set in antique gold which dropped from her small ears. Her face was oval, her eyebrows, a little darker than her hair, arched over long, almond eyes. Her mouth was very red.

Edward, with Blanche and Stanley Norton, had dined elsewhere that evening and came on, with their party, arriving just after Céline's recital had begun. 'Of course,'

said Blanche to me, 'many of those present knew of
the earlier connection between Rochester and Madame
Varens, and had heard of a child born of that union,
so that as we arrived there was in the room what might
vulgarly be called – a quiet sensation. As we entered
heads turned. Those observing Rochester to be of the
party speculated as to what effect his presence might
have upon Céline, who, so far as anyone knew, was
unaware that he would be attending her recital or, for
aught we knew, that he was even in town. And there she
was, my dear, lovely beyond all description, speaking her
lines in that voice, so flexible and so musical that the effect
seemed to me to touch one's very soul – as does a cello,
beautifully played.

'As we entered she had come to the concluding lines
of some piece – I know not what it was,' Blanche told
me, her eyes aglow with remembered excitement. 'She
did not, then, appear to have seen Mr. Rochester, yet,
whether by coincidence or not, when she next began to
speak there was a movement, a rustle, some words quietly
exchanged in the audience, among those who recognised
the opening lines of the poem – "Oriolant en haut solier
Sospirant prist à lermoier", for this, you see,' said Blanche,
'is the opening of an old French poem in which the lady
Oriolant laments that she drove away her lover, Helier.
I believe Mr. Rochester knew the poem also, for as she
began to speak he stood there, quite still, very pale, eyes
burning and fixed on Céline as if there were no one else
in the room – in the world, one might say. She spoke
on, that mellifluous voice flowing over the transfixed
listeners and each time she spoke the refrain, "Dieus!
tant par vient sa joie lente à celui cui ele atalente!" – 'Oh
God! how slowly joy comes to one who longs for it!' –

she said those lines to Rochester and only Rochester; all could tell.

'Her head slightly thrown back, her eyes fixed on his, as his were on hers – oh Jane, I cannot describe it – the sadness. We knew we saw tragedy, the tragedy of a woman bitterly regretting the errors of her youth, the tragedy of a man recalling dead love, past days . . . Who among us could have been unmoved by that extraordinary performance?

'As Céline pronounced the last words of that poem she stood for a moment quite still, accepting the applause. And then,' said Blanche, 'down the aisle, between chairs occupied by the most handsome and distinguished men, the most beautiful and well-born women of our generation, Edward Fairfax Rochester made his way. On reaching the dais he bowed gravely to Céline and offered her his arm. Calmly, she descended, took his arm and with great dignity, almost as if they were royal personages they progressed through the room – they left it, and, as it seemed, the house, without a word. When we looked for them moments later they were gone – where, none knew.

'Next morning Edward was at home: I do not know at what hour he returned, for he had a key to the front door. Of his meeting with Céline he would say nothing but "The lady and I spoke together for some hours." Since he made it plain he wished no questions, it was for Stanley and me, for all of us, to say nothing and to behave as if nothing unusual had occurred.

'Out of his presence, of course, there was a ferment of talk and speculation. The arrival of Adèle, so like her mother, fed the flames. You see, Jane,' Blanche told me, complacently smoothing her silk dress, 'strange affairs conducted behind closed doors in our remote part of the country do not escape the attention of the metropolis.

'Adèle threw herself into London life. Imagine her, dressed simply yet in the latest style, entering our salon, which was crowded with the haut ton of London, on the arm of her distinguished and interesting father, or the man all thought to be her father. It was moving, Jane, so very moving. And she comported herself very well, marvellously, with great charm and grace. All London was fascinated – we were badgered, Jane, badgered, I assure you. We had scarce a moment to ourselves. And how Adèle adored it.' Blanche sighed happily at the memory of this past triumph, then continued with determination.

'Then came the evening when Edward insisted we visit the theatre to see Céline's Phèdre, which has been so praised. It has been called the performance of the century, and I hear that they wept in Paris, and openly, when she performed it – how extraordinary.

'Mr. Rochester had procured a box and Stanley and I were to go, Adèle, of course, and Sir George Lynn, who was in London, Parliament being in session, and Lady Jago, too.

'What a performance! Imagine that tall figure, all in black in the role of Racine's tormented heroine, helpless in the grip of an illicit passion.

'We had by then, I may say, no clearer idea than before of the relations between Mr. Rochester and Céline. He had not mentioned seeing her after that evening at Lady Jago's, which is not to say he had *not* seen her. On that subject he was as silent as the grave, and none had the temerity to raise it with him.

'So there we were in our box, Jane, overlooking a crowded auditorium. Céline launched into the heroine's great speech of love and shame. As she sank to her knees on the stage, I saw Edward, his hands clenched on the front of the box, dip his head forward and I heard him – groan. So sad, I thought it, Jane,' Blanche told me. 'Ah – that groan of sadness – for deeds that could not be undone, of remorse for the past. That was that I heard in that groan. Do you not think I was right to be moved, Jane, at such grief?'

'I do,' I answered, and said no more, for my heart was also full of sadness about which I could not speak.

Chapter XXIV

During the days after Edward's angry departure from left Thornfield, St. John did all in his power to help and console me, for I was as one bereaved. The sorrow I felt was, I believe, nearly as great as if Edward had died. Never, from the time I had first known him, had he spoken to me in such a manner, as if he hated me; never had he flung away from me in a rage as he had on the night when he left.

I feared irreparable damage had been done. I loved him still, but I dreaded – no, not his rage, not even the with-drawal of his love, but that my own trust and confidence in him had disappeared. If I could not believe in Edward, I could believe in no one and nothing. My confidence in life itself had gone. And as one day followed another without a message from him, my last hopes that our parting had been a cruel mistake he would soon regret failed, and I began to think my husband's love might be lost to me for ever.

Adèle was subdued, careful of St. John, whose character and strength I think she was trying to estimate, and alarmed by the consequences of her absconding from Thornfield.

The weary December days wore on, dark and cold. As we neared the middle of the month there was a slight thaw. The snow melted, bringing mists. A week after his departure a letter from Edward came at last. I seized it from the maid and, trembling, opened it. It was brief, too brief, saying only: 'I am at Lady Norton's and require you to send Adèle to me. She should bring a maid. Be good enough to find a reliable coachman to drive. I shall send him back when is Adèle is delivered, for I imagine you and Mr. Rivers will have need of the carriage.'

On reading this cold message, I sank into a chair, unable to move for some time. My worst fears were fulfilled – Edward had not forgiven; he remained angry. And now he wished his ward, Céline's child, to go to him in London. He sent me not one word of love; this message confirmed his resolution not to cross the chasm which had opened between us.

I said nothing to Adèle or St. John of this, merely telling Adèle she was to go to London to join her father at the Nortons', which filled her with feverish excitement not unmixed with malice, for, 'Did Papa not ask you also to go, Step-mama?' she asked with a sly, small smile, as she stood in the hall swathed in furs, trunks packed and ready. I could not answer and only shook my head. Filled with thoughts of the plays, visits and entertainment awaiting her, she might not have noticed that tears had come to my eyes, not so much for the thoughts of pleasures missed but that Edward chose to be away without me.

And so Adèle left and St. John and I continued at Thornfield. It had been planned that my cousin Mary and her husband should visit us, but she became ill with a congestion of the lungs, and a December journey would plainly have been unwise. Thus the visit had to be deferred.

For many days thereafter I existed as if in a fog, sometimes despondent to the point of wondering what value my life had. Was I to bring my child into a fatherless home, to be reared by a deserted mother? These were black moments in the long watches of the night when I wondered if it would not be better if, when my time came, both I and my child closed our eyes upon the world.

Although I made all the efforts I could to conceal my state of mind, St. John, I believe, noted it. His years as a missionary had broadened his sympathies and understanding of mankind in ways of which I could not conceive. Whatever the effect of his mission on others, that experience had transformed the righteous but narrow St. John Rivers into a man of large heart and sympathies. Patient and kindly, he comforted me in small ways. He talked when I would talk, persuaded me to drive out on good days, even assumed for me some of the burdens of the household, for Mrs. Willows was obliged to go back to Mr. Todd. I was too heart-sick and uncertain of the future to appoint another housekeeper.

It was St. John too, who, when I had been in this sad state for over a fortnight, persuaded me to go to Jonathan for, shameful though it is to confess, I had scarcely given a thought even to my son during that dark period. I did not wish him to come home to that sad, abandoned house. So when a fine day came, bright but cold with a watery blue sky, we took the carriage and set off for Ferndean.

'We were so happy at Ferndean, Edward and I,' I told St. John, 'and that is where our dear son was born.'

Blessed St. John! How many such sad remarks had he heard from me, during that bitter time. Never once did he in any way show impatience, nor did he, as people will, though often more for their own satisfaction than to afford any comfort to the sufferer, urge me to rally myself, take a cheerful view and count my blessings, or make any of those other suggestions which further depress the spirits of an afflicted individual who knows full well what he should do, but finds, try as he may, that he cannot achieve it.

The visit to Jonathan at Ferndean was of more benefit to me than can be imagined. There was my dear boy, smiling, healthy and loving, providing me with the most excellent of reasons for continuing in the mid-stream of life; there were my gentle friends the Weatherfields and all around me all the memories of earlier happiness with Edward. And such happiness! I could not believe that our union of so many years could collapse in the face of difficulties and misunderstandings, of harsh words delivered under the stress of adverse circumstances.

Therefore, after merrily eating a large tea with the Weatherfields, Jonathan and their two boys, St. John and I departed, with the promise that my friends would pay a visit to Thornfield very shortly, and I returned in much better spirits.

From that point on, slowly, I think, some courage came to me, and some hope for the future.

Sleepless might still followed sleepless night; sometimes grief still struck me like a blow. But, whatever my private griefs, I occupied the position of Mrs. Rochester of Thornfield, a position of dignity and influence in the neighbourhood and the county and, although the grandeur of this position attracted me not at all, it gave me the opportunity to do some good, to be of some use to others. And if it were to be – Heaven forbid! – that

Edward were to absent himself from me and from the house for long periods in future, as was fully in his power, as indeed he had been accustomed to do when the presence of Bertha Mason had made his home a place of dread for him, I would still be at Thornfield. But if that sad fate were what Providence had dictated for me, then I would endeavour to make this solitary, mournful life a thing of some virtue and grace. If I were forced to live as but half a woman, scorned by and useless to my husband, it might yet be that by my efforts I could do some good in my life. Harsh consolation, but consolation nevertheless.

And so it was that, not long after our visit to Ferndean I said one morning at breakfast, 'St. John, the days grow shorter; Christmas is nearly here. It will be a hard time for the poor from now on. Will you help me?'

'Of course, Cousin, and gladly,' he agreed. 'But I must tell you first that Mr. Sugden has come to me again for instructions. I have felt I ought to spare you news of his visits, but he needs orders, which I have no authority to give. If you are well enough, will you see him? A farm has fallen vacant and should be re-let. There are sheep to be slaughtered, but he knows not how many. Forgive me, Jane, for mentioning all this, if you are unable to bear it. But Sugden tells me he has been sending messages through Mr. Rochester's bankers in London, and although he knows they have been delivered there has been no reply.' He paused, then evidently decided to speak on. 'Sugden hints he has received intimations there is cause for concern about the estates' revenues. Jane, may I ask if on your marriage you caused any settlement to be drawn up reserving any of your money to yourself? Otherwise, of course, under the law all you have is your husband's.'

'No,' I told him, 'I entrusted all to Edward.'

'That is as I thought,' he said soberly. 'And tell me, do you know aught of Mr. Rochester's affairs?'

'At Ferndean I knew all. Now, nothing,' I replied.

'If you are well enough, you should see Sugden,' he said in a tone of resolve. He paused. 'I should like myself to find out how matters stand. I am not eager to do this, Jane, but it is no more than my duty. I hope you have no objection?'

'I have always thought it right for a woman to trust her husband in all things,' I answered.

'That I understand. But here is Sugden with no instructions, and you cannot deny you have a responsibility to protect your husband's interests during his absence. And without some knowledge of how matters stand, decisions cannot be correctly made.'

'Very well, then,' I answered. 'If you will sit with me, I will ask Sugden for an account of the estate, but I think, as to the factory in Manchester or any other matters – those are Edward's concerns and should remain so.'

'As you wish,' he said. 'I will ride over and get Sugden.'

'Bring Mrs. Sugden, also, if convenient,' I requested him. 'I still wish to relieve want in the village and to bring a little cheer to the children there, for Christmas.'

'Of course, Jane,' he said courteously.

We saw Sugden in my husband's study, though I did not sit behind his desk as he was wont to. Instead, St. John and I sat with Sugden by the fire. The news he brought was most unwelcome. Since Edward's departure, very large sums had been drawn from the estate accounts, on his instructions, and forwarded to him in London. But – and Sugden brought all this out with some embarrassment – for several months prior to his departure there had also been withdrawals, not explained by any work on the estate or Thornfield itself. On hearing this information, St. John became grave; and to me the position was utterly bewildering, for I could not understand why Edward had need of such large sums.

The interview concluded with St. John's agreeing, on Sugden's advice, to certain courses of action as far as the estate was concerned, and saying that, as to the more important decisions, they could not be taken without Mr. Rochester's own authority, so Sugden must manage as best he could until his return.

I then arranged with Mrs. Sugden that she, I and St. John would all visit Hay in three days' time to see what were the main necessities of the local people. Things were very bad there, she told me, for now there was sickness – fever – in almost every home, and the people had no money for medicines. I had no money of my own, only what I had saved from Edward's more than generous allowance to me; but I thought it would suffice to fill the most pressing of the people's needs.

What distressing conditions met us when we began to go from house to house in Hay! Poverty and hunger were everywhere apparent, and the people had no strength to resist the sickness. I ignored Mrs. Sugden's warning not to enter the cottages, lest I catch the fever; and what pitiful sights met my eyes. In one house five children lay sick and likely to die; in another, an old woman was starving; in a third, a recently delivered woman and her baby lay stupefied, only a day, it seemed, from death.

St. John went immediately for the doctor, who agreed to visit each desolate house and do what he could. He then set off to Millcote to procure supplies of fuel, clothing, soap, food, and everything which was wanting; though only, he insisted, on condition I would return to Thornfield, go to my bed and rest.

However, I could scarcely repose myself. The sights and scenes at Hay filled my head – poverty-stricken homes, of hopeless despair, of gentleness in the face of impossible adversity, of brutishness born of misery. Even when the fever passed, I thought, taking what toll it might, even if I contrived to relieve want from my own, alas, slender purse, what permanent solution could I supply? The people wanted work, and there was none; the weaving trade was lost to them for ever.

St. John, all his missions accomplished, was back by evening. 'The doctor is in the village,' he told me, 'and the waggons of fuel and food and all necessities will be here early tomorrow. Yet, as you say, the problems are more profound. The people need schooling, and, above all else, work.'

'There is so much to do, and my means are so small,' said I.

'Well, Jane,' he told me, 'if you have no shovel, you must dig with a teaspoon. Enlist Mr. Todd as your ally—'

'Easily said but less easily done,' I interrupted.

'No,' he said briskly. 'Todd is not a bad man. He only wants direction, which you can give, if you will. And,' he continued smiling 'you will recall a certain legacy which came some time ago to a certain Miss Eyre from her uncle – and which that Miss Eyre, appalled by the magnificence of the sum she had so unexpectedly inherited, insisted should be divided between herself and her three unworthy cousins.'

'I do recall insisting on a just distribution of my uncle's legacy, St. John,' said I.

'So then,' he persisted, 'the money was divided into four equal portions, you taking a fourth of what had been left you, Diana, Mary and myself taking the remainder. And now, I must tell you we tricked you, for we did not use the money. We retained it; we invested it and said nothing and there it lies for you, if you need it, principal and interest – you may take either or both.'

'No, St. John, no. A gift is a gift and not for returning.'

'Come, Jane,' he said earnestly. 'I am quite as prosperous as a clergyman has any right to be. Diana and Mary are married and provided for. As for you, you wish to help the people of Hay, and – let me be quite honest with you – I am disconcerted by what Sugden says about heavy withdrawals of money from the estate. We know already of a claim upon your husband by the Masons. If there is aught amiss with Mr. Rochester's finances, you may be assured that I, Diana and Mary will not see you suffer.'

'I am sure there is nothing wrong,' I said.

Chapter XXV

Next day two loaded waggons came from Millcote, and Mrs. Sugden went early to the village to arrange the distribution of goods. In the afternoon I went down to make sure all was well and to visit some of the sick. Now, at least, all Hay's chimneys smoked; laundry was boiling outside, in cauldrons; a man dug his garden with a new spade; a group of children were playing in the street.

I went to the house of the woman who had taken the fever after childbirth. The first thing I saw, on entering that sad one-roomed cottage, was a bunch of yellow jasmine on the pallet where the sick woman lay; the second was a pot of broth heating on the fire; and the third, in a dim corner of the room, was a dark-clad woman pouring something from a phial. I knew her, knew her well, and was chilled. 'Mrs. Poole!' I called out. 'What do you here?'

She turned, a beaker in her hand. 'The woman requires nursing,' she said. 'Madame Roland heard you had been in Hay and declared you were right to have gone, and that if I wished I might also go to help. She herself is too fearful, but she has supplied money. In her youth her family was made prosperous by slaves, she said, which she now thought wrong, but many of those slaves were treated no worse than the people of Hay.' She went to the woman and gave her a drink from the beaker. 'Head up, Mary, drink. Fight, have nothing to fear. Your neighbour is guarding the children, your man is helping dig a garden plot. And here is Mrs. Rochester, come to see how you are.'

'Do not trouble to say anything,' said I. 'Lie still and rest.' A useless order, for the poor woman was unable to do anything else. She lay on her bed, her face pinched and her eyes bright with fever.

Who would have thought that Grace Poole and I would have found ourselves standing side by side by the bed of a sick woman, both feeling the same sensation of pity for the poor sufferer, who, we both knew, had almost no prospect of recovery? But we tended her as best we could.

Then Mrs. Poole said to me, in a low voice, 'This is not the time, I know it, but I must speak to you. I know you hate me, yet I must still speak. You are not a foolish woman, Mrs. Rochester, so you understand already, deny it as you will, that there is something wrong with your husband's account of his first wife's death. Who should know it better than I, who was trapped in that room with her on the night of the fire?

'Will you tell me how it was on that night?' I said softly.

'Yes,' she said, I will. Know then that when I smelled smoke and began to feel the heat of the fire, I searched high and low with increasing desperation to find the key to our rooms. I had not got it, nor had Bertha; nor was it to be found anywhere else in our small apartments. Yet the door was locked – locked, madam – and the key gone. Who had it? Who had locked the door?

'As the smoke thickened I saw no chance for us but the

roof, so I assisted Bertha through the window and she, strangely calm, got herself up on to the parapet of the roof. I could hear the sounds of fire below; the smoke grew even thicker and I saw to my great alarm that flames were beginning to lick up from below through the floorboards under the window, my only way of escape.

'I had almost given myself up for lost when the door opened with a crash and Mr. Rochester stood there, silhouetted, flames behind him. And in his hand he had the key, madam! *He had the key!*'

I could say nothing. I stood in that windowless cottage, the stertorous breathing of the dying woman in my ears. This could not be the truth – could not.

Mrs. Poole said, her tone less harsh than customarily, 'I escaped, madam, down the staircase, which was in flames – my clothes were alight when I ran from the house.

'Meanwhile, Mr. Rochester must have burst through the window and gone up on the roof to try to save his unfortunate wife. Madame Roland thinks he made no such attempt that, in fact, he pushed her to her death. But I am not so persuaded. If he planned to burn his wife to death, he was very close to achieving his ends, so why did he risk his life by entering a burning building and climbing on to the roof, where she was trapped, in order to save her? You may say he came back to save me, but would a man prepared to burn his wife to death scruple to burn another person with her?

'No – there is another explanation, I think, but I cannot tell what it is. I cannot tell what happened on that night. But there has been an attempt to kill you, madam, by tampering with your horse's saddle,' she continued earnestly. 'Mrs. Rochester, we stand by the bedside of a woman who may not be much longer for the world. Standing here in the face of death, I would not deceive you, nor could I forgive myself if I did not warn you. Go. For your safety – leave Thornfield. Leave at once.'

The sick woman on the bed gave a groan and begin indeed now to embark on the journey carrying her from this world. We did what we could to relieve her sufferings until, at last, those sufferings ended – and she was gone. Then we commended her to the care of neighbours waiting outside, and left the cottage. I extended my hand to Mrs. Poole, who shook it gravely, and we parted, without another word.

I said nothing of this to St. John, for I was shocked and confused. I did not know what to believe of Mrs. Poole's account of the fire, yet it seemed candid enough. She had even confessed to being uncertain herself about what exactly had occurred. She had most earnestly advised me to leave Thornfield, yet could I believe this was disinterested or might it be yet another act of malice – her own and Madame Roland's plot to separate me from my husband?

However, I had little time to contemplate the matter, for in the ensuing week the sickness reached its greatest height in the village, and all the hours my health would permit were spent in Hay. Mrs. Poole was ever there, providing help and assistance. I learned, if not to trust Grace Poole completely, at least to trust her more. And still there was no word from London.

Chapter XXVI

I will return to Lady Norton's account of Edward's visit to London.

Edward still said nothing to Blanche of Céline, but one night she saw them together, Adèle, Céline and Edward, in a restaurant to which she, her husband and a small party of friends had gone after the theatre.

'Hardly had we taken our seats,' Blanche told me, 'when Lady Jago grasped my arm and whispered, "See – over there – in the alcove!" There was a recess at the back of the long dining-room, a kind of den, papered in dark red. On the table was a shaded gilt lamp, which lit up the lovely faces of Céline and her daughter and Rochester's saturnine visage. Quite a vision, dear Jane,' Blanche laughed. 'I assure you it was like some scene from mythology – Pan with nymphs, or something of that kind.

'They were so engrossed, my dear, Madame Varens leaning forward, looking intently into Rochester's eyes, he all attention, the lovely Adèle laughing. I do not think they noticed us at all. We pretended to ignore them, though we were agog, my dear, quite agog, as you will imagine.

'Not long after, when I glanced over, they were gone.

They had not left by the main entrance or they would have passed us. They must have been allowed out by some secret door at the back of the restaurant, so as not to be remarked by the other diners, I surmised. I thought it odd – so odd that I did not mention, next day, having seen them. Nor did I ever find out if Rochester had seen our party there that night. But such beauty they had, my dear, such enchantment.'

At Thornfield I knew little beauty and less enchantment at that time. Christmas was but two weeks off, and no word had come from Edward as to the arrangements. It began to seem he would not return to Thornfield for Christmas. We had never before been apart on that day of celebrations and the prospect of his absence filled me with melancholy.

St. John, I think, understood this and therefore, without asking questions as to any plan which might have been made, suggested my cousins Diana and Mary and their husbands be invited for the holiday. I seized gratefully on this idea, for if Edward were not to return their company would be most pleasant for myself and Jonathan. Indeed, the prospect of the two of us, mother and son, alone and melancholy at Christmas, was a sad one.

And so invitations were sent. But only days later, as I sat at breakfast with St. John, a letter at last came from Edward in London.

'My dearest Jane,' he wrote, and even those first words caused my heart to leap within me, caused me to hope that he had begun to feel his old love for me. As I read on, that hope became certainty and I rejoiced. 'I have been long,' he wrote, 'all too long, in town and yearn to be back at Thornfield with you. Now, dearest heart, will you forgive a miserable exile and then forgive again, for I have invited for the holiday Sir George Lynn as well as some new acquaintances, of whom I am sure you will approve, Lord and Lady Jago and their son Henry. The Nortons also have said they will be happy to be with us for a while at that time, so we shall be quite a party coming down. I propose also that there should be a ball at Thornfield, to take place after the Boxing Day meet, which will depart from Thornfield this year as it always used to. I believe we owe it to ourselves and to Thornfield to celebrate our return with some pomp and ceremony.

'I know you are not one for such things but you deserve some society after having been alone so long, with your neglectful husband away. I know that at present you are not always strong and there will be preparations to be made, so I have taken the step of writing to Mrs. Poole to come and help. Adèle has told me she is at Madame Roland's. Mrs. Poole is not a bad woman, Jane – though Madame Roland most certainly is, and Mrs. Poole should remain no longer under her roof. At all events, her assistance will take from your shoulders some of the burden of the preparations suitable for our guests and – dare I say it, Janet, my little democrat? – suited to our dignity. Thus, preparations can be made without trying your strength too far.

'The talk in town, dearest, is of how much you have done to help in the village during the sickness. Those of us who have estates in the north have been much concerned by news of widespread disease and it has been a joy to know, and have it known, that at Hay my own lady has been at work to relieve the suffering.

'I break off now for this note must go straight away. I am not sure of the precise time of my arrival but will send later to inform you.

'Jane, my love, I believe fortune smiles at last. I long to see you and tell you all the news – which at present I have no time to do.

'I am yours, my darling, now and ever – eternally.' And below these words he had signed his dear name.

My overriding sensation was one of joy. The affectionate tone of this letter, his generous acknowledgement of what I had done – all relieved my mind of the anxiety which had so long possessed it. I put the letter down, blissfully happy and said, 'Oh, St. John, Edward returns for Christmas. He will be here soon.'

'I am very pleased, Jane,' he said gravely.

'He brings a party from London and requires me to make arrangements for a ball – Oh, St. John, he is coming home!'

'I am pleased for you, Jane,' said he again. But I noted some restraint in his tone. 'Now,' he continued, 'it is plain that with the many other guests and their servants, and with all the careful plans which must be made, I, Diana and Mary and their husbands will be an additional burden to you. What would have been a pleasant but tranquil occasion becomes suddenly a most exciting affair and for that, I suspect, you do not need five more guests. So I will return to Gateshead, where I stay with Diana, within a few days.'

'No, St. John,' I cried. 'I have been so looking forward to spending the holiday with you all.'

He gave me a wry look. 'Jane – when you have paused for perhaps two minutes to reflect on the capacity of your house, the nature of the supplies you will need and the breadth of the arrangements you must make at comparatively short notice, I think you will agree with me. Let us settle that I, Diana and Captain Fitzjames, Mary and Mr. Wharton will come to you in the New Year. We shall be sure our visit will that way be a pleasure, not a burden.'

It was true that our Christmas party as constituted would number over a dozen, and there would be other guests, no doubt, on Christmas Day and many more for the ball. Yet Thornfield was a large house and there was ample room – as was well understood by St. John. But I sensed he had no great wish to spend Christmas in the house with Edward, for they had parted on bad terms and Edward, in his letter, had made no mention of St. John, nor sent him any message.

I hesitated, whereupon St. John concluded vigorously, 'I must say, too, I am not sure that the Fitzjameses and the Whartons would welcome being flung suddenly into a large assembly of the kind Edward will bring from London. If you are going to become so very grand, Jane, you must introduce your country cousins to your high-up guests little by little, so that we may slowly accustom ourselves to their grandeur. I'm afraid if we had to meet such a party we might be quite put out of countenance.'

I did not, to tell the truth, believe any of my cousins would feel out of place among Edward's London friends but St. John had spoken forcefully so I accepted his diplomatic refusal as truth. Sir John's only encounter with my husband had been unpleasant, he, conciliatory and Edward, angry. I could not press him to join the party for the festivities.

And alas, I fear that at that time my delight at the prospect of my husband's return, and my contemplation of the great preparations required to provide fit hospitality for a large company, led me to express far less gratitude and affection to St. John than was his due – and more than his due.

He stayed two days longer and as he was on the point of departure thrust into my hands a packet, smiled and said, 'Here, madam, is your school.'

'Why, Cousin,' said I in amazement, 'what is this?' Opening the packet, I found it to contain the purchased lease of one of the two large empty houses at the edge of Hay, together with details of all the repairs St. John had ordered to make the building fit and comfortable for its purpose.

Overwhelmed with affection and gratitude, I was near to weeping as he left. I believe I saw a tear, also, in his eye. He pressed my hands, saying, 'Farewell, Jane, and remember if you have need of us, your cousins, at any time, we will not fail you.'

'We will meet very soon,' I replied. He turned then, and left me.

As the sound of his horse's hooves faded I felt heavy-hearted, for I had become accustomed to the gentle and unfailing comfort of St. John's presence and now there was no one with whom to share my days. I sustained myself, however, with the thought that the coming weeks would be full of occupation. In Hay, though the fever had passed, it had left much distress in its wake – and at Thornfield preparations for the Christmas entertainments must be speedily made.

St. John had not been gone an hour when Mrs. Poole arrived. She stood in the hall clutching her bag and looking at me doubtfully. 'Mr. Rochester wrote asking me to return to the house to help with a party for Christmas. And I gather there is to be a ball, also. I have taken the liberty of bringing my things, but should you wish me to go, I will.'

I was not sure of her, felt no warmth for her, but,

knowing I required her assistance, said, 'Will you stay, Mrs. Poole? There is much to do here.'

The sympathy we had experienced by the bedside of the dying woman had gone. Once again I and this woman were beneath the same roof, and I think neither of us took much pleasure in it.

She looked at me coldly. 'I would as soon not be employed where I am not wanted, Mrs. Rochester,' she told me.

'Mrs. Poole, Mr. Rochester has re-appointed you and I am content with that. There is no time for argument. We need more servants, maids and men. I do not think we will find them in Hay. Will you go to Millcote and see if you can find suitable persons there?'

'Very well,' she said, and, turning, silently took her bag upstairs.

The next week was bright but frosty. There was snow on the mountains and, below, the ground was icy. Nevertheless in mid-morning one day the first carriage, containing Edward and Adèle, rolled up and stopped before the house. Edward descended, hastened to where I stood waiting and embraced me almost more warmly than was suitable on such an occasion.

He said in my ear, 'Oh Jane, my Jane. How glad I am to be home at last.' I gazed joyfully up at him. His face held all his old vivid affection. Truly, he had come home.

Then came Adèle with an outstretched hand and a smile less than warm. 'Step-mama, is all ready for the ball?' were her first words.

'Youth, youth,' murmured Edward to me and I smiled.

'Here they come!' cried Adèle. 'We left London in convoy, like an army.'

And like an army they were. Sir George Lynn and

Blanche and Stanley Norton descended from the second carriage wreathed in smiles, anticipating pleasure to come, and minutes later from the third stepped Lord and Lady Jago, she slender and fashionable, he bluff and firm of countenance, bearing a mark of authority about him, for the Jagos were great land-owners, and Lord Jago was high in the government. Also in their carriage was their son Hal, a young man little more than twenty years old, pale, languid and, it seemed to me, as sophisticated as a man twice his age. He glanced up at Thornfield, surveying the house as if he planned to buy it, and I heard him observe to Adèle, 'A fine place, but a very poor location.' Behind the guests came their servants and baggage in two more carriages.

We all entered the hall, which I had caused to be decked, country-fashion, with holly and greenery of every kind. Mrs. Poole stepped forward and assisted the manservant in taking the hats and cloaks of the guests. We repaired to the drawing-room, where I had placed a new mirror, and paintings from Ferndean and, along one wall a beautiful sideboard, in red lacquer, painted in gold in the Chinese style.

'My dear,' cried Blanche, 'how charming everything is.'

Then Jonathan came in to be introduced, and stood next to Edward, before the fire, imitating his father's masterful stance and smiling his father's broad and cordial smile. We were many at lunch, all in high spirits and I, even I, shy Jane, made some contribution, I believe, to the gaiety.

Mr. Sugden had come up before luncheon to offer the gentlemen what rough shooting the estate could provide and nothing would prevent Sir Stanley Norton, Lord Jago and Sir George Lynn from going out with their guns that afternoon. Jonathan was permitted to go also, under the supervision of Sugden.

Edward, though, declared he would spend his afternoon with me and, informing the ladies in the drawing-room that I was under orders to rest after luncheon, took me upstairs, offering me his shoulder to lean on, bade me lie down, pulled a chair to my bedside, flung himself into it and gazed around him in happy appreciation, saying, 'How glad I am to be home. What you have done in my absence – relieved the sufferings of the village, perfected Thornfield for our guests – such a tiny person it is, Janet, yet so busy. And now you must tell me all that has been happening.'

And so I told him all, though not of the despair his departure had caused me, for that was as if it had never been.

'You should not have entered the cottages when there was sickness, though,' he told me. 'Yet you were ever brave – so brave.'

'And what of you?' I said. 'What passed in London?'

Reassured that his affections for me had not changed, I was nevertheless anxious to hear if he had seen Céline or if Adèle had been united with her mother. The thought of the miniature haunted me and I would have been glad if he had not met Céline in town. But the hoped-for words were not spoken.

He said, 'You will have observed our little Frenchwoman, Adèle, has emerged from her chrysalis to become the brightest butterfly in the garden. Her talent for pleasure is no news to us who know her, but now it reaches new heights. Young Hal Jago has taken a great fancy to her – but then, so have many gentlemen.'

'Perhaps she will marry soon?' I questioned.

'Perhaps.' He frowned. 'She will need a good dowry, due to her position' was all he said, and although I considered his words with all due seriousness I did not realise then their true import, what tragedy they masked.

'Well, we shall be rich soon, my darling. I had not told you, but I have sold out to Jessop and with the money acquired a sloop and cargo to trade in the West Indies. I have recently had favourable news of the early part of the voyage. When the *Janus* returns, I shall be on my way to becoming a rich man. But I know this is not a matter to concern my modest wife, who has less craving for grandeur and luxury than any woman living.' He gazed at me with love, pressed my hand and kissed my brow. Then he stood up, 'I shall go and steal an hour for business, then attend our guests. Will you rest, and we shall be together in a few short hours.'

Though I own I became increasingly fatigued by the demands of hospitality on such a scale – for of course I was not accustomed to such a life, nor had I my full strength – my days thereafter were filled with happiness. The society was stimulating, for Lord Jago, a minister in the government, was a well-read and interesting man, while Sir Stanley Norton, when released from the claims of a wife addicted to society, was a passionate local antiquarian.

Edward reproached me humorously, 'You spend more time talking to the gentlemen than to the ladies. If you continue these conversations about history and statecraft, there will be gossip.' I did not say how much I regretted that ladies, owing to the small opportunities available to them, are obliged to limit their interests to the small world about them, or, if they do not, are persuaded to pretend they do.

And now Christmas approached. As the day of the Boxing Day ball came closer, Adèle was ever at my shoulder with a dozen questions about the guests, the orchestra, the choice of dances – 'More waltzing! We must have more waltzing!' was her constant cry. Preoccupied by thoughts of the ball, memories of London and the promise of a return to the city in early spring, and enjoying the attentions of Hal Jago, she seemed happier than I had ever known her. My own conception of happiness, I reflected, was not hers, nor could I impose it on her.

Christmas Day came and it was decided we should attend the morning service, so, on that cold, bright day, with blue sky overhead, we entered our carriages. In the leading one Edward, Jonathan and Lord and Lady Jago were seated. In the other carriage came the Nortons, Adèle and Hal Jago, who had made sure to be of the party including Adèle.

The evening before, I had been down to Hay with little gifts for each child there. On our journey through the village it was a joy to see some of them outside their houses, playing – with a ball or skipping-rope, a top or a doll – and a greater one, perhaps, to see each chimney smoking and know that on that day there would be food on every plate.

Edward noted my keen and gleaming eye as I detected these signs. He patted my knee, causing me to blush a little. 'You see before you the saviour of Hay, your Mama,' he told Jonathan.

'Beware,' said I, 'for I have more plans for Hay.'

He cast up his eyes. 'To discover one is married to the Lady Bountiful,' he exclaimed.

Lord Jago, during an earlier conversation had coaxed from me what I wished to do and indeed had assisted me to understand more clearly what could and should be done. He said now in my defence, 'Do not protest, Rochester, for it is often the country gentlewoman who relieves want, and who may unwittingly be the means of preventing disaffection in agricultural areas.'

'I think for that purpose I would sooner rely on the militia than on my wife,' he replied.

'Will you gentlemen be kind enough not to alarm us with talk of rebellions and calling on soldiers?' protested Lady Jago. 'And besides, it is all fiddlesticks.'

I laughed. 'I confess I do not see the question so broadly. My intention is merely to relieve want.'

'And provide the needy with the means eventually to relieve their own want, or so you have said, Mrs. Rochester,' said Lord Jago.

'Or so you persuaded me to think, sir,' replied I. 'For as we spoke, you took me several miles further than I had thought to go.'

'Well,' said my husband, leaning back in the carriage, 'I am glad you two have set our little world to rights. And here we are, at church, so we must put all this behind us, and concentrate our minds on higher things.'

'Just so,' said Lady Jago. 'And I am paying you the compliment of believing you will do so, though secretly I know you are too wicked.'

'Never wicked,' he said in the same light tone, 'only misled. But Jane will keep me straight.'

And so we entered the church, which, bedecked with greenery, and with the organ playing, did, in truth, set my mind to thinking of a better world, beyond our troubles and our pains.

The children of the village began to sing a carol. We rose to sing too. Our pew was crowded, so I could not see the congregation, but Blanche Norton, who was seated next to me, turned as the young voices were raised in 'Adeste Fideles', and whispered, 'Who is that lady gazing so strangely at Mr. Rochester?'

I shook my head, murmuring, 'I cannot see.'

'She is very well dressed, dark and very commanding,' she persisted, though still in a low tone.

I was forced to reply, 'It is most probably Madame Roland, the woman telling these untruths about my husband.'

As we left the church, Madame Roland was outside, having placed herself deliberately, as it seemed, in our path. She looked at Edward, and smiled an unpleasant, gloating smile. Her gaze swept over me and back to him. 'You look happy today, Mr. Edward Rochester, but I predict your happiness will not last a day.'

Lord Jago had evidently overheard her words and, as we reached our carriages, he asked Edward, 'Who is that woman? I observed her staring fixedly at you during the service.'

'She is a madwoman,' Edward informed him coldly. 'I shall deal with her in the New Year.' Then to me he said, 'Come, Jane, get in,' and he helped me into the carriage.

Nevertheless, the journey back to Thornfield was not as pleasant as the earlier one, for Madame Roland's words had upset me. That she should threaten was not perhaps surprising, but there had been a confidence, almost a triumph, in her dreadful smile and malicious words – though perhaps, I thought, being advanced in pregnancy and indeed very fatigued, this anxiety might have been no more than my fancy.

We ate our Christmas dinner with much talk and laughter. Later I played the piano and we sang and had games. We were destined for the Nortons' for supper and evening entertainment, but as the day advanced I began to feel very tired and weak and, although I struggled against it, eventually I was forced to ask Edward if I might remain behind. He was deeply concerned and offered to remain with me. However, I refused, urging him vigorously to go to the party, so that finally he agreed, saying, 'Of course, my dear, I will go if you wish, and you must rest. You have been entertaining us royally and tomorrow is the ball, for which you must be at your best.'

After the party had gaily left for Raybeck Hall, I put Jonathan, who was overcome with excitement and fatigue, to bed, read to him for a little and returned to sit with my own book in the drawing-room for a while before retiring.

My quietude however, was short-lived, for less than an hour after the carriages had departed Grace Poole announced a visitor. 'He is a gentleman from London,' she told me, 'who says he must see Mr. Rochester urgently. I have told him Mr. Rochester is away from home for the evening and he desires to await him. Will you see him, madam, and find out what he wants?'

'He has come from London to arrive here on Christmas Day?' I asked. This seemed to me extraordinary.

'That is what he says,' she told me impassively. But she was grave, for some reason, and suddenly I recalled Madame Roland's triumphant smile, and there was a voice in my ears saying, as if aloud, 'This man brings bad news, and Grace Poole knows what it is.' And at the same time I felt as if all the blood had rushed from my body and I was sorely afraid.

'What is his name?' I asked.

'Phillips,' she told me.

'Show Mr. Phillips in,' I ordered. It was as though I already knew some disaster had fallen upon us, as one may know, before the doctor speaks, that he is about to deliver a death sentence.

Phillips himself did not at first sight look like one who has come to tell of tragedy. He was a small, clerkly man, tired after his journey but resolute. Awed by the grandeur of Thornfield, he gazed about the drawing-room, covertly, and said, 'This is most certainly a magnificent house, Mrs. Rochester.'

'It is,' I said, 'but it was not to examine our house that you came here on Christmas Day, surely? You had better tell me who you are, and what is your business.'

'I am a clerk in the offices of Grover and Sims, ships' owners,' he told me, 'but as to my business, I think, with respect, madam, I must communicate that first to Mr. Rochester.'

Already I began to fear some accident to my husband's ship and cargo, that venture he had been so confident would enrich us. But I felt I could not press this man for information. It was his duty first to speak to my husband.

I told him, 'Mr Rochester is at a neighbour's house. I'm afraid you will have to wait until he returns. Will you please go to his study? I will have refreshment brought to you and he will be told you are there as soon as he returns.'

The news Phillips brought Edward that night, though I was not to know it then, or for many a long day after, was that his ship, the *Janus*, and the cargo in which he had invested all the profits from selling the Manchester business to his partner, and much more besides, had sailed for the West Indies. She had fair weather throughout her voyage until by reason of a sudden storm the captain had been forced to put in at Kingston, Jamaica, against my husband's express commands. The reason he had given the ship's captain was fear of anticipated riots and disorder. The real reason was that Jamaica was the home of the Masons, his late wife's family, and that, though in reduced circumstances, they still had a name and influence there. He therefore thought it wise for the ship to stay clear of the island, in case it came to their ears that the *Janus* and her cargo were the property of Mr. Rochester of Thornfield. But, alas, wind and tide were against her, and she was forced to put in at Kingston. The harbour authorities learned of the ship, her cargo and to whom they belonged, and that information was not long in reaching the Masons. This numerous and impoverished tribe, incensed by the notion of my husband's presumed wealth, roused up all their other connections on the island and descended by night on the harbour. None could prevent them from looting the cargo and firing the ship. On that one night in the Caribbean the ship, the cargo and all my husband's hopes were destroyed.

When this intelligence reached the ships' owners in London, they saw the disaster as grave enough to be imparted immediately to my husband and so Mr. Phillips was despatched. But it was plain from her triumphant manner outside the church that Madame Roland had received the news from the Masons even earlier.

Having settled Mr. Phillips in the study I went upstairs, but I did not sleep for, if the news were grave, as I supposed, I imagined Edward might wish to speak about it to me later.

Late, at one o'clock, I heard the carriages returning from Raybeck Hall. Then came the noisy descent, the entry into the house and the animated talk of those who had come back from the party. The Nortons had stayed behind in their house that night, but would both return early next morning for the hunt, which was due to meet at Thornfield, as Edward had ordained.

I heard Adèle's high voice, my husband's deep one, Lord Jago's laugh, all the sounds of a happy group coming home after an entertainment. There came the banging of doors, more voices, then a diminution in the sound, then feet coming upstairs, then silence. Downstairs, I knew, Mr. Phillips and my husband must be in conversation.

I waited for fifteen minutes, allowing time for the imparting of the chief news, then went downstairs. The drawing-room was empty; the fire burned low; a fan, Adèle's, lay on a chair. I went then to Edward's study and entered it. The two men, Edward and Phillips, sat in chairs on either side of the fire, some papers scattered on the floor between them. The light was dim; only one lamp burned, that on Edward's desk.

Edward was lying back in his chair, his hand over his eyes, while Phillips, seated on the other side of the hearth, leaned towards him as if concerned. At the sound of the door opening, Edward started violently, his hand dropping from his face. He sat bolt upright, then rose to his feet. 'Jane! Why are you not upstairs?'

'I could not sleep,' I said. 'And, the servants being abed, I must tell Mr. Phillips where his room is. You are pale, Edward? Are you well?'

'As well as any man who has received a blow may be,' he responded. His manner was controlled – too much so, I thought – and his voice was clear and even. But it was plain he had mastered himself with difficulty. He continued, 'Before you enquire, Jane, may I request you to ask me no questions. This is a matter for Mr. Phillips and myself.'

'I ask nothing,' I told him, 'though, as your wife, aught that concerns you must concern me.'

'More's the pity,' he said in a low, bitter tone, as if to himself. 'More's the pity.' There was a silence then, broken by his saying, in a calmer voice, 'You had better give your message to Mr. Phillips and retire, Jane. The meet will take place tomorrow, and the ball. You must take your rest.'

I stepped forward. 'Edward—' I appealed.

'Jane!' he said in that tone of command he had so seldom used to me. 'Phillips and I have more to discuss.'

I said, quietly, 'Very well, Edward,' told Mr. Phillips where he was to sleep and left the room.

I went upstairs, wishing with all my heart that Edward had wished to confide in me; required my support in whatever trial he was facing. Still anxious, indeed, about the exact nature of the disaster, I could only hope that the morning would bring him to me. But this was not to be.

Chapter XXVII

Boxing Day dawned frosty and clear. The hills stood out sharp against a blue sky. It was a bright day for the hunt, the hard, frozen ground promising fast though dangerous going for those ready to take a risk.

The meet began to assemble on the drive outside. Servants moved among the horses handing up stirrup cups to the riders, horses blew out frosty air and all the while men and women came and went through the house, where a great breakfast was laid out in the dining-room. All was cheerful confusion.

I, however, was uneasy in my mind. There are small signs given out by those one knows intimately. To one who knew him less well, Edward, strong and active in his riding-dress, must have seemed amicable, hospitable and expansive, entirely at ease. Yet I, who know him so well, noted in him, below the surface, a turbulence and a hard desperation. I did not think he was in a mood to ride safely; he might be reckless, endanger himself.

I was unable to speak to him on that or any other subject. It was evident he had nothing to say to me; indeed, he evaded me, though in the politest way, so that I alone, I think, noticed this. It was clear that he wished no questions abut the message brought by Mr. Phillips.

That gentleman, dressed for travelling, found me in the morning-room as I was giving some instructions to one of the maids. 'I wished to thank you for your hospitality before departing, Mrs. Rochester,' he said to me.

There was gentleness in his face and this emboldened me. If Edward would tell me nothing of his troubles, then I would make one last attempt to get information from Mr. Phillips.

'Would you come with me into the study, Mr. Phillips? I would like to talk to you,' I said. He gazed at me for a moment and then agreed. In the study I confronted him. 'Mr. Phillips, there is some news adversely affecting my husband's fortunes which he has not told me. I wish so much to help him – yet I cannot unless I know what you have told him. Will you pity me, and say what has occurred?'

He looked at me with sympathy and then said regretfully, 'How can I, Mrs. Rochester, if he has not? Believe me, if I felt I could I would be pleased to do so. But you must see this is your husband's business, and he must decide when to confide in you. I am sorry.'

'I too am sorry,' said I, 'if I have demanded of you something you find you cannot do. You will understand, it is only concern for my husband which impels me to ask.'

'I do understand, Mrs. Rochester,' he told me sincerely.

'Well then, you are eager to get away. The carriage will be at the end of the drive for you and I have had put in it some provisions for your journey.' I held out my hand to him and he took it. 'Goodbye, Mr. Phillips.'

We shook hands and he turned to go. Then he turned

back and earnestly said, 'Mrs. Rochester – it would be wrong for me to inform you of any details but I will tell you what I believe you already suspect and what I am afraid inevitably you will soon know. I fear your husband is ruined. I am sorry.'

Gravely I thanked him and took him to the front door. As we arrived, Edward was in the hall with Jonathan and I heard him say, 'Whatever they said to you yesterday about your following the hunt, today I say you may not do so. Go upstairs now and take off your riding-clothes.' Jonathan bit his lip, turned and went upstairs.

Mr. Phillips, meanwhile, left the house and began to make his way through the crowd of riders and hounds milling beside the front door and over the lawn.

Now my husband was behind me. 'Jane, I would prefer you to attend to our guests rather than withdraw to the study, to have a private interview with a ship-owner's clerk.' I believe Mr. Phillips heard these words, for, though he did not turn round as he trudged onwards, I saw his shoulders stiffen.

'I am sorry, Edward,' I said softly, but as I spoke he strode past me to where a groom stood holding his horse, grasped the reins, flung them over his horse's back and mounted up. The others, who had been inside the house, crowded past.

'Wish us a good day, Jane,' Blanche Norton, stately in her riding-dress, called as she went past and I did, but my heart was heavy.

Edward had chosen not to confide in me a disaster which I now knew absolutely to have taken place. He had seen me leave the morning-room with Mr. Phillips and, angered, had publicly rebuked me. Though this behaviour stung me, as it would any woman, I guessed it to be connected with the bad news imparted to him by Mr. Phillips and I dreaded his beginning the hunt in such a passionate mood; such violence of feeling might impel him to ride too wildly.

The horn blew and the riders, some twenty of them, streamed across the lawn and down towards the road. Sir Stanley Norton's gamekeeper had singled out a place, near the boundary between his land and the Rochesters', where he thought they would get a scent and it was there the hunt was heading. I saw Edward in front, amid the baying pack, and moments later the hunt had gone from sight, the sounds of horn, hooves and hounds receding into the clear, cold air.

Heavy-hearted, I turned to go, Jonathan beside me. He had changed out of his riding-clothes. 'Why did Papa forbid me to follow the hunt?' he asked. 'He told me yesterday that I might.'

'The ground is frozen hard. It will be dangerous riding today,' said I, 'and he will be ahead and so not able to watch you.'

He sighed. 'I think Papa was angry,' he told me.

'Gentlemen sometimes have anxieties they cannot share or explain,' said I.

A long day ensued, shared with Adèle, Lady Jago, who like myself was no rider, and the doctor and his wife, whose son had gone out with the hunt. After our meal, the doctor took me to one side saying, 'Mrs. Rochester – I am quite concerned for you. You appear fatigued. Will you promise that from now on, until your child is born, you will exert yourself less?' And so I promised him, but still he was not satisfied. 'Will you promise me also that you will keep your mind at ease, that you will not allow yourself to become unduly anxious, nor allow the woes

Mrs Rochester

of others to overwhelm you, for I know that is something
you are prone to do? Will you promise me that?'

To that I replied, 'I wish that were a promise I could
make, but sadly I cannot, for I am not sure I would be
able to keep it.'

Then he told me soberly, 'Very well, but do your best,
Mrs. Rochester, for a new life hangs on it.'

The afternoon was longer, even, than the morning and
full of comings and goings, for the final preparations for
the ball were being made and Adèle ran to and fro, full
of commands and requests, while I attempted to keep my
patience with her. 'You will be exhausted before the ball,
child,' said Lady Jago at one point, suppressing her own
irritation.

The others played cards, I read, and soon it was growing
dark. Seated at the piano by the drawing-room window
I thought I heard, as I concluded a piece and the last
tones died away, the sound of a horn. It seemed to
come from high in the hills above Thornfield, where
the ground was rocky and dangerous and very icy –
higher still, the snow lay thick and deep. At dusk, unable
to suppress my anxiety I put down the piano lid and said,
attempting to sound quite calm, 'I will go out to see if I
can view the hunt.'

The doctor caught my eye and I assured him, 'I shall
be very well alone, for I am only going for ten minutes,
to clear my head.'

And so I put on my cloak and went forth into the failing
light, walking behind the house and past the elms to where
I could look up into the hills. I heard the horn along the
hillside, again, from that direction and, gazing upwards,
just made out the long line of horses strung out along the
hillside, Edward's big grey in front. Such light made riding

dangerous and I was sure the Master would soon call off the hunt.

As they moved, I followed them, paralleling their progress, and this took me to the verge of the thorn field where, eager to descry again the pale shape I thought must be my husband's horse, I entered that strange place through an open gate and found myself on the rough ground, amid those bare, distorted trees. Bright stars were emerging in the darkening skies. I followed the hunt, which still moved along the side of the hill, hearing faintly but clearly over the distance the blowing of the horn and the yelping of the hounds. Yet I thought I must turn back soon from this dreadful place. It grew ever darker and I had overstayed my time.

I was passing through a small grove of trees, which were formed in a crude circle of five, when a shape, a tall shape, rushed at me through the trees and, instead of stopping on seeing me in its path, came on. Too late, I realised that this person, now almost on me, had no intention of pausing. I saw too a raised arm, a fist clenched about something. In that terrifying instant I caught the glint of steel and realised that, unthinkable as it was, here in this fearful field, bare of aught but twisted trees, I was being attacked.

I saw only the white blur of a face, a covered head, a dark cloak, before my assailant was on me, gripping my shoulder firmly with one strong hand. The other arm, grasping the knife, was high above my head. Even as I felt the weapon plunging down towards me I pulled to one side, still unable to free myself from my attacker's grasp but avoiding the knife. As it met empty air I felt my enemy to be off balance and, wrenching myself free, fled, stumbling down the darkened field in the direction of the road. Slow and heavy, terrified all the while of falling, I pushed forward, hearing behind the sound of my pursuer coming after me over the uneven ground.

On I went, terrified, gasping my own breath so loud in my ears it drowned out all other sound.

As I reached the wall by the road and fell against it, spent and breathing hard. I became aware that the sounds of feet behind me, the clatter of dislodged stones, had disappeared; what I could hear nearby, now, was the sound of the hunting-horn, the baying of dogs, horses' hooves coming down the field towards me.

I leaned against the wall, still sobbing for breath. When the hunt passed me, bound for the gate and the road beyond, I was too weak even to cry out. Yet as they went by I understood it must have been only the sound of their coming which had deterred my attacker, he must be still lurking there in the darkness and as soon as the riders were far enough away – would strike again.

I forced myself to move towards the gate, hugging the wall for concealment, then go through and out on to the road. The hunt, though moving slowly, was far ahead of me now; in the darkness I could barely see the hindmost riders,

Fearful every moment of a renewed attack, I limped slowly down the dark road towards Thornfield. I was shaking with cold and fear by the time I gained the drive. I stumbled across the lawn.

From the open front doors of the house, light flooded; outside were the horses; riders were going into the house; two men were mustering the excited hounds for their return to the kennels. All was light, noise, movement and activity.

Shocked and exhausted, seeking, like some wounded

animal, only rest and darkness, I went in by the side door next to Edward's study and made my way unobserved by the back stair to my chamber. There I cast myself on my bed. Only one lamp burned, in a corner; the fire was low. From the rest of the house I could hear voices, laughter, footsteps on the stairs and along the gallery outside my room. There was the sound of the orchestra tuning their instruments. Below, supper would be being laid out, candles lit. Upstairs, maids would be going to and fro with hot water. Soon, more guests for the ball would arrive.

Yet I was still in the dark thorn field in fear of my life. I lay there long, hardly able to believe what had just occurred. I had been attacked, on my husband's own land, by someone whose intention was almost certainly to kill me. I had no clue as to whom it might have been, whether a vagrant, a tenant resentful of some supposed injustice or – heaven forbid! – someone close to me. In reason and common sense, I could not think of anyone who wished me harm, whether at home or abroad. And yet a month before someone had cut my horse's girths and left her saddled in the yard for me to ride, I could not believe I had an enemy. Yet I had.

There came a tap on the door.

'Come in,' said I.

'Mrs. Rochester?' Grace Poole stood in the doorway. She observed my dishevelled state, my pallor, and asked, 'Mrs. Rochester – are you well? Is something the matter?'

I could not trust her – where trouble was for me, there was Grace Poole; it had always been so.

'Shall I make up the fire?' she asked me.

'If you please,' I told her. She bent to the grate, then

went about the room with a taper, lighting the lamps, and pools of light appeared; and as she did so she ever glanced at me. I lay there, still not looking at her. Then she came up to me, looked down and said grimly, 'I have warned you once, Mrs. Rochester. You are not safe in this house. And now I warn you again – you should go, go anywhere, but go, and go quickly.' And then she left the room.

I lay for some time, scarcely thinking, and those thoughts I had were not rational, yet from somewhere, it was as if a voice spoke in my head, I knew that, yes, if only for a time, if only until my child came, I would – I must – leave this house. I would explain all to Edward, crave his forgiveness if need be – but I *would* leave. Curiously, what hardened my resolve was not so much the thought that here in this place there was one who had, twice now, I believed, tried to kill me, but that now over Thornfield Hall, magnificent as it was, hovered a cloud of mystery and confusion. I could no longer bear that in spite of its new brick, fresh paint and paper, odours of lavender and rosemary and good scents of all description, and in spite of all the care I had put into its re-creation, this house, Thornfield, was as rank, as tainted as corrupt as any place in the land, however vile. I determined that as soon as morning came I would leave go to my cousin Diana's, and there I would remain in peace until my child was born.

This resolve, shocking as it was, was all the more startling because it came to me so suddenly, almost like an order given to me by another. Only now did I understand how, day by day, event by event, culminating in that attack in the thorn field, had my strength and endurance been worn away until now, as in one blinding flash, I saw all the mysteries and dangers of Thornfield and found I could bear no more. Who or what I was fighting, I did not know; involuntarily it seemed, I had made my decision that the battle was too much for me. A voice was crying ever more urgently, 'Leave this place!'

A maid, no doubt told by Mrs. Poole where I could be found, came in with hot water. 'Will you dress now, madam?' she asked.

Well, I will, I thought. For as long as I am here I will not be found wanting in hospitality, or courtesy towards my guests. And later, when the ball is ended, I will tell Edward about the attack, explain I can stay at Thornfield no longer and he, I suppose, will understand. Therefore, 'Return in ten minutes, please,' I requested. I washed, and laid out my dress and my jewels, but rather than begin to put on my grey lace ball-gown began to take from my cupboards those few simple articles I would need to take to Gateshead with me. One valise would suffice.

I determined that only when I had packed would I put on my dress, and put in my ears and round my throat those earrings and the matching parure of bright rubies said once to have been worn by the last Queen of France. I would wear these, not for myself – for those brilliant and costly crimson jewels always imparted to me a sense of unease, as if they had been created from great drops of blood. No – I would wear the rubies for Edward, who some days before had suggested my dress would be well set off by their colour and splendour.

When the maid came to help me dress, I had in my valise all I would require when I left Thornfield. Her eyebrows went up, but she said nothing, and silently picked up my dress and helped me into it.

How cold I felt, now that my resolution to go was made. I was seated before my dressing-table, the maid having assisted me in dressing my hair, and she was about to place the circle of bright jewels around my neck, when the door opened and Edward came in, dressed for the ball, handsome and commanding. I began to tell him of the attack on me, but almost immediately his eye hit on my packed valise, which was standing by the bed, and his expression darkened.

'Leave us,' he said to the maid. She, with one swift glance at his lowering countenance, dropped the necklace of rubies into my hand and left the room. Edward came to stand behind me so that as he spoke I saw, not him, but his reflection above me in the long mirror. 'Jane – is this what I think – are you leaving here?'

'I must,' I said. 'Dreadful things are happening and I afraid. Oh, Edward, it is not for lack of love for you, but this place has become a nightmare to me. I fear for myself and for my coming child's life. I must go, Edward, I must.'

'I am astonished,' he said vigorously. 'I am astonished you can consider leaving me, and without telling me, asking me.'

'I did not suppose you were going to forbid me a visit to my cousin's, like a Turk,' said I, but I think my voice was shaking. 'Nor have you asked why I wish to go. I have good reason, I assure you. Do you think I would lightly separate myself from you? You, who are as much to me as life itself?'

'Then why go?' he asked coldly.

'It is that I am afraid for myself and the coming child. Edward – there have been two attempts to kill me. I know you were unsure of what was intended when Ruby's girths were cut and she threw me. But just now – just now – while I was in the thorn field looking out for the hunt, someone attacked me with a knife, I believe, and tried to kill me – and would have, had I not broken free at the moment when the hunt came past, allowing my attacker to escape.'

He uttered an oath. 'I cannot believe it. But who did this thing?'

'The attack was sudden and in near-darkness. I could not tell.'

He gazed at me and slowly, to my horror, I saw him become doubtful. 'Are you sure, Jane? Could you not have been mistaken? Could you not have become caught in the thorns, in the darkness, and become afraid?'

'Edward,' I burst out, 'you must believe me! Twice, someone has tried to kill me. Can you not see how this life at Thornfield is affecting me? I truly believe that if I stay I and the child I am carrying will not survive.'

He gazed at me. 'This is sore news to receive when I have just had such a blow.'

'But what is it?' I cried. 'You will not tell me. How can I help you and comfort you when I do not know what ails you? What is it, Edward?'

But he said, 'I do not require you to bear my burdens. That would be unmanly. What I should like is for you to be with me as I bear them. Is that an unreasonable thing for a husband to ask of his wife?'

I bent my head. 'Oh, Edward – I am so afraid.'

'You imply that I cannot protect you.'

'No – *no!*' I said.

'You will forgive me if that is how I interpret your words.'

'But you are not always here – you cannot always be here,' I cried wildly.

'I shall be with you from now on,' he told me gravely,

'for my disappearances are over. Now, Jane – my dearest. Our guests are arriving and we must greet them. Listen to me. Perhaps your imagination has been playing tricks, for ladies in your condition are said to be subject to fancies. But, be that as it may, you need fear nothing – henceforth I shall always be near you, protecting you. You will be safe. But you must not, you shall not, leave me. Beauty – you must stay by your monster's side, for what kind of sad beast would he be without you?

'And now,' he said in a practical tone, 'the guests await and the mistress in her rubies must attend.' He leaned forward, took the rubies from my hand, put them round my throat and fastened the clasp; then, smiling, he took my hand and raised me from my seat. 'I would not live if you were not with me. Stay, Jane. You will stay.' He kissed my brow, then led me to the head of the great staircase, and, as we descended, the guests in all their beauty, dignity and worth looked up at us, master and lady of Thornfield Hall.

I could not forget that fierce assault in the dark, the pang of horror as I saw that upraised knife and knew I was close to death. But Edward's firmness, and his reassurance that he would stay with me and protect me, had weakened my resolve to leave Thornfield. And, though he had been too proud to appeal to me, how could I leave him? My heart failed me. But had he not told me I had imagined not one but two attacks on my life? And I knew full well they were not fancy, but horrid reality. But was it not hard for a man with the pride of Edward Rochester to believe any would dare lay hands on that which was dearest to him?

I suppressed my fears and anxieties as he led me out into the ballroom, which gleamed with light. Some twenty couples joined us, circling the shining floor before the long mirrors which fringed the walls. The ladies' dresses billowed out like petals and the music was very sweet.

By supper time I was tired and good Sir George Lynn, remarking it, took my arm and led me into the supper-room, where he sat me down at a table and fetched me some refreshment.

He said, 'Eat and drink, Mrs. Rochester, I beg you. What a splendid occasion you have made for us and how gratifying it is to see Thornfield opened up again, to know that one of the great houses of the county is once again functioning as it should, as a bedrock, a stay and support to the little world it dominates.'

I was barely able to understand his words. I felt as if the wine I supped was some strong opiate. I saw the tables, the feast laid out on long tables, the spotless linen, shining cutlery. I heard the music and the talk of the guests – and remembered again that terrifying assault in the thorn field. Mr. Phillips's voice said again, 'I fear your husband is ruined.' Where did reality lie? In this entertainment under the mighty roof of Thornfield, where men and women of distinction danced and ate and talked and greeted each other, or elsewhere, in a world of violence, assaults, rumour of unnatural death and sudden, unpredictable events?

Sir George spoke on and I attempted to listen and reply, but I had one impulse now, to speak fully to Edward for he and only he could solve the mysteries, he and only he could provide explanations, give me back a sense of what was real and what was not, settle my mind, which seemed wandering, independent of my control, like some lost creature roaming through mist seeking home, light and security.

'Sir George,' I said, 'will you escort me back to the ballroom? I wish to find Edward.' And he conducted me back.

There was a dance in progress and I sat in an alcove with Sir George, watching Adèle dancing with my husband. She, exquisite creature, smiled up at him radiantly. As she did so, Lady Norton came past, arm in arm with Lady Jago, the two of them watching the dancers so that they did not observe Sir George and me.

In her clear voice Blanche Norton said, 'How splendid Rochester and Adèle look together. What a wonderful creature she is. Your son must beware, my dear, for Jane is not looking well. Childbirth is hazardous and if she were, sadly to succumb – well, how can I best put it? – there would be no obstacle to a marriage between Rochester and Adèle. She is his ward, not his daughter, after all, and she loves him well enough, that is plain.'

Lady Jago's response was cold. 'More than enough, I should say. Too much.'

These were dreadful words, yet in some strange manner my dreamlike state protected me from feeling the pain they would otherwise have caused. I even understood Blanche's motives in so speaking. At no time did she feel the necessity to believe what she was saying; she did it merely to rouse her own dull spirit and the interest of others.

I was conscious of Sir George, who had not, I think, caught what was said, asking me anxiously, 'Mrs. Rochester – are you well?'

I replied, calmly, I believe, 'I am a little tired. Perhaps I will go and sit quietly in my husband's study.' For all I desired at that moment was some solitude for a little while.

And as Edward and Adèle still danced, Sir George led me from the room. Mrs. Poole caught up with us. 'Mrs. Poole will look after me now, Sir George,' I said. 'I order you away to do your duty and ask a lady to dance.'

Mrs. Poole helped me to the library and brought me water, and I sat numb yet clear-headed for half an hour and knew again the compulsion to leave Thornfield, that mighty house which had turned itself, for me, into a place of danger and torment. And yet, could I leave, in the face of Edward's opposition – and his sore need of me?

Then above the sound of the music came cries – and abruptly, the music ceased. Then a woman screamed, and another. I smelled smoke.

Chapter XXVIII

It was as if I had expected it. I rose and left the study and the moment I opened the door heard hubbub. The hall was full of smoke and people; the front door gaped open; figures staggered blindly out on to the lawn. The drawing-room was a red glow, the staircase alight, flames shooting up from the treads and places on the banisters. The entire gallery upstairs was ablaze.

I fought my way through the smoke into the freezing air outside, quickly finding Jonathan on the grass. Mrs. Poole was beside him, holding his hand but not regarding him. Instead, her gaze was fixed on the upper windows, from which flames now leaped. As I bent down to reassure Jonathan, I heard her say, 'So it has come.'

As the ladies in their ball dresses huddled on the lawn, and the men formed a bucket-chain from the stables to the door, Sir George counted us all, checking that everyone was present and safe. Then suddenly I heard Hal Jago's cry of alarm: 'Adèle! Where is Adèle?'

I gave Jonathan into the care of a maid and ran to Edward. Bucket after bucket of water was being emptied on to the blaze in the hall but the flames still burned.

'She must be inside still,' he said desperately. 'Oh – dear God, dear God.'

He declared, 'I will go in.'

'No, Edward. It is an inferno,' I cried.

'I have no choice,' he told me.

Even as he spoke I saw, through the open doorway, halfway up the stairs, in all the flame and smoke, Adèle, engulfed in flames, her mouth open in a scream.

Edward ran into the house. He hurled himself across the hall and up the burning stairs, flung Adèle over his shoulder and came down.

I, too, had run into the flames. At the foot of the stairs he put down his burden – together we dragged her from the house. Lord Jago tore off his coat and flung it over her body to smother the flames.

As we bent over her, I took from the convulsive grasp of her blackened hand – a key, an old, dark key.

Chapter XXIX

And so I come to the end of my story, which I write, as I have said, in the window of my room overlooking the lawn and garden at Thornfield. My little daughter lies beside me in her cradle, asleep, pale lashes showing on her creamy, perfect skin, her head crowned with gold. Who would have believed that dark Rochester and I could have between us such golden children? Yet we have, and rejoice in this new daughter, whose birth followed tragedy, as if to redeem us after much pain.

We came to Thornfield without her and soon, very soon now, we shall be taking her away, for the house must be let as we are much poorer. We will go back to Ferndean.

And so I must complete my story before we go, conclude the sad tale which began at Thornfield and, there, ended.

Poor Adèle is dead. She lived only a week after the fire, in much pain, and then died. It was better so.

Following the fire I was taken straight to Mr. Todd's by night and there forced to rest for several weeks, recovering my strength, which had been so much taxed at the time of the fire and, indeed, for many months before it – during that period which I now look back on as a trial, a trial of courage and love.

During the early days at Mr. Todd's Edward was ever with me, save for the visits he made to Adèle, who lay opposite, at Old House, devotedly nursed by Grace Poole.

Was it not strange that Madame Roland gave Adèle shelter so close to where I lay, recovering? Some might find it so. Edward, indeed, spoke to me tenderly after I had been a day at Mr. Todd's and, holding my hand asked gently, 'Jane – does it disturb you, my darling, that Adèle lies so close at Madame Roland's? Certainly, she bears me no love – nor do I for her – but she was insistent after the fire that Adèle should go to her because of the great affection she has for Céline.' – And I confess, I shuddered at that name on Edward's lips. 'It is a blessing in some ways,' he continued, 'that she insisted Adèle be carried there, for where else could she have gone to spend her last days?' For by that time we knew Adèle had not much longer to live.

'But tell me, my love, do you find the situation painful?'

And I told him, 'Edward – whatever the child needs, she must have.'

He smiled at me then, a slow, sad smile. 'Could I doubt you would show charity? And,' he went on, his eyes still fastened on mine, 'there are reasons why old enmities no longer have the same force – matters about which I must not speak while you are still so tired.'

'I know there are mysteries,' I told him softly, and said no more; for I knew that I must wait for explanations not only until I was stronger but until Edward was prepared to confide in me. And this was not the time, as Adèle took her last journey, that from this world into the next.

I believe no one knows what I saw on the night of her death.

I was in my chamber, which overlooked the road, when I was aroused by the sound of carriage wheels outside. I rose, pulled a robe about me and went to the window, where I knelt on a seat below it and gazed out into the darkness. The moon was shining, and by its light I observed the carriage draw up, horses breathing hard, their breath white on the cold air.

From the carriage there descended the figure of a tall woman, swathed in a hooded cloak of some dark fur. At the same moment the front door of Old House was flung open and light flooded out. Madame Roland ran from it, arms outstretched towards the other woman.

As the woman stood motionless, half turned towards the approaching figure of Madame Roland, her hood fell back and I saw for the first and, I imagine, the last time the beautiful profile of Céline Varens, clear as a cameo in the moonlight, and above that lovely face the cloud of fair hair.

Madame Roland gathered Céline to her and led her into the house. Though she was the shorter figure, I saw by her posture she was supporting the taller woman. They went in and the door closed behind them.

I believe thoughts of Céline had caused me some of the most anguished moments of my life. Indeed, at that time I was still uncertain of the exact relationship between her and my husband. But I am a mother; I was attending the birth of another child. How could I not pity that woman who, for all her beauty and fame, was now watching over the deathbed of her only child like the poorest of women in the humblest cottage in the land? I lay awake until dawn came and I heard the carriage depart – and then I slept.

In the morning Edward told me Adèle was dead and I said nothing of the visitor that night. It may be that none but those at Old House knew of it. My duty then was to comfort Edward as best I could. His sadness was great but, 'It is better so – much better,' he said. I thought then that it was only of Adèle's hideous injuries he spoke.

That day St. John, to my surprise, arrived and sat all morning with Edward in Mr. Todd's study. In the afternoon he took tea in my room. He told me Edward had asked him to speak to me, for he was at Old House discussing the arrangements for Adèle's interment. St. John told me that Edward thought I should be apprised of some information of great future importance.

'We have discussed certain affairs which will secure both you and Jonathan,' he told me. 'And of that I will say no more, unless you would like to ask any questions about our deliberations.' I shook my head and assured him I had all confidence in any decisions made by him and Edward.

'Then,' he said, 'I will turn to the matter of the *Janus*, as Edward has asked me to. This business – a bad business I may say – began with the arrival of Madame Roland and her fierce demands for return of the dowry of Bertha Mason, a claim which Edward still disputes but which,' St. John said with a smile, 'he, in his lordly way, decided to pay. He told me his idea was not to haggle with the woman like a tradesman but to obtain the money the lady thought she was owed, give it to her and tell her to be gone.'

St. John was still smiling as he said, 'That, I have come to realise, is the Rochester manner, grand but impatient.

Consequently, he sold his interest in the Manchester mill to his partner and chartered a vessel, the *Janus*, loading it with all manner of goods to trade in the West Indies. On her return the *Janus* would carry cotton (which Edward's partner, Mr. Jessop, had agreed to buy), also tobacco and rum. As a man of the cloth,' St. John said wryly, 'there is that in this scheme I might deplore, but although I am no man of business I see that it had every prospect of success. Then the Rochesters would have been on their way to riches and Madame Roland paid off and gone.

'He did all for the best, Jane,' my cousin earnestly assured me. 'He has confessed that during the time he was selling his share in the mill, preparing the *Janus* – and during her voyage – his anxieties often overcame him. He was hasty, impatient – well, Jane,' St. John said humorously, 'I can bear witness to that – but you see, the doctor had forbidden him to trouble you in any way, otherwise there might be danger to you or the coming child. Your husband obeyed the doctor.'

'Would that he had not,' I said. 'For I was more troubled by that ignorance than I should have been by any amount of business cares laid on me.'

St. John nodded. 'Indeed – but the doctor cannot have guessed what he was asking your husband to keep from you. He may have supposed it would have been a matter of some plates from a dinner service broken, or your boy scratched and bruised by falling from a tree. As it was, the doctor ordered and Mr. Rochester obeyed – he is not, I would guess, a man given to running back and forth to the doctor and confiding all his family business.'

'That is so,' said I ruefully. Yet I was glad to note St. John's affectionate understanding of my husband.

'Like all of us, he has the defects of his qualities.'

'But what of the *Janus*?' I was asking of my cousin, when Edward came in, clad in black and very grave.

St. John stood up. 'Will you take up the tale?' he said.

'I will. And thank you, Rivers, for beginning it for me. But before you go, may I request something of you – a kindness?'

'Aught in my power,' St. John replied.

'We shall be burying Adèle in the churchyard next to this house tomorrow. I should take it as a great favour if you would consent to conduct the service. Mr. Todd will, I am sure, have no objection.'

St. John, bowing slightly, replied, 'I should be honoured. You may count on me tomorrow.'

'I thank you,' said my husband and St. John left the room. I saw by this that the difficulties between my husband and St. John had indeed been resolved, for this request was as close as Edward could come to an apology for his hasty treatment of my cousin – and would be seen as such by St. John.

'You will consent to my rising for luncheon,' I said to Edward. 'And then, when you have taken a little refreshment, will you continue the tale of the *Janus*?'

He agreed, adding with bitter humour, 'For it is a story best not told on an empty stomach.'

That afternoon, in Mr. Todd's drawing-room, before a brightly burning fire, he said, 'St. John has, I expect, told you of my dissolving the partnership with Jessop to invest in the West Indies trade, and he may also have mentioned that to make good the shortfall I took money from the estate's funds. Anyway – there it was – business gone, estate plundered and all hanging on the success of the *Janus*. Now, before she sailed I gave strict instructions to the master on no account to put in at Kingston in Jamaica, giving to him to understand that I had private information from friends in high places that riot and disturbance were expected there and I feared the loss of ship and cargo. This was not the real reason – as my intelligent little wife will have guessed,' and he looked at me quizzically.

'He could not put in at Kingston for fear of the Masons?' I hazarded.

'Just so,' he said. 'I suspected that if the *Janus* put in at Kingston and word got back to the Masons they would make trouble. And,' he said, in a tone of calm resignation, 'they did, Jane, they did.'

Then he told me the tale of the ship being forced to put in at Kingston and how the news rapidly circulated that this was Edward Rochester's ship and cargo. He described the arrival of a mob led by the Masons which, carrying torches, swords and cutlasses, rapidly overpowered all who stood in their way, fired the ship and destroyed her completely.

'What I chiefly wanted from this scheme,' my husband told me, 'was a sufficient sum to pay Madame Roland so that she would cease to distress you, my Jane, and cease to blemish the name of Rochester, which would in turn affect our son. And is it not an irony that, by causing me to charter the *Janus*, which was then destroyed by her family, Madame Roland has managed to ruin not just the Masons – but me?'

'Well, we are not quite ruined yet,' said I.

'Not quite,' he agreed, 'but Thornfield will have to be let if it can be restored without too much cost. Shall you mind that, Jane?'

I shook my head. 'I mind nothing, so long as we are together.'

Edward's head dropped to his breast. 'Oh, Jane – oh, Jane – what should I do without you, so brave, so loyal?'

In the course of one short week Edward had found himself ruined, seen his house in flames – and on the following day he would bury Adèle . Such events, coming so quickly, one upon the other, can crush the strongest spirit. I feared my husband would break under the strain – and suspected, too, he carried a further burden, which he would not let me know. With the intention of confronting what might have been one of his nightmares, I said, 'Edward – I think we must go to Thornfield to estimate the damage. Shall we visit the house together, soon?'

There was defeat in his tone as he said, 'Let me first bury my daughter.'

'Of course, Edward,' I said. I stood, bent to kiss him and quietly left the room, knowing he needed solitude.

As did I. I found myself outside the house, then walking towards the church. I entered and sat alone in a pew near the back and did not pray but allowed the peace to flow over me. I had been shocked when Edward named Adèle 'daughter' for though she was dead it roused in me all my old doubts and fears concerning Edward's meetings with Adèle and Céline – and with Céline alone in London. Perhaps it was wrong to sit in that holy place thinking anxious, jealous thoughts but I could not help myself. Adèle was dead; Adèle *had* been Edward's daughter by the beautiful Frenchwoman; Céline was in England still – that I knew. What if their shared grief for their unfortunate child brought them closer together?

I told myself I was wrong to think such thoughts in that place at that time, before poor Adèle had even been laid to rest. But a jealous heart cares not for time and place. I knew Edward loved me but a man may love two women at once – I feared Céline.

And then – like a miracle – I calmed. Peace came to me and some kind of knowledge the source of which I did not recognise. It was as if a voice said to me, 'The secret lies with Adèle. Ask Edward about Adèle.' And I resolved to do this, even though I did not understand.

Next day we laid Adèle to rest, near the grave of Bertha Mason, and on the following day Edward said, 'Well, Jane – will you come with me to Thornfield?' We walked there through the fields. The day was bright and sunny and warm for the time of year. We stood on the lawn gazing up at the house, which was streaked with black. The windows were holed and cracked.

Inside all smelled of smoke. I stayed below in the hall, surveying the dirtied walls and pillars; beneath my feet the marble floor was still puddled with water. Edward, meanwhile, went as far up the staircase as was safe and peered upwards at the gallery, then, sighing, descended. Arm in arm we entered the drawing-room – the walls were blackened, and one of the long windows had been broken to admit the men carrying water. The curtains hung at the windows like dirty rags; my cherished pale carpet with the pattern of roses was sooty and footmarked.

'Do not grieve for your pretty room, Jane,' he said.

'I do not,' I said. 'What damage there is can be repaired.'

'From what I have seen there will be a good deal to be done upstairs. But, nevertheless, it can be managed,' he told me. His tone was spiritless and I looked at him and saw desolation in his face – but the cause, I knew, was not the wretched condition of his house.

'The fire began upstairs, it seems,' I said quietly. 'Shall we go outside?'

We walked down the lawn a little and then, without discussing it, turned into the walled garden. There I said to him, 'Edward – I beg you – there is a mystery here. You are like a man carrying a heavy burden – share it with me. I am your wife; I am not made of sugar or of glass. Do not hurt me by considering me unfit to confide in.'

'I would rather not—' he began, but I interrupted him: 'I would rather not live with a husband trying to bear an awful secret – for that is what I think it is – alone.'

'It is too sad,' he told me. 'What of your health and the child you carry?'

'What of my mind, Edward?' I asked. 'Can you imagine what anxiety I shall suffer knowing only that you are unhappy and uneasy, but not the reason?' I remembered that voice I seemed to have heard alone in the church only two days before - 'The secret lies with Adèle.' 'You think of Adèle, do you not?' I asked. 'Tell me, why was she upstairs when the fire began?' – for this question had puzzled me for some time.

He gazed at me, as if stricken, then smiled, unhappily. 'You were ever a mind-reader where I am concerned,' he told me. And a great chill came over me as I said, 'Edward – Adèle started the fire, did she not? That is why she went upstairs, why the worst damage was there, where she was.' And then, as if a fresh pattern of events came suddenly into my mind, I asked him, 'Edward – did she start the earlier fire also? Edward – please tell me – how did Bertha die?'

His voice was very low as he spoke. 'I see you have found me out. Very well, I will explain, God help me, though I fear the consequences for you and the child. Yet you have gone so far now that we reach the point where silence may do more harm than speech. It is a dreadful tale I have to tell, that of a secret I have kept for more than ten years.

'The beginning of these sorry events was when Adèle was but eight years old, shortly before you came to us, Jane. You must imagine our situation – she and I alone at Thornfield, but for a nursemaid – a local girl who proved to have been neglectful of her charge. And that was when this little girl, whose pretty tricks, as you know, had such power to disarm me, spoke to me one evening.

'We were by the fire and as she sat caressing the great body of Pilot, who lay beside her on the rug, she gazed up at me charmingly from under lowered lids, the very model of a little coquette, and asked me, "Papa – could it be that one day you will marry my Mama, and bring her here, as your wife, so that we may all live together?"

'I replied, "Alas no, Adèle, for as you know, you Mama is dead."

'To which she returned, all innocence, "But if she were not dead, Papa?" For she knew even then, Jane – how, I cannot tell – that Céline was alive. When I say "knew" perhaps that is wrong. She may have had a fantasy, as children do, that what she most dearly wished – that she had a living mother to love her – was true. And as it happened, it was indeed true, though I myself did not know it then.

'I told her, with as little attention as one gives to the innocent and ill-informed questions of children, "No, child. Even if your Mama were alive it would still not be possible for me to marry her."

'And that remark,' Edward said sombrely, 'of which I took so little account, began the whole obsession in Adèle which was to lead to the fire at Thornfield and Bertha's death. How could I know, how could I have guess that this child, at large in the house and improperly supervised by her nurse, had discovered the presence of my wife in the upper rooms? Who could have imagined that by eavesdropping on the servants, and listening to the mutterings of Grace Poole when she had taken drink, that she would discover that the prisoner was my wife?

'It was a short step for this careful, intelligent child, whose nature was nevertheless twisted and distorted beyond any imagination, to conceive that if Bertha were dead I would be at liberty to marry her mother and thus she would gain what she so violently desired.

'And so, by studying the habits of the household and discovering my wife's capacity to release herself from her place of confinement and roam the house, Adèle made her plans. One evening she watched Bertha release herself from her room and begin her roaming and crying out from room to room. But when Bertha re-mounted the stairs to re-enter her prison, lock the door and pretend to Grace Poole, when she awoke, that she had not escaped from the room, Adèle, who had followed her upstairs, snatched the key from Bertha as she re-entered the room – and locked her in. And then she, Adèle, crept downstairs, lit her fire and waited for it to burn the house down – and kill my wife.

'After the blaze had taken full hold I found her outside the house with the others gazing up at the house, which was in flames. And she said, "When Bertha is dead, Papa, you can marry Mama" – and Jane,' he said in a tone of horror, 'she held out to me the key to Bertha's door! Held it out, as if presenting me with a trophy. I snatched it from her and ran inside. She had not calculated in her warped, but still childish mind that I would go to the rescue of Bertha, whom she knew to be my bane. Standing outside with the others, she became hysterical and tried, they said, to run in after me, into the fire.' And Edward gave a great shudder.

After a pause, he continued, 'Very well – I will finish. After those long months of illness I sustained after the fire, she came to me. She was quite unrepentant. She felt no remorse for what she had done.' Edward's voice dropped low. 'In the ruins she had found a key, half melted by the heat. She chose to believe it was the key to the upper storey where Bertha had been kept. She showed it to me as if she treasured it, as if it were a symbol of success – our success! She confessed all, speaking of her deed quite calmly, as if it were nothing and asked me, "Will you now marry my Mama?" What could I have done? Could I reveal to anyone the truth about this child so young, my own flesh and blood, tell anyone of the monster I knew her to be? I decided to protect her and in so doing I have caused great distress and destruction to you, in particular, my darling whom I love more than anything else in the world; you have suffered more than anyone for my foolish protection of Adèle.'

I put my hand in his. 'You did what you thought best. Perhaps you thought she would change. It cannot have been an easy burden to bear alone.'

Edward sighed. 'I am happy it is over, that you know all at last. For it has been a sore burden to bear alone over the years. Only I knew this story; only I watched and patiently hoped Adèle would begin to improve. Only I mourned when she did not. Behind the peace and contentment at Ferndean there was always something else – that deadly knowledge I could not share, even with you.'

'Poor Adèle,' I said.

He kissed me there, in the wintry garden. 'You are an angel, I think.'

I did not reply, knowing that I was far from an angel but that all this pain and woe had changed me, perhaps, into something a little better than I was.

'It grows cold,' he said. 'Shall we walk back to Todd's?'

As we went he said, 'When she came back to Thornfield I continued to hope she would change but it took little time to detect that she would not – she had merely become a more polished version of the evil little creature she had been. I continued, though, to hope – foolishly, as I now see. I treated her indulgently, hoping that kindness and, perhaps above all, daily contact with you, my Jane, would moderate the ferocity and all-consuming selfishness I saw in her, hidden behind the mask of sweetness. That was why I forgave her for taking the carriage that day – but my anxiety over her, combined with my business worries, was too much for me, alas. I punished Jeremy instead.'

We stood beneath a great, bare horse chestnut which grew close to the path. He drew me to him and kissed my brow. 'Jane,' he said tenderly, 'I know you feared I had sought out Céline and had renewed my love for her. I knew – I grieved – but what could I tell you? That I went to her to discover if Adèle was indeed my child? And if she was not – was there some taint in her blood, some family madness which might explain what she was? That I went to my old mistress and besought her to tell me aught that might have created Adèle Rochester? I had kept the secret of Adèle for years. Was I to reveal it in all its horror to you when you were ill and expecting our child? I did not know, of course, that she had tried to kill you – that I could not believe, even of her – until the second time in the thorn field.

'So,' he continued, and bitter humour entered his tone. 'I went to Madame Varens and asked her, was Adèle indeed my child? She told me yes – she told me no – she told me yes again. When I became impatient, she tapped me with her fan and murmured something about life having been very complicated at that time. "More complicated than *I* ever supposed," said I to myself.' He sobered. 'But there – she has now lost the only child she had or is ever likely to have, poor woman.

'Having earlier kept my very great fears and doubts about Adèle's nature from her, I was forced to reveal them, to appeal to Céline. Was there aught in Adèle's parentage, or in her earlier life, which gave any clue as to her perverse disposition? But,' he sighed, 'Céline is a star in our firmament Jane, no longer a creature of flesh and blood. She could not help, she had no help to give – she began to babble of Greek drama. The Greeks, Jane!' he exclaimed. 'At such a moment! It angered me – but I calmed myself, thinking, Rochester – you were foolish – how could you have imagined Céline Varens would help you? And meanwhile,' he said regretfully, 'I had left my poor little wife in bad health in a great, lonely house in the country. And she responded gallantly.'

'Not so gallantly,' I murmured, recalling the long hours spent mourning my husband's absences and brooding on the beauty and charm of Céline Varens. But of this I said nothing.

We had reached the churchyard and went to Adèle's grave, a poor heap of earth, for no headstone had yet been raised, and on it were only such scanty blooms as winter could provide.

As we stood there he told me, 'Grace Poole knew all, of course.'

'I see,' said I. 'And that was why you employed her?'

He nodded. 'When I came on Mrs. Poole in Manchester,

in the sad condition of which I told you, she told me she knew Adèle had caused the fire in which Bertha perished. Her employment was the price of her silence.

'You see, at first, after the fire, Grace Poole believed herself solely responsible for Bertha's escape and the destruction of the house, not to mention my own injuries. She fled. It was only later, when she gave up drink and got her life in order, that she recognised the complete impossibility of Bertha's having caused the fire. If neither she nor Bertha had the key to their place of confinement, some other person had it, and that person had locked them in. She ruled out the servants, and concluded, logically enough, that I was the person with most to gain by my wife's death – and yet did me the justice of not believing me responsible.

'But she knew Adèle, and her ways, hit on her as culprit by instinct as well as reason, and when she spoke to me had the cunning to put it to me that she positively knew the child to have been guilty of all. And I, off guard and foolish, very shocked by the notion that another person knew this horrible secret, did not realise that she only guessed at facts of which she was not certain, confirmed her suspicions – and then, of course, she had me in her power.

'Ah, Jane,' he said, his hand still in mine, 'how could I imagine the girl would grow up and became not better but worse, infinitely worse? That her obsession would grow, that, having disposed of one wife to make, as she supposed, room for her mother, she would not scruple to attempt the life of the other? She saddled the horse for you, with the intention you should fall and be killed, though I could not, would not, believe at first that was what had happened. Then she attacked you that night in the thorn field. When you told me that, my darling, I felt as if a knife had been plunged into my own breast. To you, I swore I would never again leave you alone. To myself I vowed that now I must deal with Adèle, once and for all.

'I could not tell you all this, on the night of the ball. My guilt was extreme, for had I not tried to protect her all those years ago, she would not have grown up to believe she could commit any atrocity and go unpunished.'

'There was ever a kind of madness in her,' I murmured. 'She was one of those whom nature creates perfectly egotistical. They are rare, very rare, those who are born with no sense of the value of the existence of others, and therefore no sense of right conduct towards them. I do not think there was anything you could have done to change her, Edward. You must not reproach yourself.'

'Only that in protecting Adèle I allowed suspicions to rise among the Masons as to the true facts of Bertha's death, and thereby began a whole chain of dreadful events. I did not respond to Mason's importunities. There was no agreement between us as to the dowry – never had been – yet, in my desire to rid myself of Madame Roland I resolved to repay what they alleged I owed – and thus matters grew worse – and worse.'

'It is over now,' I said. 'And perhaps if there is any consolation at all, it is that through these awful trials we have become, I hope, wiser?'

'And closer and closer,' Edward said. 'Shall we go in?' And hand in hand we returned to Mr. Todd's.

'I believe there might be a place for Mrs. Poole at the Nortons',' I said. 'I know their housekeeper is retiring.'

'We certainly shall not need her at Ferndean,' he said. Then he laughed. 'I should enjoy the thought of Blanche babbling on thoughtlessly, as she does, under the steely gaze of Mrs. Poole.'

There was, however, to be one last, unpleasant event before we recovered our former peace. This came some two days later. Edward had risen early to go out with Mr. Sugden, for the land had to be attended to as usual, though we were to leave Thornfield. Mr. Todd was away on some parish business, so that I was alone in the house when Madame Roland called.

I had heard she was leaving the neighbourhood but I had no wish to bid her farewell. Yet I could not refuse to see her, since it was at her house that Adèle had been cared for before her death.

She came, dressed for travelling, into the parlour where I was sitting. When I invited her to sit down she refused. 'I would not come to you, Mrs. Rochester, for I know you dislike me, but I leave England today and wished to speak to you before I go.'

'And I owe you a great debt for your care of Adèle,' I told her.

'I did that for Céline, not for you or Rochester' was her uncompromising reply.

'Then there can be little else for us to say to each other – only goodbye,' I answered.

'Not quite,' she said. 'I could not leave without a warning to you. You must realise all Mr. Rochester's explanations are untrue. Whatever he has said of the past is lies – lies!' she exclaimed passionately. 'He will have laid the blame for all on the shoulders of that young girl, a child, indeed. Well, she is dead,' the woman said contemptuously, 'and is it not fortunate that once again the explanations are all Rochester's? Adèle can tell us nothing now.

'Look at it! Look at it!' she exclaimed. 'There is nothing said to have been done by Adèle which could not have been done just as easily by himself. Is it likely an eight-year-old child would deliberately set light to a house? A girl of eighteen, with a life ahead of her, try to kill her step-mother? No – in all things Rochester had a motive, even for killing you, so that he could marry Céline. He talked to her of it, I can assure you of that.'

I stood up. 'I will hear you no longer. Go,' I said.

She turned as if to go, then turned back. 'I did not come to trouble you. But even as Adèle was breathing her last, I heard him begin to rehearse his explanations. Let me beg you, in the name of my dead sister, if ever you have further cause to suspect your husband – look to yourself, Mrs. Rochester. Be warned.'

And she went, her malignancy unabated, sweeping off in a cloud of dark skirts. I stood in the doorway as she put her hand on the latch of the front door. 'Go, crow – fly back to France,' I cried. She did not look back at me, but left the house.

I did not tell Edward, on his return, of that vile woman's visit.

Later, I sat down to my plans. Though we are going from Thornfield, I shall not leave it completely behind. The first of the big abandoned houses outside the village will be the village school, as St. John planned. The other will become a small factory, with the most modern equipment, for the weaving of wool. It will not be so profitable as the great mills of Halifax or Bradford, but it will do well enough and will suffice to help the people of Hay.

Our time at Thornfield was one of tragedy and tragedy overcome, but neither of us will abandon the neighbourhood completely. Some good must come from the worst, I believe. In this we will be helped by St. John, who will become Mr. Todd's curate and will eventually, I imagine, when Mr. Todd retires, take over the responsibility for the parish.

Soon we shall be at Ferndean, and leading again our old, modest life. Perhaps, some little corner of ambition in me regrets leaving behind the title of Mrs. Rochester of Thornfield, but a greater part of my soul rejoices at the thought of having under our old, familiar, friendly, roof, after so much tribulation, those closest to me – my children and my most dearly loved husband, Edward, love of my life, half my soul, chief reason for my existence – and all my happiness.